THE STRANGEWORLDS

· TRAVEL AGENCY ·

Also by L.D. Lapinski

THE STRANGEWORLDS

· TRAVEL AGENCY ·

The Edge of the Ocean

THE STRANGEWORLDS

TRAVEL AGENCY

L. D. LAPINSKI

Orion

ORION CHILDREN'S BOOKS

First published in Great Britain in 2020
by Hodder and Stoughton

7 9 10 8

A CIP catalogue record for this book
is available from the British Library.

ISBN 978 1 51010 594 2

Printed and bound in Great Britain by Clays Ltd, Elcograf S.p.A.

The paper and board used in this book are made
from wood from responsible sources.

Orion Children's Books
An imprint of
Hachette Children's Group
Part of Hodder and Stoughton
Carmelite House
50 Victoria Embankment
London EC4Y 0DZ

An Hachette UK Company

www.hachette.co.uk
www.hachettechildrens.co.uk

for Joseph

'Everybody has a secret world inside
of them. I mean everybody.

All of the people in the whole
world, I mean everybody —

no matter how dull and boring
they are on the outside.

Inside them they've all got
unimaginable, magnificent, wonderful,
stupid, amazing worlds . . .

Not just one world. Hundreds of them.
Thousands, maybe.'

– Neil Gaiman, *A Game of You*

The Sandman: A Game of You © 1991 DC Comics.
Written by Neil Gaiman.

CHAPTER ONE

There have always been places in our world where magic gathers.

You can see it, if you look close enough.

You might see an ancient horse and cart passing down a modern high-street; or a cobbled alleyway that people walk into, but never out of. Now and again, you might see it in a person – someone who looks like they've stepped straight out of an old photograph. Or, perhaps, someone whose bag seems to hover off the ground catches your eye in a coffee shop. And when you look again they, and their bag, have disappeared.

And, occasionally, you see magic in shops.

Squashed between brand name stores and fancy displays, the shops soaked in magic are never eye-catching, or ostentatious. Their windows are stained with dirt and dust, and sometimes their signs have peeled away so much that it looks as though ghost letters are trying to work their way through. Magic does not wish to be noticed, you see. And most people are happy to pretend it does not exist.

The Strangeworlds Travel Agency was very much like a magical shop should be.

The leaded windows were dirty and cracked. There was peeling paint on the front door and it hardly ever seemed to be open. However, there was one element of the shop that refused to fade into the background: the sign over the window. It was always clearly painted, in silky gold letters embellished with black against a ruby-red background. There was one globe at the beginning of the sign and another at the end. The shop was out of its time, for certain, and yet the name was blazoned for all to see.

In the time between the agency opening almost one hundred and fifty years ago and the summer everything changed, the only thing that altered about the frontage was the globes – they were repainted occasionally, to reflect the shifting borders of various countries.

So, a change was overdue. And it was a new visitor coming into Strangeworlds that ultimately saved the business.

As well as other things.

*

Jonathan Mercator was working. At least, that's what he would claim to be doing, if you asked him. What he was actually doing was sitting at the shop desk, ankles crossed on the surface as he leaned back in his chair, reading.

A number of open journals lay on the desk beside his shoes, and the sound of several out-of-sync clocks, ticking to their own distinct rhythms, filled the otherwise silent air. Jonathan paid them no attention.

It was going to be, by his standards, a very busy day.

A shadow crossed in front of the large bay window. And then it passed again, this time pausing in the region of the front door. After a moment the door opened, scraping over the swollen floorboards, and a boy came in, curling not so much his lip as his entire face at the sight of the shop interior.

Jonathan raised his eyes over the edge of his novel and watched the boy with interest.

'Um . . .' The boy looked around. 'This isn't Games Warehouse, is it?'

The interest slipped from Jonathan's face like water vanishing through a sieve, and he gazed around in false astonishment. 'Isn't it? Whatever gave you that idea?'

The boy pulled his phone out. 'It's supposed to be here.'

'Ah, well then. If your *phone* says this is the place, it must be correct. Don't trust your own eyes, whatever you do.' Jonathan reached into the inside pocket of his jacket and fished out a very small magnifying glass. It was made of a bronze metal, with a thick glass lens. He tossed it at the boy, who caught it uncertainly. 'Have a good look around, make absolutely certain, why don't you?'

'What's this for?'

'Humour me.'

The boy frowned and lifted the magnifying glass to his face. 'What am I supposed to see? Does this even work? Everything's blurry.' He put the glass back on the desk. 'What sort of place is this?' His loud voice was absorbed by the room, so the sound of it fell rather flat.

Jonathan sighed, picking up the magnifying glass and putting it back in his pocket. 'The sign over the window wasn't enough of a clue? We're a travel agency.'

The boy snorted. 'All right, maybe it does say *travel agency* over the door, but you don't even have a computer.'

Jonathan looked at his desk, before taking his legs off it. As well as the pile of journals, there was a half-drunk mug of tea and a plate with the crumby remains of toast and peanut butter still on it. He put the novel he was reading down, fanned open to save the page. 'What on earth would I need a computer for?'

'Er ... don't you need to book flights? Arrange holidays?'

Jonathan smiled. A smile full of secrets. 'I'm not that sort of travel agent.'

The boy frowned. 'What *do* you do, then?'

Jonathan pushed his glasses up his nose and folded his hands, his fingers interlocking like gears.

But he was saved the trouble of answering by the suitcase to his left springing open.

Perhaps, before things become too complicated, we should clarify precisely *why* this young man was so sceptical about The Strangeworlds Travel Agency.

First of all, the visitor was correct in pointing out that the place was a technological relic. Indeed, the most modern item in Jonathan Mercator's possession was a typewriter from the 1960s. He liked to type passive-aggressive notes on it and hide them in library books. The desk the typewriter sat upon wouldn't have been out of place in the office of a Victorian headmaster, and even Jonathan's clothes looked old. You got the feeling someone might well have died in some of his tweed suits. They were not the sort of thing you'd expect an eighteen-year-old to be wearing.

Then there was the fact that the travel agency had no fancy posters of Disneyland, or the Algarve, or anywhere else you might have wanted to visit. There were no posters at all, in fact. Only a few globes and atlases. And something that was like a globe, except the sphere was shaped more like a pear than a ball.

And then there were the suitcases.

They filled an entire wall of the travel agency, sitting in neat wooden slots that had been built right into the wall. The shelves went from floor to ceiling, each suitcase snug in a niche of its own, its handle waiting to be grasped and pulled down. There were more suitcases stacked between two fireside armchairs like a coffee table, others neatly arranged in piles against the far wall and a couple leaning against Jonathan's desk.

You could count at least fifty of them stacked in the wall, and not a single one was alike. There were leather ones, heavy cardboard ones, shining crocodile hide ones, and some made of skins that would make even the most learned of zoologists scratch their heads. Some had stamps on their edges, some had splashes of paint, and at least a dozen had paper labels tied onto their handles with string.

The Strangeworlds Travel Agency looked more like a lost and found office, or a rather specialist antique shop, than a travel agency. So it was hardly surprising that the boy was suspicious – even before the suitcase sprang open.

At the sound of the suitcase bursting open, Jonathan turned around, startled, his wood-and-leather swivel chair screeching on its casters. The suitcase lid flew back and a torrent of water splashed out of it.

'What's happening?' the boy gasped, backing quickly away from the flood.

Seconds later, a man climbed out of the suitcase as if it were a trap-door. He was soaking wet and coughing. A collapsed telescope was hanging from his belt in a leather hoop. He quickly reached back down into the case and heaved until a woman half-clambered, half-tumbled out as well. She landed on her hands and knees, her many-layered dress dripping onto the floorboards. She had three pairs of spectacles hanging around her neck, and thick black hair that was braided and decorated with little strips of ribbons and lace.

And around her right ankle was wrapped a bright red and very slimy-looking tentacle.

'The blasted thing's still got hold of me, Hudspeth,' she huffed, sounding more annoyed than frightened, even as the tentacle wrapped itself higher around her leg.

Her partner gave a sort of mild slap to the tendril. 'Get off. Pick on something with the same number of legs, why don't you?'

The tentacle clenched tighter and went redder.

'Kindly disentangle yourself,' Jonathan sighed. 'I can't have anything coming back with you. You know the rules.'

The woman kicked again, and at last the tentacle let go of her ankle and fell back into the case with a splash.

The suitcase jumped, and the lid snapped shut with a *CLUNK*.

The couple lay on the floor, wet through, catching their breath and grinning like no one who had just climbed out of a suitcase along with an overly affectionate octopus had any right to. Then they looked at each other and started laughing.

Jonathan pulled one of the journals towards himself. He flipped through it to the right page, and picked up a pen. 'Welcome back, both of you. Mori and Alfred Hudspeth . . .'

'Just Hudspeth, if you don't mind,' the man winced.

'Fine. Hm,' Jonathan pouted. 'Your registration doesn't mark you as due back for another week. Didn't you have a jolly old time?'

'Jolly's not the word I'd use.' The woman, Mori, ruffled her hair, and lifted a pair of glasses to her face, before taking them off and trying a second pair which she kept on, apparently liking them better. 'The weather's taken a turn for the worse – you wouldn't believe the size of the waves. There was talk of ships being blown off the edge of the map entirely.'

Hudspeth nodded. 'Worst storm I've seen for a long time. The ports were all but shut down on the lower half of the world. And they've swapped currency again, did you know that?'

'Oh, for heaven's sake.' Jonathan picked up a piece of paper and wrote on it, shaking his head. 'They do it so often they'll be back to a barter system next time someone visits. Did you at least get some decent notes?'

'Decent enough.' Hudspeth pulled a damp-looking book from inside his shirt and put it on the desk.

Jonathan raised an eyebrow at it. 'You realise that each one of these guidebooks is extremely valuable? Not to mention unique to each suitcase?' He picked it up between thumb and finger. It dripped. 'This is not how I expect Society members to treat documents in their care.'

'Hey, there wasn't a lot of time for sitting and writing essays,' Hudspeth laughed.

Jonathan didn't join in.

Hudspeth held his fringe back. A cut was visible on his forehead, white where the water had made the wound swell. 'See that? More than a slight fracas by the time we got to the Cove of Voices. Captain Nyfe doesn't want to give passage to anyone she doesn't know, not with how things are at the moment, so we had to catch a lift off one of the smaller vessels to try and get around to The Break. And we almost lost the suitcase when the storm started . . .'

'And then the – the octopus things.' Mori wiped at her eyeliner with a manicured finger. 'What did she call them?'

'*Hafgufa*,' Hudspeth said. 'Monsters of the mist.'

'That's it.' Mori dabbed at her makeup again. The makeup around her eyes was somehow still immaculate. 'They seemed to be attracted to the suitcase. We had to jump overboard when the beast got hold of the ship. Never seen that before. We were picked up by one of the lifeboats, but finding somewhere to open the case was a nightmare.'

'Doesn't mean we wouldn't do it again.' Hudspeth grinned.

'Well, thank heavens you managed to wade back through that ocean of excuses,' Jonathan said drily. He opened the damp book, and gave it a read. 'All of one single paragraph written, too.' He looked up. 'You know this really isn't good enough.'

The couple blushed.

'There wasn't really time—'

'We – we nearly lost the suitcase, you know.'

'*Don't Lose Your Luggage*,' Jonathan snapped. 'That's Rule Number One. If you wear that badge on your arm,' Jonathan nodded at a very faded and torn patch on Hudspeth's sleeve, 'you abide by the rules and requirements. This isn't just an opportunity for you to—'

'We'll do better, next time,' Hudspeth interrupted dismissively, helping his wife to her feet. 'You all right, Mori?'

'Just about.' She checked her clothes, fixing them back into position.

As she moved her skirt, a magnifying glass attached to a ring swung down from where it had been tucked into her belt.

This magnifying glass was not as small as the one Jonathan had returned to his jacket pocket. This one was the size of a hairbrush, and had a heavy sort of look about it. The handle was a stained red wood, trimmed with polished brass. The circle of brass that held the lens in place was gleaming, and the glass itself was thick. It was attached to Mori's belt by a metal loop, like the sort of ring you put your keys on, only much stronger and nicer to look at.

Jonathan stared, his face going from polite to outraged like the flick of a switch. 'You – you took a magnifying lens with you?'

'Only as a precaution,' Hudspeth said quickly. 'You never know—'

'I *do* know,' Jonathan snapped, drawing himself up so he seemed much taller than his usually unimpressive five-foot-eight. 'How – how *dare* you? You know full well you do not have the authority to wield that.'

'Listen—'

'No, *you* listen.' Jonathan came around the desk, his eyes flashing dangerously behind his glasses. 'You're Society members. You know the history of the agency, and you know *why* those lenses are a restricted item. How dare you keep one, let alone take it with you? I am your Head Custodian. I should strike your names off the ledger right this second.'

Mori blushed redder than ever. 'It was just in case—'

'In case of *what*?'

'Sorry.' Hudspeth raised his hands. 'Jonathan . . . Mr Mercator . . . We're sorry. We got it in Five Lights, and thought it might come in useful.'

Jonathan held his hand out. 'Hand it over.'

The couple looked at each other.

'I am your Head Custodian,' he repeated. 'Unless you want a lifetime ban, hand it over. Now.'

Reluctantly, Mori unhooked the ring from her belt, and put the magnifying glass into Jonathan's hand.

Hudspeth scowled. 'Cost me an arm and a leg, that did.'

'You're lucky it's not costing you more,' Jonathan said ominously. He dropped it into his desk drawer. 'If you don't trust yourselves to use a suitcase – and only a suitcase – don't bother coming back here. This isn't a game.'

'All right,' Mori said gently. 'We're sorry. We didn't think. And we'll do better with the guidebook, next time. And the suitcase. Not come as close to losing it, I mean.'

Jonathan shut the desk drawer, and nodded. 'Thank you.'

'Taking your responsibilities seriously, I see,' Hudspeth said, with grudging admiration. 'No offence meant, er . . .'

'I'm quite sure.'

Mori's dress dripped water onto the floorboards.

'Until next time, then.' Jonathan pushed the ledger towards the edge of the desk and placed a pen into the groove where the pages met.

The two travellers signed their names on the open page. And then there were quick handshakes and smiles, before Mori and her husband excused themselves. They walked inelegantly outside, their clothes still soaked.

The bell over the door shook silently, the tongue long since torn out.

Jonathan fetched a mop and bucket from behind the doorway that led to the back of the shop. He pulled it through on its three remaining wheels, before slapping the mop onto the floor.

He noticed the boy, whose mouth was flapping like he was a goldfish at feeding time. 'Oh. Are you still here?'

The boy shook his head, snapped his mouth shut, and ran out of the door.

The bell wobbled violently.

Jonathan tutted, and carried on mopping the floor. Once it was dry, he picked up the wet suitcase in one hand, testing the weight and shaking off a few droplets of sea-water. There was a faint scent of cold and salt in the air.

Jonathan gave the suitcase an affectionate pat. Then he put it carefully back into its empty space on the shelves. He went over to the desk, and took out the large magnifying glass, holding it up to the light and examining the lens for a moment. It really was beautiful. Highly crafted. Made by someone who loved it, and would have done wonderful things with it.

A look of anger suddenly crossed over Jonathan's face.

He dropped the magnifying glass to the floor, and brought his foot down hard.

The glass cracked in two under his heel.

He relaxed a bit. Better to have it broken than at risk of falling into the wrong hands.

He gave a small laugh, barely more than a breath with sound in it, and turned to say something. 'Did you—'

Then quickly he shut his mouth again, in the way people do when they remember that the person they wanted to speak to is no longer there.

He was quite alone.

And he felt it.

CHAPTER TWO

Flick should have been excited.

Her parents were. They were laughing and singing along with the radio like no one was watching. Even Freddy, the baby, was waving his sticky hands and kicking his legs as they drove up the motorway. It wasn't that Flick didn't understand the excitement over the new house ('A garden!' her mum had squealed for the ninetieth time, 'and two toilets!'), and it was true it was going to make things a lot easier for them all with Freddy having his own bedroom from now on . . . but she'd been born in the old flat (quite literally, as the paramedics were still hauling their equipment up the stairs because the lifts were broken that day), and she'd watched her mum and dad turn it into a proper home, with window boxes that had actual flowers in them and a customisable doorbell instead of a buzzer – even if it did get stuck chiming *We Will Rock You* once the rain got into it.

'It'll be good to get away from the city and to somewhere with a bit of green around it,' her dad had said.

Flick disagreed. She *liked* living in the city. And anyway, it wasn't like the St Bosco's estate had been right in the centre. It had been great living high up and above everyone else, with a panoramic view over town. In the cold weather, you could watch the cooling towers of the power station belching out steam and smoke. Flick's mum used to tell stories about the towers, and say they were hiding dragons inside. Not that Flick believed that sort of rubbish any more.

She glanced at her backpack, beside her. It was brand new, because, once September rolled around, she'd be going to a new school. She'd spent a year getting used to the size of Lawrence Academy, where the Year Sevens moved in packs like prey animals, and now she was going to be attending Byron Hall, where there were less than 400 kids in the whole school. And she had to wear a tie. The only bit about it that didn't sound awful to Flick was the fact they let students use real pianos for music lessons.

They turned off the motorway onto a tree-flanked road, following it past some very posh houses. The new Elm Tree Estate had been built right on the edge of the village of Little Wyverns, and apparently there'd been a lot of complaints about it. When the road narrowed to the width of about one and a half cars, Flick breathed in, as though she could make their old Corolla thinner. Another turning, and abruptly the houses of the new estate seemed to spring up around them, lining the pavements and filing backwards, each one perfectly placed behind the other, like dominoes.

Flick shut one eye, and poked her finger at one of the buildings, imagining it collapsing backwards and taking the whole estate with it.

'This is us,' Flick's dad said, pulling onto the driveway. 'Crikey. The garden looks a bit different to the show-home . . .'

Flick thought that was the understatement of the century. The picture on the front of their housing association brochure had shown the sort of lawn that got cut with nail-scissors. But there was no neat grass in front of their new house. In fact, there was no grass to be seen at all. There were, however, weeds. It looked like someone had played a bad game of Jumanji in the yard. Some of the nettles were as tall as Flick. Freddy, freshly released from his car-seat prison, made a grab for one of them, but was quickly yanked back by their mum. He howled, and a cat shot out of the undergrowth and down the street like a ginger-and-white rocket. The cats around the flats had got used to Freddy's in-built siren. These new ones would have to learn fast.

*

'This is my room,' Flick said, holding Freddy in front of her. He burbled, and rammed a fist in his mouth. 'I'll assume that means you understand. My room. Not ours, any more. Your room . . .' she walked back across the landing, 'is this one. Nice and small, because you're a small person.' Using the word *small* about the bedroom was being generous. Once Freddy needed a single bed he wouldn't even have room to stand up beside it.

The baby kicked his legs to get down. Flick put him on the carpet, which still smelled of the carpet shop, and let him crawl away, leaving a fine trail of crumbs as he went, like a specialised snail.

There was a baby gate at the top of the stairs, which Flick had no doubt her brother was going to learn to scale before the week was out. Like everything else in the house, it was new. New carpets, new paint, new oven, even new plug sockets, which were crisp-white and smooth – nothing like the ones in the old place that sometimes crackled alarmingly when you put a plug into them.

Flick sighed as she put Freddy's night light on to charge. You couldn't pretend to be controlling the electricity with your mind if the plugs didn't crackle.

Downstairs, the two removal people were leaving. Flick's dad was giving each of them a tip and thanking them for their help. Flick gave them a smile as she carried Freddy over to the baby-jail (or playpen) her mum had put up to keep him away from the boxes and bags.

'So, what do you think of your room?' her mum asked.

'It's nice,' Flick said, flexing her arms after putting Freddy down. 'It's a bit beige.'

'The whole house is beige,' her mum said. 'Cream paint and beige carpets. If we ever get round to changing them, we can choose something more cheerful. I suppose they think it looks clean.'

'It *is* clean. There's a plastic wrapper on the toilet.' Flick went over to the box labelled 'Felicity's Clothes' and picked it up. 'I'll start taking things up, then?'

'Thank you, sweetheart.' Her mum handed the baby a rusk. 'Be careful on the stairs, won't you.'

*

By the end of the day, most of the boxes had been sorted through. Freddy's cot was assembled, and everyone's bed was made, but they hadn't got a dining table or chairs yet, so they were having fish and chips on the living room floor 'as a treat'. Though Flick's mum was still making them eat off plates with cutlery, even if Flick insisted that the wooden forks from the chip shop made everything taste nicer.

Flick's dad sat picking at his fish. Isaac Hudson didn't trust anything that came out of the sea. 'There's a free plastic bag comes with every fish,' he would say loudly when they walked past the fish counter in Morrisons, 'and it's inside it.' Flick was sure she would die of embarrassment before she ever got to leave home.

'It's a shame we won't get a full day at it tomorrow,' her dad said, abandoning his dissection of the haddock. 'But we've made a dent in it. I can carry on unpacking tomorrow afternoon.'

'You've got Freddy,' her mum reminded him. 'His new childcare doesn't start for a day or so.'

Flick rolled her eyes. Her parents were rarely under the same roof. Her dad worked as a refuse collector, and was out the door at 4am, coming back as her mum left for her afternoon shift as a post office clerk. Her mum would come home just in time to bath Freddy and was sometimes so tired that she would go to bed at the same time as the baby. Flick's dad would try to stay up to keep Flick company, but often fell asleep in front of the TV. Most of the time, Flick would wake him up and make sure he went to bed, but sometimes she covered him with a blanket and left him.

'What are your plans for tomorrow, Felicity?' Her mum put her plate down.

This was a trap. Flick knew she should offer to help her dad unpack, but she'd been unpacking all day. She'd seen enough brown tape and cardboard to last a lifetime. She couldn't say so without sounding like the most ungrateful daughter in the universe though.

She stirred a chip through what was left of her ketchup. 'Um . . .'

Her dad saved her. 'I think you should have a wander,' he said. 'See what's happening in this little place. You could find out where your school is.'

'I don't think it'll be difficult to find,' Flick said. 'There's like ten buildings in the whole village, if you don't count these new ones.' She put her cutlery down. 'But yeah, I'll go and find it. See where the library is, and stuff, for after school.'

Her mum nodded. 'That's very sensible. You can unpack your toys and things in the evening.'

Flick scowled. She was twelve. She didn't have toys. She had Collectables, and Items of Sentimental Value. But not toys. 'Sure.'

Freddy stretched from his position on the playmat, managing to yawn and fart simultaneously, and looked immensely pleased with himself.

*

Flick drew her new (beige) curtains and switched on the lamp she'd brought with her from the old place. It was shaped like a mushroom and had been a present from Nanna and Grandad Pitchford when she was very small. There was a mouse at the base of it, and Flick used to pretend it was alive. She didn't do that any more, but she loved the memory of being able to pretend like that. Sadly, the lamp now had a big crack in the dome where Freddy had smacked it with a full bottle. It made the light form a sort of zig-zag pattern across the ceiling.

24

There were half a dozen boxes against the wall, each with her name on. Flick picked up the smallest one and lifted the lid. As she expected, there wasn't only her stuff in it – at the end of the packing, her dad had panicked and started to throw things into any box that still had space.

On the top, though, was the last thing Flick had packed. She lifted out a poster that had been folded over and over, and held it by a corner to let it flop open. The poster had been a Christmas present, and Flick stuck it straight onto the wall, the Blu-Tack from the old house still on the paper.

It was a very impressive poster, Flick thought. It was a map of the world, and the idea was to put a sticker onto each country you visited. Flick didn't have the stickers that had come with it any more – one memorable Saturday Freddy had found them and stuck them all over himself – but it didn't matter. The only country she'd managed to mark off the map was the United Kingdom, anyway.

Flick pressed two of her fingers to the UK, and made them walk like legs over the Channel to France, and then onwards through different countries, right until she got to China, and the land ran out. She sighed, a little seed of sadness sprouting in her chest. China might as well be Jupiter – she had about as much chance of ever getting there.

She went back to unpacking, lifting out a battered-looking shoe-box that she didn't think she'd seen before. There was a crossed-out address on it, and a faded sticker on the front said 'I. T. Hudson' – her dad's name. She opened it and tutted in despair at the folded bits of paper, the expired key-card, and the broken and dry pens her dad seemed incapable of throwing away. There was a wooden jewellery box at the bottom, with a gold catch.

Flick pulled it out. It was heavy. Her mum didn't have a lot of jewellery, and her dad had worn the same Casio watch for as long as she could remember. Maybe this box held some sort of family secret, she thought excitedly. A box full of jewellery, or money, or proof that they were somehow related to a royal family halfway around the world.

She flicked the catch up.

And sighed in disappointment. The inside was stuffed full of yet more envelopes and paperwork. If she found the library, she really needed to get her dad that Magical Tidying Up book she'd heard people talking about.

She closed the wooden box, put it to one side and went back to searching through her things. At last she found what she was looking for – a slice of agate crystal.

The agate was one of the few precious things Flick owned that had survived her baby brother. Her dad had bought it for her when they went to the Blue-John Mines together, just the two of them, a couple of years ago. The agate was as thin as drinking glass and swirled through with pink and purple.

She put it on top of her lamp and the zig-zagged light turned into an aurora on the ceiling.

Flick smiled and got into bed, letting the colours of the light paint themselves into her dreams.

CHAPTER THREE

Flick didn't feel even slightly guilty as she escaped out of the house the next day. Her mum had given her some change, and told her not to stay out late, but to have fun. Flick wondered how often kids were told to 'have fun', and whether or not they did in the end. There was probably an interesting statistic there. Flick liked numbers. Maths was much simpler than English, where you could have lots of right answers depending on how you wrote them down. Maths you were either right or wrong.

'Ah.' Mr Kalil, Flick's favourite Maths teacher had smiled when she pointed this out. 'But numbers don't always mean one thing alone. For instance, you can use numbers to lie.'

'How?'

He'd shown her some of the statistics work from the year above and how those same numbers could be used to prove different things by different people. Flick hadn't known whether to be pleased or not that her precious straightforward numbers could be made to seem more (or less) important, depending on who was using them.

Her parents had quickly got tired of her pointing this out when they watched the news.

Now, she went around the back of the house, followed the paths between the gardens, and walked past two more families who were unpacking removal vans. She ducked under the curtains of a wild silver birch, brushing at her dark curls in case some spiders had decided to hitch-hike on her head, and came out at the pedestrian crossing that led to the high-street.

Flick felt quite surprised as she walked to the market-place. For such a small village, Little Wyverns was busy. There were crowds of people, open shop doors, and stalls and canopies everywhere.

Flick had never minded crowds – it was impossible to avoid them in the city, after all. But this crowd felt like one she didn't belong in. People were glancing at her, clocking her as someone from the new estate. She had a weird sensation – like she'd turned up to a football match wearing the wrong colour shirt.

In a village as small as this, any stranger would be like an interesting specimen in a jar.

Flick peeled away from the market, and went to lean against one of the buildings, pretending to check her phone. The sun was already beating down, and the air was full of that strange sour tang from the fake plastic grass stallholders put their strawberry punnets on. There were a lot of swinging shopping bags and even more babies squalling in prams.

The groups of chattering villagers were making her feel like she was standing awkwardly at the edge of a party she hadn't been invited to. Flick was tempted to go back home, where there was only one squalling baby, and he at least was easily distracted with a banana, but she felt she'd quite like at least one baby-free day in the whole summer holidays. Freddy had been what their parents called 'a surprise'. Flick thought 'a shock' was probably more accurate. He'd been hogging attention since before he was even born.

She started walking again, veering off the high-street, trying to put some distance between herself and the tiny Freddy-reminders, and turned down a quiet Victorian arcade. The arcade was made of old stone on all sides, and it seemed to suck the heat out of the air completely. Flick shivered. She passed a busy haberdashery and an empty bar and came out beside a bridal shop. The bustle of the village was in the distance now. There was a small church ringed with a sharp arrow-like fence directly opposite where she stood.

And beside the church, leaning drunkenly into the alleyway, was a tiny, squashed-looking shop with a big bay window. It had a shiny black door and a corner porch with a stone step so worn it appeared to be melting into the pavement.

Flick looked up at the sign.

The Strangeworlds Travel Agency

Something prickled under her skin. The feeling wasn't unpleasant; if she'd had to describe it, she would have said it was curiosity mixed with oranges. She felt her fingers curl into her palms in an involuntary clench that sent an electric sort of feeling through her bones. She wanted to get closer to that shop.

She couldn't say exactly why.

The travel agency, if that's what it really was, looked the same as the other shops on the street: old, unpopular, rather unloved, and as though it might have a bit of a weird smell. It did have fresh red and gold paint spelling out its name, though, and a gleaming glossy globe at either end of the sign. There was also a brass plaque beside the door, though at this distance Flick couldn't make out what it said.

Her legs, moving almost without permission, took her across the cobblestoned road, and up to the shop door before she could think of a reason not to.

The porch had a bit of an overhang, to shelter people from rain, and once under it Flick felt as if she was standing in a little cocoon. She brushed a hand against the sandy brickwork, and some of the dusty masonry clung to her fingers. She rubbed it off on the leg of her jeans, and touched the brass plaque bolted to the outside wall. It was dented and scratched. It had also been vandalised – the letters were scoured as though they had been attacked with a chisel. Flick could just make out the letters: 'ociety'.

She studied the big bay window. The glass, shining in the sunlight, seemed to look back at her. And Flick realised the shop wasn't really so grubby, after all.

It was . . . sort of beautiful. Like a book that's been read so many times the cover has fallen off and the pages have started to curl, or a soft bear that's had all its fur loved away.

Flick felt a smile tugging at the corners of her mouth. There was a soft, affectionate feeling growing in her chest that she couldn't explain. Like the feeling you get when you see a photograph of a person taken before you met them. You recognise them, and you know you're going to meet them someday, but it's as though they're not quite . . . ready. Not yet.

She put a hand on the door and pushed.

The door swung open easily, and she stepped in after it, catching it before it could bang against the wall. It closed softly behind her, letting out a dusty sigh as it settled back into place.

Flick looked around.

She had never seen anywhere that seemed less like a travel agency in her life. The air was slightly dusty, almost as though the place seemed to have a sepia filter thrown over it. The wall to Flick's left was a mosaic of luggage. Dozens of different sized suitcases were slotted into perfectly proportioned holes of varnished dark wood; only one single cavity was empty.

To her right, in the corner behind the door, was a glass-and-wood cabinet stuffed to bursting with books and files and tiny knick-knacks and a glass case of insects. Beside this corner-cabinet was a stretch of wood-panelled wall that was home to a dozen photographs in heavy, dark frames. The pictures were all of people. Flick frowned as she looked at them closely. There were tiny brass plaques beneath each picture, with barely readable names engraved into them.

To the back of the room there was a bookcase, stuffed into a corner beneath the stairs. In front of the bookcase was a desk. There was enough space between it and the bookcase for a leather-cushioned swivel chair. The desk was littered with books and papers, and a wrapper from a packet of custard creams.

Gooseflesh rose on Flick's arms as she stared at the suitcases, the twin armchairs either side of the empty fireplace to the right, and the mantelpiece with a synchronous of clocks on the top of it. There was a faint smell of blown-out candle and something like damp paper.

It felt familiar and new at the same time. It felt like somewhere she probably shouldn't be, and yet Flick didn't even think once about going for the door. She walked carefully over to the mantelpiece. The clocks on it were all ticking at different speeds. The hands of some were whizzing around the faces; others seemed barely to be moving at all. Each one had a label.

'Cove of Voices,' Flick read aloud. 'Aquata Minor. Crystal Forest . . .'

She picked up one of the clocks. The label on it read *City of Five Lights*. It was ticking merrily and quickly.

It was small, black and round like a cartoon alarm clock, but so heavy and greasy that when she turned it over, it immediately slipped from her fingers. She scrambled and bent to catch it just before it could crash onto a couple of leather-bound suitcases that were stacked between two chairs.

She breathed a sigh of relief and shook her head at the clock, as if it had decided to jump out of her hands on its own. She carefully put it back where it belonged.

'That was close.'

Flick jumped like she'd been stung and looked around to see who had spoken.

The shopkeeper (who was, of course, Jonathan Mercator) stood in the doorway between the travel agency's front room and the back. He was holding a china cup in one hand, and a saucer in the other. There was a custard cream on the saucer. 'May I help you?' he asked.

'Um . . .' Flick felt herself going extremely red. 'I'm sorry about the clock. It didn't smash, or anything. I was just . . . looking around.'

'Well, mission accomplished,' Jonathan said sarcastically. He put his cup and saucer down. 'I've been suffering from a terrible lack of people coming in to waste my time. Thank heavens you arrived when you did, Miss . . .?'

'Flick.'

'Miss Flick?'

'Flick Hudson. Well, Felicity, but—'

'Hudson . . .' Jonathan narrowed his eyes, and Flick had the impression he was trying to see through her eyes clean to the back of her head and possibly several yards beyond it as well.

'Any relation?'

Flick blinked. 'Well, I've got a mum and dad.' *And a brother*, she added, silently.

'No, I meant to Henry Hudson, the explorer.'

'Oh,' Flick smiled, pleased to share a surname with an explorer. 'I don't know. Maybe.'

'Maybe. Well, that's as good as a no, isn't it?' He picked up the custard cream, and bit into it. 'Did someone send you here for something?' he asked, mouth full.

'No, I was just walking past and—'

He waved a hand at her to be quiet. 'Very well. Now, if you wouldn't mind . . .' He pointed at the door with the remaining half of his biscuit, before popping it into his mouth.

Flick stayed where she was. Her feet seemed extremely reluctant to move. She looked back at the suitcases. 'What are all those bags for?'

'We're a travel agency,' Jonathan said, in the special slow voice people use when talking to children they think don't understand them. 'The best in the world. Old family firm.'

'The best in the world?' Flick repeated sceptically.

'Yes. We send you where you want to go.' He tapped the desk with a finger. 'It isn't cheap.'

The vague smile evaporated off Flick's face. No doubt this young man lived in one of the huge posh houses they'd driven past on the way in. He probably had special poor-person detection abilities. She shrugged, trying to look like that didn't matter to her. 'I didn't think it would be.'

'So don't linger on my account.'

Flick still didn't move. She looked back at the suitcases. They were very striking, but it didn't make sense for there to be so many of them in one travel agency. 'So you save people's bags? Until they go on a trip or something?'

'Oh, no.' Jonathan followed her gaze. 'No, these are all mine.'

'Yours? Why are there so many?'

For the first time, Jonathan paused, searching for a believable lie the way one searches for their keys in an overstuffed bag. 'They're atmospheric.'

Flick folded her arms.

Jonathan folded his arms right back, and he did it with a great deal more style. 'Was there anything else, miss?'

There wasn't, of course. But Flick still didn't leave. She went over to one of the smaller suitcase piles and reached for the one on the top.

'Don't touch that,' Jonathan snapped.

'Why?' she asked, instantly wanting to touch it, maybe write her name in the dust. 'Is it old?'

'It's – yes. They all are. Look, I don't mean to be rude –'

Flick pulled an incredulous face.

'– but this is my business, and I really don't see how I can help you.'

'Seems to me like you're the one who needs help,' she said, closing her mouth quickly after the words had escaped.

Jonathan stared, his eyes boggling behind his glasses. 'I beg your par—'

'Are you here on your own?' Flick blurted out. 'Or looking after the place for your dad, or something?'

'I am here by myself. This is my travel agency. I inherited it.'

Flick wasn't entirely sure that sounded right. 'Don't you need to be eighteen to inherit things?'

'I *am* eighteen,' Jonathan said indignantly.

'Really?' asked Flick, disbelievingly. He didn't seem more than a couple of years older than she was. He was white, and his black hair seemed to be a stranger to combs and brushes; the soft dark curls coiled haphazardly over the arms of his glasses. He wasn't very tall, and he didn't look like he was shaving yet, but – now she really stared at him – there was a sort of *oldness* in his eyes. She'd seen her mum's eyes like that, not long after Freddy was born. They were the eyes of someone who wasn't sleeping and had too much to think about. He was wearing a suit with a plum tie, and a blue waistcoat that needed an iron.

Jonathan bit his bottom lip for a moment. 'If you must know, I'm the only one the shop could go to. I'm not awash with family.'

Flick didn't quite know what to say to that. She suddenly felt rather guilty about her questions. 'That makes sense,' she risked. 'So . . . I'm sorry.'

'Whatever for?'

'Well, if you inherited it . . .' The implication hung in the air.

Jonathan let her words fester for a moment, before nodding. 'Thank you.'

There was an uneasy silence.

Flick took her hand off the suitcase. 'It must be tiring,' she said, stepping carefully around the implication that he looked tired. 'Taking care of the place on your own.'

'I suppose it can be.'

Flick could feel her heart beating very fast. She wanted to say something, but also didn't want to speak. For some reason, she felt as if she had to stay in this travel agency. And if she couldn't be a customer . . .

She brightened, a solution popping into her head. 'You could do with an assistant.'

'An assistant?' Jonathan spluttered. 'I don't employ people; no, not even for a summer job, and especially not some – some child who's wandered in from goodness knows where. And another thing . . .'

Flick's face burned with embarrassment. She hadn't necessarily expected a delighted 'Yes!' and a handshake, but this boy seemed to enjoy going out of his way to be hurtful and rude. She focussed on her shoes to hide her face, concentrating on the dusty floorboards and the spilled ash coming from the fireplace.

Then, something caught her eye. She blinked in surprise. In the grate of the fire, she could see several pieces of broken glass. Smashed. She knelt down to see them more clearly.

Jonathan was bustling around his desk, still wittering away. '. . . perfectly capable of running this place by myself, and more to the point, this isn't a child-friendly environment. I appreciate you think we've formed some sort of deep sentimental bond in the last four minutes, but . . .' he trailed off as Flick stood, a piece of glass between her fingers.

The room seemed to have gone very, very still, as if even the dust motes were frozen in the stuffy air.

'What's this from?' she asked, turning the glass over in her fingers. It was very thick and smooth and there was something pleasing about holding it.

'Be careful,' Jonathan said. 'It's sharp.'

'It feels nice.' Flick lifted it up to see better.

In the fractured triangle of glass, something glittered.

No – *everything* glittered.

A tight feeling of excitement clenched between her ribs. She forgot to breathe.

She raised the glass to her eye.

Through the glass, the world sparkled and shone, shimmered and blurred. It was like looking through a kaleidoscope made of brightly coloured lights. Golden and white droplets floated randomly through the air like snow, drifting this way and that, up and down, left and right. The golden-white flakes twisted as Flick raised a hand to brush through them. The sparkles clung to her skin as she moved her hand, then drifted away again, like fireflies.

Flick felt something like static electricity crackle beneath her skin, and anticipation rose for a moment in her chest, before softening into gentle wonderment.

'What is it?' She lowered the glass and turned slowly, on the spot.

Jonathan was staring at her in open-mouthed astonishment. 'What can you see?'

Flick hesitated. 'It was like . . . like glitter. Shining stuff. What is it?'

'It's a secret.'

The excited feeling in her chest spiralled quickly down her arms and legs. 'A secret?' Flick raised the glass to look through it again. She laughed softly, delight making her feel giddy as the sparkling flakes gathered on her palm before taking off again. It was like catching snow that didn't melt. Like glitter underwater, swirling against an invisible current.

'It's beautiful.' She stopped. Outside the shop, in the yard beyond the bay window, amongst the gentle shimmer of the air, was something else . . . something more. It made her pause and take a step closer, for a better look.

It looked like a crack in some invisible mid-air rock, except that it was *glowing*, like a frozen bolt of lightning. Glowing the same gilded white as the flakes in the air. The jagged bolt hung a few feet off the ground as drops of the glittering stuff floated into it and away from it at the same time.

Flick lowered the shard of glass.

The line in the air vanished.

She raised the glass, and once again the line was there, like a jagged scar in the middle of the street. As she watched, a man walked past, head down as he looked at his phone, and brushed against the glowing line. Flick gasped. The lightning bolt glowed brightly for a moment, but then settled again into soft luminescence. The man didn't seem to have noticed – he didn't even flinch.

Flick turned around to look at Jonathan. 'There's something out there.'

He was staring at her as if she'd fallen through his ceiling. His mouth was still hanging open. He shut it, and seemed to shake himself. 'Out there? More . . . shining stuff?' he said.

'No.' Flick shook her head. 'Well, yeah, there's a lot of that, but there's something else as well. It looks like a lightning bolt in the air. It's a crack. A glowing crack.'

The effect of her words on Jonathan was instantaneous. His hands slipped on the polished wood of the desk, and he almost fell clean out of his chair as he tried to stand up, his legs apparently forgetting how to work. He steadied himself on the desk, and took a deliberate deep breath. 'A crack? In the air?' His voice sounded as though he'd been punched.

Flick nodded, uncertainty taking hold of the excited feeling and squashing it. 'Right there.' She squinted through the glass again, and pointed. 'Out in the street.'

Jonathan swallowed audibly. He came over to the window and fished around in his inside pocket before taking out a very small magnifying glass. He raised it to his own eye, in front of his glasses and squinted through it. 'Right out there, you say?'

'Right there. Above the manhole cover.' Flick watched him, her nerves prickling as he moved the magnifying glass back and forth.

Eventually, he lowered the magnifying glass, and a blank look settled over his face. 'That piece of glass in your hand is from a curiosity. Broken, now. Unfortunately.' He held his hand out for it. 'Swap?'

Flick handed the shard of glass over, and he put the little brass magnifying glass into her palm. It was the size of something you might get out of a Christmas cracker, except when Jonathan put it in Flick's palm she could tell it was made of glass, not plastic. The handle was swirled tortoiseshell and trimmed with brass. The lens itself was shining and yet cloudy at the same time, without a single scratch on it.

Jonathan nodded at it. 'See if that works any better,' he said.

Jonathan was quiet for a moment. There was a tiny frown between his eyebrows, as though he was thinking. 'You can honestly see something in the street?'

'Yes,' she said, starting to get annoyed. 'What is it?'

Jonathan took the tiny instrument back, his eyes unfocussed. 'You can see.' He shook his head as if dislodging the thought. 'Who are you? Where did you come from?'

'I'm Felicity Hudson,' Flick said uncertainly. 'Like I said. We just moved here. We're up on the new estate. I only came in to look around. What's wrong? Is that crack something important?'

Jonathan nodded to himself, as if coming to a decision. 'You will have to take my word for it that it is nothing to be concerned about.' He stood and held out his hand. 'I, er, don't believe I've properly introduced myself. My name's Jonathan Mercator. It's an absolute delight to meet you, Felicity, it really is.'

Flick shook his hand. 'Nice to meet you too.'

'Absolutely,' he said, still shaking her hand. 'You're . . . Well, you're . . .'

She stared.

'You're brilliant,' he said. 'I'm sorry, I'm making a mess of this. I've never actually had to welcome anyone new before. I never thought . . . Well, there's all sorts of formalities, you see. There's things to give you, things to go through, and—'

'What do you mean?' Flick stared.

Jonathan stepped back and held his arms out, as if trying to show off the whole shop at once. 'Welcome,' he grinned, 'to The Strangeworlds Society.'

CHAPTER FOUR

he *what* society?' Flick stared at Jonathan. 'Are you winding me up? Is this going on YouTube?'

Jonathan looked insulted. 'This isn't a joke, I promise you. Not at all. Please, let me explain.' He indicated one of the armchairs for Flick and sat in the other himself. 'You gazed through the lenses and you saw glittery-ness, correct?'

'That's right.' Flick sat on the edge of the cushion, hands gripping the seam. She wondered if she ought to feel nervous, but really she was practically vibrating on the seat with excitement. 'It was everywhere. What is it – a filter?'

'The glass doesn't create the glitter,' he said. 'The glitter is already in the air. The glass merely reveals it.'

Flick glanced around the quiet travel agency. 'Reveals what?'

Jonathan gave a tiny smile. 'Why, magic, of course.'

Flick didn't say anything for a good few seconds. Then she burst out laughing.

Jonathan simply sat there, watching her laugh at him, waiting patiently for her to finish, before shrugging. 'You don't believe in magic.' It wasn't a question. His eyes sparkled behind his spectacles.

Flick instantly felt bad about laughing. 'Magic isn't real,' she said. 'I'm not a kid. You can tell me the truth, you know.'

'Actually, it's adults who often require lies,' he said. 'You've probably been told that magic isn't real because the average person wandering the world believes that to be true. But I can assure you that it is extremely real. It's what you saw through the magnifying glass.'

Flick felt as if she'd missed a step going down the stairs. She shook her head. 'If it was real, everyone would know about it. Everyone would know about those magnifying glasses. They'd be on the news.'

'Not everyone can use them.' Jonathan took the tiny instrument out from his pocket and twirled it in his fingers. 'You see – anyone can walk into this travel agency. The door is opened at nine and locked at five. But not everyone can become a member of The Strangeworlds Society.'

'And what does the society do?'

'We travel.'

'Oh.' Flick stared up at the cases in their pigeon-holes. 'So that's what the cases are for? They really are people's luggage? But what does that have to do with, um, magic?' She tried to sound pleasantly curious, but she was starting to wonder if Jonathan was entirely sane. She glanced at the door, half-wondering if she should get up and leave. Even saying the word 'magic' out loud made her want to squirm.

Jonathan patted a case that was stacked in a tower to the height of the side-table. 'You saw magic in this very room, didn't you? That's because the suitcases are magical.'

'Magical?'

'Indeed.' Jonathan leaned forward, his fingers in a steeple. 'The Strangeworlds Travel Agency doesn't send you to the seaside, or indeed to anywhere you can get to by boat, train or air. We send you to other worlds.'

Flick fought down the temptation to laugh again. 'Other worlds,' she repeated.

'Yes. Each of these suitcases can send you to a different magical world.'

'Right.' She looked up at the wall of suitcases. 'There's one missing,' she pointed out.

'Yes.' Jonathan glanced up. 'It's . . . in use, at the moment.'

She watched his face. He looked entirely serious. And, the embarrassing thing was, Flick actually *wanted* this to be real. She was a heartbeat away from believing him. But . . . 'This is just pretend, isn't it?' she asked.

He shook his head. 'It isn't a game, Felicity. Use the magnifying glass again, if you wish. You're too clever not to trust your own eyes.'

'But magic isn't real!'

'Says who?'

'Says everyone!' Flick folded her arms. She wasn't about to let Jonathan make fun of her. 'I'm not stupid and I'm not a baby. I don't believe in magical suitcases. Or other worlds. Whatever those bits of glass show, it's not magic. It's a trick. Like when someone's grandad makes coins appear from behind your ears. Pulling rabbits out of hats.'

Jonathan grinned. 'I can see you're an expert, so I won't hide anything from you. Let us consider the rabbit-out-of-the-hat trick. Where, let me ask you, does the rabbit come from?'

'Out of the hat,' she frowned.

'But how does it get in there?'

She hesitated. 'I guess . . . someone puts it in? Or it's in the magician's pocket? Or something?'

'Or something.' Jonathan nodded. He got up, went behind the desk, and opened the cabinet-door below the drawers. He stood again, holding an old top hat.

'What's that?' Flick asked.

'Magician's hat,' Jonathan said, giving the crown a quick dust with his hand. 'Obviously. My grandfather found it in the back room. We think it was probably a practical joke from when the travel agency first opened. He used to try and supplement the shop's income by doing children's parties. All that went belly-up when one of the kids stuck their arm into the hat when he left it unattended. Now . . .' Jonathan put the hat down on the desk, made a show of twirling his fingers dramatically, and then stuck a hand inside.

Then his forearm. And then all the way up to his shoulder.

Flick gasped.

Jonathan rummaged around for a moment, then pulled his arm back out; alas, without anything in his hand.

'Must be a slow rabbit day.' He inspected the hat crossly.

Flick shot out of the chair feeling like her whole body was buzzing with shock or fear. 'How . . . how did you do that?' she demanded. 'You stuck your whole arm in!'

He raised his eyebrows. 'How do you think I did it?'

'It's a trick.' Flick shook her head. 'There's a sliding bit on the desk or something.'

He tossed her the hat. 'You try it then.'

Flick stuck her hand in, feeling for the top of the hat, the trick bit that would twist away into a trick compartment where it rested on the desk.

Except it never came. Her hand dropped down into nothing. Her arm was in right up to her shoulder and yet somehow her hand wasn't sticking out of the top. Her fingers brushed against something spiky yet soft. She yelped, and flung the hat away. 'There's something in there!'

'It's only grass,' Jonathan said. 'The rabbits eat it, I expect.'

Flick bent down and picked the hat up. It was slightly dusty, with a faded green velvet ribbon above the brim. Ordinary. But . . . she thought again about the glittering dust in the air. The stuff Jonathan had said was magic.

This is real, a voice said inside her. *This is actually, properly, real.*

Flick didn't know whether to laugh or cry. She could feel a sort of kernel of hysteria threatening to pop in her chest. She peeped into the hat, half-expecting to see floppy ears and whiskers pointing back at her. 'You're telling me that rabbits live in that hat?'

'Don't be so absurd. Of course they don't live *in* the hat,' Jonathan said, picking the hat up and waving it around impatiently. 'Use your head.'

Flick stared at the twirling headgear. If it had shot into the air like a helicopter she wouldn't have been surprised. 'It *goes* somewhere?' she said.

'Yes. In a manner of speaking,' Jonathan said. He put the hat down and cast a hand around at the suitcase-stacked shelves. 'And it isn't the only thing that goes somewhere. Every single one of these suitcases leads to a different place.'

The excitement-kernel in Flick's chest exploded. She gripped the back of one of the armchairs, her legs feeling as though they might give way in shock. She knew her mouth was open, but she didn't care. 'The suitcases take you to other places? How?'

'You simply step inside.'

Disbelief gave way to fiery curiosity and Flick shot over to the wall of suitcases as though she was on a track. *They take you to other places*? 'And you go to ... like ... like ... to another dimension?' She touched one of the handles with the tips of her fingers.

'Don't be absurd,' Jonathan snorted. 'You go to other worlds in the multiverse.'

'Multiverse. Not *uni*verse?'

'Correct. Within each case is a schism – a tear in the fabric of reality – that acts as a gateway from our world to another.' He put his hand back into the hat. This time, his eyes went wide, and he drew his arm out.

In his hand, caught by the scruff of the neck, was a white rabbit, looking somewhat nonplussed, a dandelion hanging out of its mouth.

'There,' Jonathan said proudly. 'I told you so.'

CHAPTER FIVE

Once the rabbit was safely returned to the top
hat, Flick sat in the window-seat and
considered her options. Her first instinct was
to ask one hundred million questions. Her
second was to try and be logical, to try and make sense
of it all. *If magic was real . . .* It felt as if her entire
world had been knocked off-balance. She wanted to
run out of the travel agency and ask everyone if they
knew. Could there really be a secret this big?

Jonathan watched her internal wrangling for a
moment, and then went to put the kettle on. He made a
pot of tea and brought it out on a tray with some cups
and an actual milk jug, like he was someone's grandma.
After going through a complicated routine with a
tea-strainer and half a dozen spoons, he held out a china

cup of tea. 'For the shock,' he said, presenting Flick with it and a plate of plastic-pink ring biscuits.

Flick swallowed some of the tea, wishing there was sugar in it and fewer flecks of black from the loose-leaf tea. She looked around her, at the piles of cases, the suitcases set into the walls, the big trunk on the floor. Flick thought it felt quite homely. And yet hiding such a secret. A secret she knew! Flick squashed down the urge to wriggle in delight. She felt as if she was carrying the secret in her pocket, like a pet. 'So,' she said at last.

'So.' Jonathan folded himself back into the opposite armchair.

'These suitcases are full of other worlds?' Saying it out loud made Flick want to laugh nervously, but Jonathan looked utterly serious.

'Yes.' He sipped from his own cup. 'It's my responsibility to look after them. I'm the Head Custodian.'

'Just you? I thought you said there was a Society?'

'Oh, there is.' He nodded. 'But only one Head Custodian. I make sure everyone else in the Society does as they're meant to.'

'And what's that?'

'To "*do right by all manner of worlds with regards to the laws and practices of their realm and ours*",' he reeled off. 'That's part of the pledge members take when they become part of The Strangeworlds Society.'

Flick stared in confusion. 'And what does that mean?'

Jonathan's mouth twitched. 'It means that Society members promise to look after all the worlds they visit, as well as this one. And to respect the laws or rules of wherever they travel to.'

Flick pointed at the neatly framed photographs on the wall. 'Were they all members of The Strangeworlds Society?'

'Yes, some of the very first. The Society is one hundred and forty-seven years old, you know.'

Flick gazed at the people in their walking boots, knitted hats and weatherproof coats. 'They look like explorers.'

'That's because they are. Were,' Jonathan corrected himself. 'There are hundreds of suitcases here, and therefore hundreds of worlds. They all need to be taken care of. That wall commemorates some of the bravest explorers The Strangeworlds Society has ever had. They discovered worlds, had adventures . . .'

'Had adventures?' Flick repeated, before she could stop herself.

Jonathan nodded. 'A lot of adventures.'

Flick sipped her tea. *Adventures* . . . She thought of the map on her bedroom wall, with one single country ticked off, and a hot feeling of *want* made her grip the china cup tight in her hands.

Jonathan flicked a speck of something off the arm of the chair. 'I can't tell what you're thinking. Are you planning to leave and never come back?'

Flick put her cup down. 'I don't know.'

Jonathan's face fell slightly.

'Look, this is all bonkers,' Flick said. 'And if it's real then it changes everything, doesn't it?'

Jonathan didn't say anything.

Flick thought for a moment. 'You said not everyone sees glitter through those magnifying glasses, right?'

'Correct.'

'But I can.' Flick looked at her hands, remembering the delight of weaving them through the white-gold sparkles in the air. 'What does that mean?'

Jonathan crossed his legs. 'It means you're special, Felicity. Magically gifted, like me. Like everyone in those pictures. You're one of us. You're part of The Strangeworlds Society. Or you could be,' he added. 'If you wanted to.'

Flick swallowed. She felt as if she was starting to drown in information. 'Do I have to? I mean, what would happen if I walked out and left, like you said?'

Jonathan's face twitched. 'I'd be disappointed. It's been a long, long time since anyone new came into the travel agency and saw magic. I was beginning to think I was the last.'

Flick bit her lip to hide a smile. She was special. The feeling made her chest fizz. She was bursting to know everything – what powers she had, how the suitcases worked. But it was as though the questions in her head were like butterflies battering themselves at a window, unable to find the way out. 'This is so weird,' she said instead.

Jonathan raised an eyebrow. 'And what's wrong with weird, Felicity? What would you rather have? An average life? What's that, exactly? Washing dishes? Going shopping? Watching the television? Going to a job you hate and falling asleep on the sofa at the end of the day, never doing half the things you dream about?'

Flick could feel a blush creeping over her cheeks. 'No,' she said quietly. 'No, I know what that's like, already.'

Jonathan gave her a look she couldn't quite read. 'Wait one moment, please.' He got up, and went over to the bookcase behind the desk, selecting a very worn-looking book with a soft leather cover and bringing it back over. 'Here. I would like you to borrow this. Forgive the condition; it's quite old.'

'What's this?' Flick opened it. A striking title page greeted her, printed in several different fonts. '*A Study of Particulars In Regards to The Strangeworlds Society.*'

'Exactly.' Jonathan smiled.

'What's *A Study of Particulars*?' Flick turned a few more pages. The book was filled with pages of printed text and maps and charts, and occasionally there was tight copperplate handwriting in the margins.

'It's a guide to The Strangeworlds Society, to the travel agency, to suitcases, and magic. It was quite thin, to begin with.' He leaned over and carefully turned the pages back to the start. 'Look.' Flick saw that there was a section of pages that looked quite different – a slim volume with age-softened pages stuck, with thick yellow glue, into the newer leather cover. 'The society members expanded on it as they went along, having new pages printed, updating it as their numbers and responsibilities grew. You'll need to read it, to become a Strangeworlds Society member.'

Flick turned the pages, and saw a couple of pencilled maps, as well as properly printed names and lists and charts of all kinds alongside the professionally printed pages. Jonathan was beaming at her as though he'd given her a wonderful present, but Flick felt rather unsure about it. The book somehow felt very heavy in her hands, as though it was weighted down with expectation. 'I don't know if I should take this,' she said.

Jonathan's delight blinked into surprise. 'Why ever not? Don't you want to know more about what makes you special?'

'I'm not sure I am, though.' She held the book out. 'I'm not . . . magical.'

Jonathan ignored the offered book. 'You saw the magic with your own eyes.'

'I only saw some special glass,' Flick said, knowing even as she said it that that wasn't true.

Jonathan raked a hand through his hair. 'You saw magic through those magnifying lenses, Felicity. You know you did. Look. I understand this must be overwhelming, but I don't think either of us wants you to walk out of that door and never return.'

They stared at one another.

Jonathan sighed. 'Please, just read it.' He pushed the book back towards her. 'You don't have to agree to join the Society right away. You can even come back and ask more questions, if you're not sure.'

'But I don't know if I want—'

'Something made you come into the travel agency,' he interrupted. 'I'm too much of a cynic to believe in fate. But you took that shard of glass from the ashes. You saw magic through it. Those are the facts, Felicity. This . . . this is a place you belong.'

Flick looked at the book in her hands. She didn't know what to do. And the fact she didn't know made her feel strange. This wasn't a problem to be solved; this was choosing to be part of something she didn't really understand.

'I can show you what's *inside* the cases, Felicity,' Jonathan said softly. 'You could travel to places you could never have imagined, see worlds on the edge of the multiverse. You could watch blue suns rise over mountains of red glass, see flowers the size of houses, hear the crunch of the ground as dragons hatch from hidden caverns, and feel the heat in the emptiness of space as a ship cruises close to a dying star. You could see it all, Felicity. And more.' He spread his hands. 'You've got something, Felicity. I am pleased to have met you, even if this is to be but a very short friendship.'

Flick tried to think. None of this made sense. But there was no denying she'd seen a rabbit pulled out of a hat in the middle of a dusty old travel agency, and something magical afloat on the air. And then there were all these suitcases . . .

She gripped the book tight.

This was madness. The farthest her family had been on holiday was to the seaside, a couple of hours away. She wanted to travel yes, but she'd thought she'd start by going to France or maybe Spain. The idea of travelling to whole other worlds was ridiculous. And besides, she didn't have the time. She had to help her parents sort the house and take care of Freddy and prepare for school in the autumn –

No.

Flick shook her head. That was her parents talking. That's what they expected her to do. She looked again at the leather-bound book in her hands. She ran a thumb over the cover, feeling the softness of the grain. The pages creaked as she moved it in her hands.

What would it be like, she wondered, *to watch a blue sun rise over a mountain of red glass?* A spark of something like excitement rose in her belly, as if the glittering magic in the air was inside her.

'So . . . what happens if I do come back?'

'I'll show you what magic can really do,' Jonathan said.

Flick stood, holding the book in both hands. 'I'll think about it.'

'Do,' Jonathan said.

Flick gave him a nod. She went out without looking back, flinching slightly at the heavy clunk of the door as it closed behind her.

She stepped onto the pavement and blinked as the noise of the road, the thunderous chatter of people, and the smells of *busyness* all smashed into her like a wave knocking against a ship.

She stared back at the travel agency with the wall of cases just visible inside and then at the book she held in her hands.

It felt as though she had already stepped into a different world.

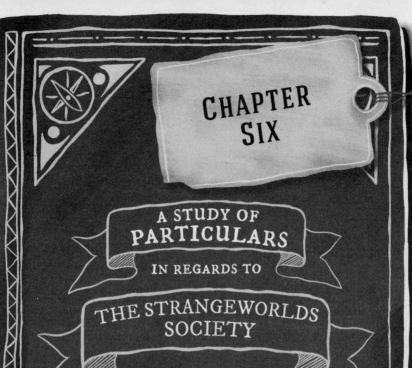

CHAPTER SIX

A STUDY OF PARTICULARS

IN REGARDS TO

THE STRANGEWORLDS SOCIETY

Being a Treatise of Rules and Regulations
laid down by Founder Members Miss Elara Mercator
& Mister Henry L'Estrange of Little Wyverns,
in the County of Nottinghamshire

A HOST OF IMPORTANT FACTS TO
CONSIDER AND STANDARDS TO MAINTAIN
WHEN EMBARKING ON YOUR VOYAGE
AS A MEMBER OF
THE STRANGEWORLDS SOCIETY

Welcome, traveller,
for you are amongst friends.

The Strangeworlds Society is an organisation established and maintained for the purposes of exploring and preserving new worlds. The responsibility of our cause and purpose is demonstrated by the oath below, which must be taken by each new member of the Society, once they have proven their Sight:

> *I, [applicant's full name], do hereby swear that I will well and truly serve The Strangeworlds Society. I will uphold its secrets and do right by all manner of worlds with regards to the laws and practices of their realm and ours. I will chart, respect and protect new worlds without fear, favour, ill will or affection.*

To be a Custodian of new worlds is a duty and a privilege given to few. It is a chance offered only to those who have proved they possess the ability to see magic, via the lenses in the possession of existing members. Travellers to new worlds have an obligation to record facts and evidences about the world, for future consumption by other Society members.

Flick turned the page.

Established in 1873 by Miss Elara Mercator and Mister Henry L'Estrange, The Strangeworlds Society has been based at the travel agency of the same name, in Little Wyverns, since 1895. The travel agency has existed as both a gathering place and a home for the suitcases that enable other-worldly travel (see page 10).

She quickly turned to page ten.

ON THE SUBJECT OF SUITCASES AND THE SCHISM PHENOMENON

The phenomenon of schisms is one that continues to demand study. We currently understand the following:

1. Schisms are gateways to other worlds.
2. Schisms are alive and feed on magical energy.
3. Schisms can be contained (for example, within suitcases). Note: to date, only Elara Mercator has possessed the ability to move a schism and to contain it within a suitcase.
4. Schisms are known to (and used by) others outside of the Society.

Let us examine each point above in more detail.

1. Schisms are gateways to other worlds.

We do not, despite what modern science claims, live in a singular universe. Rather, our world (which includes our planet, sun, stars, et cetera) is part of a much broader multiverse. There are many other worlds besides our own in the multiverse, and each one must be properly explored and written about in a non-romantic fashion. We are not, as some have assumed, the rightful lords of new lands – we are merely travellers. seeking peace and understanding.

Flick read the page twice. Those suitcases at Strangeworlds ... each one was a gateway to somewhere magical. Every single one.

She continued reading.

2. Schisms are alive and feed on magical energy.

Schisms are wounds in the skin of the world. They bleed magic to and fro. If left loose in the air, they will eventually clot and close, much like a wound in human skin.

3. Schisms can be contained (for example, within suitcases).

If given a durable and fixed space to inhabit, schisms become dormant and restful. During her lifetime Miss Mercator enclosed in excess of 100 schisms in suitcases, allowing safe and reliable travel to other worlds in the multiverse. The ability to move and contain schisms has not yet been demonstrated by anyone else.

Flick wondered about Elara Mercator. Imagine being the only person who could do something so extraordinary. Had she tried to teach people? And who had taught *her*?

4. Schisms are known to (and used by) others outside of the Society. There is more to the purpose of The Strangeworlds Travel Agency than tourism and exploration. This study has a purpose. For although humans cannot use schisms to travel without having them first contained within a suitcase, we are not the only travellers between worlds. There are others, outside our Society and our home world, who also travel the multiverse, using magic more fearsome than our own.

And it is The Strangeworlds Society's sworn duty to protect every world we know of.

Flick's stomach went cold. There was something very menacing about that last part. Fearsome magic did not sound impressive – it sounded like something to be wary of. Feeling more than a little nervous, she quickly turned a few more pages, wanting some distance between herself and those words. She was still intrigued by Elara Mercator and wanted to find out more about her, but there didn't seem to be a page dedicated to the mysterious travel agency founder's life. Flick flipped through the book again, and this time a different heading caught her eye.

On the Subject of Magical Sight

Not everyone possesses the ability to see magic. And magic may only be seen through using one of Miss Mercator's magnifying glasses. Many believe that the talent for Magical Sight is inherited – and that certainly seems to be true of The Strangeworlds Society members. Seeing magic through a magnifying lens is not something that can be taught. Those who cannot see magic may still be granted membership of The Strangeworlds Society – this is at the discretion of the currently serving Head Custodian.

Magical Sight has been a feature of folklore for many centuries. In the northern countries of the world in particular, a belief in the faerie and the elvish still exists. In Icelandic legend, seers believed they could look through hag-stones, horses' bridles or even under their own arm to reveal what they called the *Unseen*. Our magnifying lenses have taken the place of such superstition, though these old traditions bring to mind the question of whether or not these people knew of schisms, and who or what they were referring to by the *Unseen*.

It is possible that there are greater mysteries out in the multiverse still to be revealed.

A sudden chill ran down Flick's spine and over her

skin like a breath of cold wind. She remembered the sight of that glittering scar in the air and the dusting of magic floating around it like fireflies drifting on a breeze. It hadn't felt eerie at the time, but rather calming, satisfying almost, like when she applied a formula to a maths problem and saw all the numbers fall into place.

But what were the *Unseen*? Were they real? Or nothing but an old bit of folklore?

She turned back to the start of the book and scanned to the bottom of one of the pages.

. . . we are not the only travellers between worlds.

Flick touched a finger to the word 'we'. *That's me, as well*, she thought. *I'm one of them. I could be.* She looked over at her map, at all those places she had never been, and felt an ache in her chest.

'I will be,' she whispered.

CHAPTER SEVEN

'**Y**ou came back,' Jonathan said as Flick walked into the shop the next day. He looked up from sweeping the floor to give her a wide and slightly self-satisfied smile. He was wearing brown tartan trousers, with a mustard-coloured shirt and a waistcoat that was a bit too big for him. It had an embroidered peacock on the back.

Flick closed the door behind her. It had been easy to come back. Her parents were at work, and Freddy was at day-care. As soon as her mother's bus had vanished down the road, she'd almost run through the estate to get into the village. She had *A Study of Particulars* in her backpack, along with a water bottle and a banana. There was a box of plasters in the front zip pocket, as well as a change of socks and pants. If she was going travelling today, she wanted to be ready. 'Yes. Is that sand on the floor?' Flick asked, as she stepped forward and it crunched under her purple Converse.

'Oh, yes,' Jonathan sighed despondently.

'Did you go to a beach or something?'

'Heavens, no. Not so much a beach as a desert. Some people can't even be trusted to give their boots a shake out before they come back.'

Jonathan tapped the dustpan out into a steel waste-bin and put it and the broom to one side. Flick tried to think of what to say.

'I read that book,' she said.

'And?'

There was a beat of silence. The travel agency stirred in the warm summer air, and above their heads, the floorboards creaked.

Flick took a deep breath. 'I want to travel.'

Without saying a word, Jonathan came around the desk, and went over to the suitcase wall. He took hold of a handle and pulled. A suitcase of dark blue, with bright violet trim, came free from the wall. Jonathan looked at Flick. 'This is as good a place as any to start.'

'We're going now?' she asked, her bravado deflating like an escaped balloon in the face of how fast things seemed to be moving. 'Right this second?

Jonathan put the case down. 'It's not dangerous,' he promised. He tried to open the case, then realised it was back to front and had to turn it over. 'Good start.' He rolled his eyes at himself, and Flick hid a grin, despite the cloud of butterflies starting to swarm in her stomach. Jonathan pressed the silvery catches again and this time the lid of the suitcase popped open. A cool sort of emptiness floated from within the case, as though he had opened a window in the musty shop, and fresh air was filtering through.

Flick stepped forward and stopped, blinking as light cascaded out of the case. It was the same sort of swirling pink that her slice of agate created when it was on the top of her bedside lamp. It felt familiar and yet eerie, like seeing your reflection in the mirror move one fraction of a second too late.

'Don't be frightened,' said Jonathan, misreading her wide eyes.

Flick stood in front of the case, letting the breeze from another world kiss her face. She could hear her own heartbeat thumping in her ears. 'So, how do I get inside? Jump?'

'*We* just climb in,' Jonathan said, tucking the blade of his tie between two shirt buttons. 'One foot at a time. Feel for the ground before you take a second step. And keep your eyes open, even if you feel dizzy.'

'All right.' Flick gritted her teeth and stood, raising a foot to step into the case. 'Sounds easy enough. Which probably means it's incredibly difficult.'

'You'll be absolutely fine. Try not to overthink it. And when you get through, don't wander off,' Jonathan warned. 'You go first. I'll be right behind you.'

Flick nodded.

She took a deep breath, gripped the straps of her backpack tight, and stepped down into the suitcase.

The world tipped on its axis.

She went from stepping down to stepping *up* without changing the motion of her legs, so she was both simultaneously climbing into the suitcase and out of it. She could smell trees and woodland, but she could hear Jonathan back in Strangeworlds, and she could somehow see both places at once, and –

A hand gently pushed at her back, and she stepped again; this time her legs were going both into and out of the case at the same time, and everything was doubled and there were two of Flick and two of the worlds, and then –

Then she was standing.

Standing alone, in a different world.

CHAPTER EIGHT

It was a beautiful woodland, though unlike any forest Flick had ever seen before.

It was hot, almost tropical in temperature, and the air was heavy with moisture. The sky, where it could be seen through the thick canopy of oversized, violet-veined leaves, was a blue so deep it was almost black, though it wasn't night.

Flick looked down at her feet, and realised she wasn't standing on the ground at all. She had stepped onto a very thick, flat section of black tree branch. Looking down further, she could see that the thick boughs of the trees snaked and knotted below her, each of the branches wide and smooth enough to be a walkway.

The ground could have been three hundred feet below.

The smooth, dark trunks of the trees, each one wider than a bus, grew up through the interlocking web of branches. And growing on the bark, like moss or lichen, were small glowing crystals. Some were tiny, no bigger than a grain of sand, but others were as long as a pencil, and growing upward, their cloudy, cracked interiors glimmering delicately.

Flick laughed softly in wonder. The crystals glowed brighter as she reached for them, as if delighted to see her, happy to put on a show of illumination. When she touched them, she was surprised to find them cool and smooth under her fingers.

Behind her, there was a gentle cry and the soft sound of feathers. She turned to see a bird, no larger than a magpie, but with purple and gold tail feathers as long as she was tall, watching her from a branch. It ruffled its wings, the long feathers glittering as if they too were made of crystal.

Perhaps they were.

Jonathan stepped out of the case then, unfolding himself like a particularly well-dressed deckchair and staggering upright. 'Oh, it's not changed much,' he smiled, smoothing his hair down.

The bird squawked and took off, sailing over their heads before disappearing amongst the twisted tree branches. The crystals on the trees glowed a deep plum.

'We're in another world.' Flick stared around, the truth of the matter starting to feel a bit heavy. She wanted to sit down. 'We're in a whole other world. Just like you said. Where – where are we?'

'I don't know if it has a proper name,' Jonathan said. 'But I always called it the Crystal Forest.'

The quartz encrusted on the tree bark seemed to twinkle appreciatively, brightening from peach to pink as he spoke.

Flick touched a leaf that was the size of a table. 'How do we know what time it is? Is it night?'

'Remember the clocks on the mantelpiece, back at the travel agency? Each one of those corresponds to a different world time. My watch,' Jonathan tapped his wrist, 'is permanently set to our own time.' He showed her the watch face and she saw that the second hand was speeding around faster than normal. 'Time here moves slower than our own time, so my watch ticks faster. A minute here might be the equivalent of a quarter of an hour back home. It's essential to keep track of the time at home to avoid going missing for days without realising.'

'Are all worlds slower than our own?'

'Oh, no. Some are the same. A great many are faster.' He gazed around at the leaves reaching out all around them. 'What do you think?'

'It's beautiful. It's so . . .' She couldn't think of anything else to say. The new world was wrapped around her, welcoming and divine. The heavy air smelled of heat and leaves, like the inside of a greenhouse, and the gentle chatter of birdsong floated through the air. The darkness of the Crystal Forest whispered to her of mystery, of hidden adventure.

The crystals glimmered again, in a pleased sort of way.

Flick sudden burst out laughing. 'I'm in another world!' she cried, grabbing hold of the closest tree branch and hugging it. She felt as if she might burst from the sheer joy of it. She couldn't remember the last time she'd felt this happy. Flick squeezed the branch again, before letting go, and looking up at the umbrella of leaves hiding the sky. 'It's really real!'

'As real as anything else,' Jonathan said. 'Now, before we go anywhere, I have to show you something important.' He knelt down in front of the case. 'Reach with me.'

Flick did as she was told, feeling into the nothingness in the case. And then, she felt something smooth and wooden. 'Is that the floorboards of the agency?' she asked. The sensation of touching her own world through another was utterly bizarre.

'Yes. Now, come back this way ...' Jonathan's hand touched her own, pushed her fingers back, guiding her over to –

'The suitcase handle?' Flick frowned. 'But how can the handle be—'

'Grab it. And pull. Now!'

She did so, gripping onto the handle, Jonathan's hand next to her own.

Their hands drew back into the Crystal Forest world, the suitcase handle still grasped tight. The case turned inside out, yet somehow right way round at the same time, as it was dragged into the crystal world with a *SNAP*. The catches closed, and the two of them stood, smiling in a dazed sort of way, holding the suitcase they had stepped into.

'See?' Jonathan beamed. 'Easy as that.'

'And ... that's the case we just went into?' Flick frowned, letting go.

'Yes. And we'll go through it to get back.' Jonathan adjusted his grip. 'Think of the suitcase as a hallway between two doors. By pulling the suitcase through after us, we've closed one of the doors. Now no one can follow us, see?'

Flick's brain was trying so hard to keep up it was making her go cross-eyed. 'So we could have left it in Strangeworlds?'

'Correct. But, when I travel, I don't like my suitcase to be in two places at once, so I try to remember to pull it through with me. I like the security.'

'But how can it be here, if this world was inside it? And now our world is inside it?' She blinked. 'What happens if someone sits on it?' Flick's train of logic had derailed several minutes ago.

Jonathan rolled his eyes. 'Honestly, Felicity. If you want sense, you've come to the wrong place. Now, take this.' He handed her the magnifying glass that she had looked through on her first visit to the agency.

'Lift it.'

Flick turned the little instrument over in her fingers. It felt so comfortable in her grip. She held it up to her eye.

The dark world of crystal exploded into a kaleidoscope of drifting colour. Each stick of quartz shone brilliantly, rainbows dancing from every facet. The dark trees looked bolder, brightness poured from the enormous leaves of the trees like liquid light and the world dripped with colour.

'It's gorgeous,' she whispered. She looked up at the canopy of branches, the joy of seeing magic pouring through the air making her smile wide. 'Can you see this?'

'I could, if I used that instrument. That magnifying glass is made using these crystals,' Jonathan said. 'It reacts to them. It's like coming home . . .' He put his hands in his pockets. 'This is an intensely magical place.'

Flick squinted through the lens. 'I can see something else . . .'

Amongst the tree branches, too far to reach, but close enough to see, was a shimmering line in the air. It was about the length of Flick's forearm, and thin as the edge of a knife-blade, but it glittered and shone so invitingly it was all she could do to keep her feet still on the branch.

Jonathan followed her gaze. 'What can you see?'

'I don't know.' She turned to Jonathan. 'It looks like the crack I saw in the street, outside the travel agency.'

'It's a schism,' Jonathan said.

Flick remembered what she had read in the Study of Particulars. 'And schisms are . . . gateways to other worlds?'

'Schisms are what are contained within each of the Strangeworlds suitcases. Wounds in the skin of the multiverse. They are places where the boundaries between the worlds are thin.'

She lowered the magnifying glass. 'Thin enough to step through?'

'Certainly not.' Jonathan's expression changed, and he instantly looked ferocious. 'You cannot use a schism to travel between worlds unless it is contained within a suitcase. It is absolutely beyond forbidden. For your own safety. It would almost certainly kill you, if you tried.'

Flick almost dropped the magnifying glass as undiluted fear shot through her veins. She stepped backwards, away from the schism she had seen and bumped hard into a thick branch behind her. 'Kill me? Why? How?'

Jonathan sighed. 'Like I said, schisms are wounds,' he explained. 'Wounds where worlds have collided. A cut in the skin of our reality. For a cut on your skin to heal, it bleeds and clots. Schisms heal in a similar way. They do so slowly, taking small bits of magical energy from the surrounding worlds over time to clot and close up gradually. Left alone, they are harmless.'

'But?' Flick prompted, knowing there was more.

'But,' Jonathan said, 'if you were to try to step through it, the schism would help itself to every single drop of magic from *you*, to heal itself.'

Flick shuddered. 'That's . . . evil.'

'They're not deliberately malicious,' Jonathan said. 'They're like sponges. They absorb magic they come into contact with and living things have a great deal of it. If you tried to step through, the schism would close, seal up, and you would be gone.'

'Dead?'

'Not only dead. Erased from existence. Your atoms, everything that holds you together, everything that fuels your memories would be gone. There would be nothing left of you. A gap in the multiverse, where you ought to be.'

An icy silence followed.

'But I saw a man in the street brush against one,' Flick said, after a moment. 'He didn't . . . disappear. But . . . it did glow brighter, after he touched it.'

'There is a difference between touching a schism and trying to cross through one,' Jonathan said. 'There's more to magic than accident. Whatever schisms are, they know our intentions. And to try to cross through one is to invite catastrophe.'

Flick swallowed. 'People have tried it, then?'

'Yes. In the past.' He shrugged. 'I wanted to warn you and now I have.'

Flick contemplated the precious world around her. 'So, this is what you do? You show people other worlds?'

'Correct,' said Jonathan. 'I send people travelling all over the worlds. Worlds like this. The Strangeworlds Travel Agency doesn't sell holidays. We sell wonder.'

Flick badly needed to sit down. She did so, folding her legs up and parking herself against the nearest tree trunk. It was surprisingly warm. 'But why me?' she asked. 'I'm just . . . me.'

Jonathan sat down as well and stroked a patch of crystal. It lit up bright white under his touch, then faded quickly back to a subtle glimmer. '*Just?* Felicity, you can see magic. You can see schisms. You couldn't be *just* anything if you tried. And as for the why . . .' He sighed. 'Being part of The Strangeworlds Society means taking care of what we have. We look after other worlds and the connections between them. We are Custodians. We are Cartographers.'

'Cartographers?'

'Mapmakers. We map the routes through the suitcases. No one wants to lose their way home.'

'Can that happen?'

'Not if you still have your suitcase in your hand.' He quirked an eyebrow. 'Don't lose your luggage.'

Flick had an urge to take the suitcase out of his hand, just to be sure she had it safe. Instead, she turned her face to the dark blue sky. 'You said you had to look after the worlds. What does that mean?'

'My father told me what I know. There is a balance of schism and magic. Like two weights on one of those brass scales. In most worlds, the weights are equal, or slightly in favour of magic. But,' he took a breath, 'there have been instances, on occasion, of people taking more from a world than they should.'

'Taking what?'

'Magic,' Jonathan said bluntly. 'Like all other energies, it can be used. And it can be used up.'

A queasy feeling lodged itself into Flick's stomach. 'And what happens if it's used up?'

'World-collapse.'

Flick didn't need to ask what this meant. Even the sound of it made her feel sick. 'Can't you stop them?' she asked.

'How can you stop anyone whose greed is destroying their world?' Jonathan asked. 'If you can't convince them of wrongdoing, the only course would be direct action. In one of our history books, there's an account of a Society member trapping a villain inside a suitcase. Remove the problem at the source, you see. Can you imagine what might happen if these cases were to fall into the wrong hands? The sort of carnage you could unleash if you brought back a creature from another world? Or a weapon? Or a *person*?' He shuddered.

Flick swallowed hard. 'That's . . .'

'Nothing like that has been necessary for many, *many* years,' Jonathan said quickly. 'Which is probably why The Strangeworlds Society has become almost obsolete. A long time ago, there were dozens of members, and they worked for the agency, helped to map the connections between the worlds, monitor the flow of magic to and from schisms. But now things have changed. It would be all too easy to let the whole enterprise go; but how can I, when it's my responsibility to look after everything?' He raked his fingers over his scalp.

Flick felt a jolt of sympathy. 'What would happen if you just quit Strangeworlds?' she asked.

Jonathan looked rather grim. 'There must always be a Head Custodian. There must. Can you imagine what some people would do if they had access to multiple, unguarded worlds to exploit?'

Flick's stomach clenched. She nodded. It was all too easy to imagine the sort of greed that would be inspired by the magical suitcases.

'I need help,' Jonathan said softly. 'I can't take care of Strangeworlds on my own.'

Flick glanced at the suitcase in Jonathan's hand. It suddenly looked extremely heavy.

CHAPTER NINE

They walked steadily through the woodland, the slippery smoothness of the trees' boughs making them take small, careful steps. Occasionally, one of the shimmering birds would fly across the path. As they walked, the quartz in the trees took on a pale blue hue, some of the crystals sporting little caps and rivulets of gold. The trees' leaves shrank as they climbed upwards. They were still great fanning things, the size of encyclopaedias, thick as cardboard but pliable as rubber.

'So, some people know about the agency, don't they?' Flick asked. 'The ones who pay to travel.'

'There are enough Society members to pay the bills, and that's about it. They help keep the records updated – I insist they take the book that corresponds to the suitcase they're using, so they can make notes about it. But there are so few of them, and so many worlds . . .' Jonathan rubbed absently at the curls at the back of his neck. 'My biggest worry is that someone will put something on the internet and one day I'll wake up in a tiny room with a two-way mirror staring at me.'

'Do you have a family?' Flick asked. She held tight onto the thought of her own. It was both comforting, and something she didn't want to mention. A mum, a dad, a baby brother . . . they seemed too normal to invite into this conversation, or even into this strange world.

'Until very recently, I had my father.' Jonathan stopped walking. 'However—' His mouth shut, as if he was afraid something would escape from it.

Sympathy welled up inside Flick. The little bubble of resentment she felt over Jonathan's obvious poshness went 'pop'. When it came to things that were really valuable, she had a lot more than he did. 'I'm sorry. Did your dad . . .'

'He's not dead,' Jonathan said fiercely. 'He'll come back to me. I know he will. I . . .' He stopped. 'I'm sorry. I didn't mean to snap.'

'It's OK.' Flick looked away as Jonathan gave his glasses a furious clean. She wanted to ask a lot more questions – about where Jonathan's dad had gone in the first place, for starters – but she knew now wasn't the time.

She looked back as Jonathan forced a smile.

They went a little further. The world was quiet, though not silent – the quietness seemed to come from the stillness of the air and the soft glow of the crystals.

Flick sat down on a hump of tree branch and a butterfly the size of a Labrador came and perched on her knee. It weighed almost nothing. The insect had wings like wafer-thin slices of a geode; the white crackle of the centre fanned out into mirrored, ever-increasing circles of colour.

No one in her world would believe her if she told them. She could take the butterfly home, of course, and be rich . . . but that was what Jonathan meant. Just because something was full of riches, didn't mean you had to try and take them for yourself. The suitcases did need looking after.

Jonathan pushed his glasses up his nose and checked his watch. 'Are you ready to go back?'

Flick stood, and the butterfly took off, flapping its wings in a slightly disgruntled way before vanishing beneath the twinkling trees. 'If we have to. I guess we just step in again?'

'Correct.' Jonathan opened the case. He looked at Flick and made an 'after you' gesture.

She took a breath and stepped back into her own world.

*

When they were back, Flick borrowed Jonathan's magnifying glass again, and looked around at the soft glittering glow of the travel agency. The suitcase they had travelled through seemed especially bright.

'I'll make us some tea,' said Jonathan.

Flick looked around the front room of the travel agency again while Jonathan rattled around in the kitchen. She gave a smile at the photographs on the wall, feeling a sort of camaraderie with the explorers – the Strangeworlds Society members – who looked proudly out of their frames. Though the pictures were in black and white, one or two of the subjects looked familiar. They must be Jonathan's family.

'Jonathan,' she called, 'can I ask what happened to your dad?'

Jonathan peered around the doorframe from the kitchen. 'You can ask.' He came through, drying his hands, having washed out a couple of mugs. 'I was at boarding school by then and he was working at the agency, as Head Custodian. I had a call from the bookshop next door. They hadn't seen my dad in a while. I came home to find out what had happened, and . . . he was gone.' He trailed off. 'He won't have left me.'

'How long has it been?' Flick asked quietly.

Jonathan paused, turning back to the kitchen area. 'A couple of months.' He disappeared into the back of the shop.

Months? Even Flick knew that was a long time for someone missing to come back.

Jonathan came back through, stuffing a handkerchief into his sleeve. 'Kettle's on.'

Flick decided to change the subject. 'Are all the worlds linked?'

He brightened slightly. 'In a way, all the worlds of the multiverse are linked. The trick is knowing how to get where you want to go. We wouldn't get far without a map.' He pushed his glasses up his nose, and leaned on the desk in what he probably hoped was a casual way. 'Now you've made a journey through a suitcase, I don't suppose you feel like taking a pledge, at all?'

Flick's smile twisted into an uncertainty. 'You said it can be dangerous.'

Jonathan shrugged. 'So's crossing the road.'

Flick had to agree. 'But what if—'

BEEP BEEP BEEP BEEP BEEP –

'Oh, pants, that's my alarm.' Flick fished her phone out. 'I need to get back, I've got to pick Freddy up.'

'Freddy?'

'My baby brother.'

'Oh, so you're not an only child,' Jonathan said. 'Well, that's good. For your parents, I mean.' He went to hold the door open. 'Don't stay away too long,' he said as she darted past. 'You're needed.'

CHAPTER
TEN

Flick stayed up late that night, reading more of the *Study of Particulars* by the pink agate-light of her bedside lamp.

The previous contributors to the book (and there were clearly many based on the variety of handwriting) had treated it like a scrapbook, sticking in drawings and photographs and tickets. There were three names jotted neatly on the first page:

Property of:

Anthony Mercator, 1900

Juliet Mercator, 1970

Aspen Thatcher, 1982

And there were scribbles and inky fingerprints here

and there in the margins. There was even a very faded and brown photograph of the front of Strangeworlds, with a dozen people stood outside it in what Flick thought was Victorian dress. They weren't smiling, though one of the gentlemen had his hat raised in apparent cheerfulness.

Flick only realised how late it was when she heard her dad's alarm go off at 3:30am. She hid the book under her pillow and fell asleep instantly, dreaming of the worlds she had read about.

When she woke up later, she felt as if her head was rather stuffy, filled to the brim with other worlds and other people's adventures.

She wanted one of her own. And if she could help Jonathan, even better.

'Afternoon,' her mum said drily, as she came down the stairs. 'What time do you call this?'

'It's still morning.' Flick waved at the wall clock. 'Just.'

'Put some bread in the toaster, will you? Freddy's ready for his lunch.'

Flick felt resentment bubble up inside of her. *Yes, Mum,* she thought. *I know you've been down here on your own with Freddy and I've been selfishly sleeping, but he is your baby, not mine.* She shoved four slices into the toaster and clicked the kettle on.

'Why did you sleep so late? Are you growing or something?' Her mum followed her into the kitchen and started the process of wrestling Freddy into his highchair. It was like watching someone trying to get a cat into a carpetbag.

'I hope so.' Flick poured the boiling water into the teapot, swished it around and emptied it into the sink before adding teabags. Warming the pot in the Hudson household was almost a legal requirement.

The toast popped up, and Flick's mum started buttering a couple of slices, and applying peanut butter and jam to the others. 'Was any of this for you?'

Apparently not, Flick thought, grumpiness hovering over her head like a dark cloud. 'I'll have cereal.'

'Good. You can help me in Lidl, when you're dressed. There's nothing for tea. Again.'

Flick thought about the box full of cookbooks on the landing that still needed to be unpacked, and decided not to mention them. 'I was going to go down the high-street,' she huffed, annoyed that her mum seemed to be drafting Flick into her operations without even asking if Flick had plans.

'To do what? You've hardly been home since we moved in, what're you up to?'

Well, actually, Mum, I've decided to take a pledge

to become part of a secret society that explores other worlds through magical suitcases, Flick thought to herself. 'Just stuff,' she said out loud.

Her mum looked unimpressed, and put the plastic plate of toast in front of Freddy. As soon as her back was turned, Freddy emptied it onto the floor with all the precision of a scientist conducting an experiment. '*Stuff* or not, there's things need doing here, as well. You've got enough on your plate as it is.'

Flick thought she didn't so much need a plate as a three-tier cake stand for all the things her mother expected her to be doing. 'You can't expect me to stay inside all summer and—'

'Oh, FREDDY,' her mum wailed, turning around to see the baby gleefully laughing at the pile of toast on the floor.

Flick rolled her eyes and went to eat her breakfast in the living room.

*

In the end, Flick didn't manage to escape from her mother until the next day.

Everyone had gone out before she was even dressed, so Flick left the house without saying a word to anyone.

She only had to double-back once, when she remembered she was supposed to take some chicken out of the freezer.

Sometimes, Flick thought she couldn't wait to be a grown-up if it meant getting away from other people telling her what to do all the time. But then all adults seemed to do was complain and cook and wipe things (surfaces, faces, babies' bottoms), so that didn't exactly appeal, either. And their lives were so *boring*. But they secretly liked it like that. It made them feel safe. That was the reason her parents had moved them here. In the city, there had been rolling 24-hour news projected on the side of the shopping centre. In Little Wyverns, a shed had once fallen down in a night of strong winds. People were still talking about it.

She got to Strangeworlds right as the sky started to darken, threatening a summer downpour. She darted across the road, pushed at the door –

– and it didn't move. Flick's face almost banged into it. She stepped back and tried it again. It was locked fast.

She went around to the window and peered in, cupping her hands to the glass to see through it. She could see the armchairs and the suitcases sitting neatly in their pigeon-holes and the desk at the back, which looked to have a pile of laundry on it.

No. Wait . . . Jonathan *was* the pile of laundry.

A few drops of rain started to spit down onto the pavement.

Flick banged on the window. 'Jonathan! JONATHAN!'

Jonathan sat bolt upright like someone had shoved a handful of nettles down the back of his neck. His hair was on end like a beehive and he cast around wildly for the source of the noise.

Flick banged again. 'JONATHAN!'

He caught sight of her and staggered over to the door, unlocking it just as the rain started in earnest, emptying out of the sky in a hot wash of steaming downpour. 'Come in, come in.'

Flick shot past him like an arrow. 'Thanks.' She put her damp backpack down close to the fire, though it was out. 'What were you doing? Were you asleep?'

'I don't know. What day is it?'

'Wednesday. And it's like eleven in the morning.'

'Only by your clock.' Jonathan yawned so widely he could have swallowed one of the suitcases. 'Do excuse me. Difficult night. I was working.'

He yawned again, shaking with tiredness. 'A Society member came in, you know, and I don't like to say no. I was making a note of something, and then . . . I must have nodded off. What can I do for you? Did you want to discuss the pledge?'

Flick had been about to declare that she was ready to take the Strangeworlds pledge and start jumping into suitcases left and right, but the exhausted expression on Jonathan's face made her swallow her prepared speech back down again. 'You look too tired to discuss anything.'

'I am.' He didn't bother to lie. 'I am sorry, I know you made a special trip in, but I feel as though my brain is full of dead bumblebees at the moment. Apologies.'

'You don't have to say sorry,' Flick said quickly. She tried to cover her disappointment. 'I should have texted you or something, not just turned up.'

Jonathan waved a hand. 'You weren't to know.' He rubbed his eyes beneath his glasses. 'Would you excuse me? I'd like to try and do something with . . . this.' He gestured vaguely at himself.

Flick nodded and watched him go through the kitchen to the stairs at the back of the shop. She waited a moment, and then went into the kitchen herself. There was an uncut loaf of bread and a jar of pasta

101

twists on the counter and a glass bottle of milk on the windowsill in the shade. There was no fridge.

Flick decided to do what everyone else in the country did when action was needed. She took the kettle off the hob and filled it at the sink. The kettle used a gas ring, the same as Flick's nanna had at her house. She remembered her nanna showing her how to do it and she turned the gas on, so blue flames shot out.

Putting the whistle on the spout of the kettle, she listened up the stairs and heard water starting to run. Finding some china cups in one of the tiny cupboards, she set them out before wandering back into the travel agency.

Around her, the suitcases seemed to hum with anticipation. One singular case, close to the desk, wobbled slightly as the bathroom door upstairs slammed shut. It wasn't stacked; it was leaning against the desk, looking for all the world as though it was waiting for her.

Flick pulled a face at it. The suitcase was light brown and battered, though the leather handle wasn't too worn. There was a faded red stamp on the broadest side and peeling painted letters spelling out a ghost word.

She pulled the case onto the desk. Jonathan hadn't said not to touch. And she *had* made a trip down. She could take a little peek . . .

She tested the latches, pushing the round bits of the mechanism apart.

They stayed closed and tight, and she wondered if the suitcase was locked. But it couldn't be, she realised – there was no keyhole on the fastenings and no padlock.

'Come on,' she breathed through gritted teeth, pushing on the catches again with her thumbs. 'Open up.'

The catches popped open, but only partially – Flick had to prise them from the fittings with her fingernails the rest of the way. They must be stiff from age. She gripped the edge of the lid and tried to pull. The leather stuck.

The suitcase was resisting her mightily.

In the kitchen, there was a rattle and a groan as the pipes upstairs were coaxed into giving up the last of the hot water.

Flick yanked harder.

The suitcase lid flew up.

And Flick fell down.

CHAPTER ELEVEN

Flick scrunched her eyes shut, preparing for the pain of hitting her chin on the desk.

But it didn't come.

The falling sensation whipped around her face for a moment longer than it should have. And when it stopped, she landed on her feet, not her face.

But only for a moment.

Her trainers slipped on the ground, and she opened her eyes just as her backside hit the ground. Her hands banged against the ground, and she felt sand beneath them graze her palms.

Sand.

Sand?

Flick stared at her shoes, half-buried in it. This was

distinctly not the dusty little travel agency she'd been in a moment ago.

'Oh, no . . .' She scrambled to her feet, powered by nervous uncertainty, trying not to sink into the softness underfoot. She raised a hand to shield her eyes from the yellow sun, and focussed on the dry, still, dunes.

Behind her, the suitcase lay, lid up, wedged into the sand. She turned away from it and brushed her sandy palms against her shorts. The sand trickled through her fingers. It didn't blow away through the air, though. Instead, it fell straight down.

'This is different,' she said, her voice carrying loudly. It was extremely still. There wasn't a breath of breeze to be felt. The air felt frozen, almost, though the sun overhead was warm.

Flick turned on the spot slowly.

She was standing on a pale beach that sloped down gradually towards a body of water, some fifty yards away. The water was so still it might have been a mirror. Behind her, on a slight incline easily within her ability to climb, was a browning grass-covered cliff-top.

On the top of this flat stretch of land was a lighthouse.

It looked just as a lighthouse should – a red and white striped tube, with a curved glass vessel on the top

– only it was about half the height you'd expect. It was made of painted brick, and there was a stack of leftover unpainted grey bricks to one side, resting on a collapsed wooden pallet.

Beside the lighthouse was a space where a garden might be, but there was no green whatsoever – only brown grass, sand, and stone. Flick could make out washing hung on a string line, stiff as boards and rotting from the salt in the sea air.

An uneasy feeling stirred under her skin.

Flick bent down, and fished the suitcase out of the sand, shaking it out before closing it. She peered out at the water. On the horizon, the only thing that broke the flat mirror-surface of the water was a rock.

She gripped the suitcase tight and began to walk towards the water, half-watching the stone in the sea, in case it tried anything. The sand slid heavily as she walked, making it difficult to move with any speed.

Something crunched, horribly, under her shoe.

She froze in fright, steeling herself before looking down.

The remnants of a picnic were scattered over the sand. There was a checked blanket and a wicker basket and even wineglasses (one of which Flick had stepped on and broken). The food was long gone, presumably rotted under the sun. And even though there was no breeze, the blanket was disturbed – as though several heavy footsteps had gone over it.

She wasn't the first person to have found this picnic site.

Leading away from the scattered debris were several long, deep, gouges in the sand. As though something, or someone, had been dragged off.

The drag-marks led to the sea.

Something very cold crept down into Flick's stomach.

She changed direction and, her feet digging into the sand like ineffective shovels, headed quickly for the lighthouse instead. She wanted to put as much distance between herself and those awful drag-marks as possible. The sand changed to rock as she climbed, and before long she was standing on top of the stone cliff.

The lighthouse was so still it somehow seemed to give Flick vertigo. She half-expected it to fall over at any moment and looking up at the glass dome made her head swim. She walked closer anyway, the suitcase still tight in her hand. Her footsteps in the dead grass sounded extremely loud to her own ears.

There was a red handprint on the white paint, close to the door. It had smeared a little, the fingers dragging and long, disappearing as the colour ran out.

Flick realised her legs had stopped moving. 'It's just paint,' she said to herself. 'Only paint.' She gripped the suitcase tight, as if it could protect her as she walked past the eerie handprint, and around the lighthouse to the door.

The wooden door was swollen, and it wasn't so much closed as wedged most of the way into the doorframe. The paint was a green-blue eczema of colour, peeling where the salted air had eaten into it.

Flick put her hand on the door, feeling the sharp edges of the paint coming away against her palm. She dragged her hand over to the black steel door-handle and gripped it hard. It took several hard tugs, but she eventually yanked the door free.

The door groaned and swung outwards, releasing a sour smell of yeast and coldness that made Flick wrinkle her nose as she stepped into the cool space.

Rather than the darkness she expected, the inside of the lighthouse was fairly bright from the light that filtered in through the dirt-coated windows and the dome above.

There was a spiral staircase of black metal in the centre of the circular room, and at the edges were various pieces of furniture, all curved to fit the strange space. Furthest away from the door was a desk, and above it was a collage of papers and pictures and maps and photographs.

There were no cobwebs, and no signs of mice.

Like the beach, the lighthouse was completely devoid of life.

Flick shivered. She had never been anywhere that felt more dead, and it made her very aware of her own muscles moving, the anxious rush of blood through her veins, and the way her fingers gripped tight at the leather suitcase handle.

It was noticeably colder inside the lighthouse, almost unpleasantly so, and she rubbed her bare arms as she looked about. The spiral staircase was made of iron, and dust clung to the cast shapes and patterns in great clumps, along with red-orange rust on the screw-heads and bolts. Although Flick was interested in what lay up in the glass dome, the staircase seemed too rickety to try climbing.

She walked over to the desk instead. It was littered with pens and papers. Flick put the suitcase down, and touched some of the papers. They were stiff and crispy. She felt as if they might crumble in her hands. They were the colour of tea and covered in a thin film of dust.

She cast her eyes up at the domed ceiling again. Where had the owner of this place gone? Nothing was packed, nothing was tidied away, it was just . . .

Abandoned. The whole world seemed to be abandoned.

She gave a grateful glance down at the suitcase. She had a way out of this place, at least.

There was a photograph on the wall of a couple beside the lighthouse when it was half-built, and Flick walked over to it. They were laughing and wearing overalls, and one of them was hefting one of the large bricks. Beside the photograph there were more scraps of ephemera pasted to the wall: newspaper clippings, and pages torn from books with notes scribbled on them. The writing on the paper was in a language Flick didn't recognise.

There were more photos too. The pictures all seemed to be of the same family: there was a man with long black hair, shot through with grey and tied back in a ponytail, outside a shop whose windows were filled with bottles. There was a picture of a woman with a thundercloud of tight black curls, laughing at a little girl blowing bubbles through a hoop; then a shot of all three of them on a beach not unlike the one Flick had landed on, except there were other families in the background, and there was clearly a wind blowing, as the little girl had her hand on her straw hat. The three of them looked happy, giggling at whoever was taking the picture. The man's hair didn't have any grey in it in this picture. It was tucked back, and Flick could see his ears had a point to them, rather than a rounded edge like her own. She couldn't see the ears of the other subjects, but somehow, she knew they couldn't be from her world.

A tightness gripped the back of Flick's skull, and she could hear her own heartbeat. This was a picture not meant for her eyes. Flick reached out and touched the glass covering the photo. Her fingertip came back covered in a pale dust, a clear space on the man's face.

Had those people lived here? Picnicked on that beach?

What had happened to them?

She went back to the desk and moved some of the papers, her fingers sifting through the sheets until she touched a soft-edged photograph, lifting it to get a better look.

The man and woman were in it again. They were younger, but sadder. And each of them held a baby. Two infants in matching white blankets, their tiny noses just visible.

Flick frowned at the photo. Her own mother had been grinning like a kid in a sweet shop when Freddy was born, in every photo that she hadn't been sleeping.

Flick had seen her own baby photos, and it was the same in them – her parents sporting identical goofy grins in every shot.

So, why did the woman in the photograph look so sad? And the man so solemn?

Flick looked back to the beach photograph. There was only one child in it, with the two adults. Two babies and then, later, one child.

Something must have happened to the other one.

A wave of sadness crashed into Flick without warning. She compared the photo of the girl with her parents against the one with the two tiny bundles. It felt as if a pit had opened somewhere inside her, and everything was being dragged into it. With a plummeting feeling, she thought about her own parents, and wondered what would happen if she fell into another world but never came back. The thought made her miss them terribly, and she wrapped an arm around herself in a pitiful half-a-hug that didn't do the job at all. She put the photograph down on the desk.

Of course, there was every chance the beach picture was taken by the missing child. He or she could have been holding the camera. But there was no other trace of them, not on the desk or in the frames on the wall. They were . . . gone.

All at once, Flick felt as if she was intruding on something deathly private, and she stepped back from the desk, feeling sick. She knocked the chair as she stepped away. It spun and banged against the surface of the desk, sending several books and a slim walnut box with a gold catch straight to the floor. The clatter echoed horribly in the empty space.

Flick quickly picked all the things up and put them back in their pile on the desk. The photograph with the babies was buried under the heap.

She was about to turn away from the desk, when something caught her eye.

Amongst the papers and letters covered with writing Flick could not read, was a word she most definitely could:

Mercator

Heart beating fast, Flick hurriedly pushed sheets of paper aside to uncover a very slim workbook – the sort of thing she used in school, with lined paper on the inside. And on the front cover, in neat leaning script that belonged to an adult's hand, was the name *Daniel Mercator*.

The book wasn't as dusty as the rest of the items on the desk – it hadn't been there as long. Flick hesitated. She longed to open it. But this belonged to Jonathan more than her. And even if Jonathan had said it was a bad thing to take something from another world, surely she had to make an exception for this?

As she nodded to herself, one of the framed pictures on the wall slid awkwardly to one side on its nail and hung there, wobbling strangely, barely balancing at an angle.

Without a doubt, this was her cue to leave. This place was too empty, too full of mystery, and too *sad*. Putting Daniel Mercator's book into the back pocket of her shorts, she glanced for a final time at the picture of the grey-haired man standing in front of the shop. His arms were folded, and he wore an apron with a name badge on it. How many years were there between the photograph of him holding that tiny baby, and him grey-haired and alone, in front of that store?

Was this lighthouse where he had lived? Were his family all gone?

And what had Daniel Mercator been doing in this place?

Flick left the desk, moved quickly back to the open door, opened the suitcase and hastily climbed back in.

CHAPTER TWELVE

She'd forgotten the case was on the desk. She tumbled out awkwardly, banged her hip hard on the corner, and fell to the floor swearing under her breath.

From upstairs, she heard a door close, and then footsteps come down the stairs.

Flick quickly kicked the suitcase back down the side of the desk and leaned against the wall, trying to look innocent.

Jonathan appeared in the doorway to the kitchen. 'The kettle has been whistling for quite some time,' he said. He stared deliberately at the space where the suitcase should have been, two feet to the left of where it now was, and at the sand on his previously clean floor. He raised an eyebrow.

Flick felt her face begin to heat up. The kettle was indeed screaming.

Jonathan sat himself back in the desk chair and gave Flick such a severe look it could have melted an anvil. 'I do very much hope what I think just happened did, in fact, *not*.' His voice was soft but dangerous.

The fire in Flick's face somehow grew thorns as well. 'Um.'

'On your own, no supervision, and not even a note to say where you'd gone.' He shook his head. 'I suppose it's fortunate that you failed to pull the suitcase through after yourself – at least I could have followed you, if you failed to re-materialise after a few hours.'

Flick swallowed. 'I'm sorry.'

Jonathan sniffed. 'Not to mention that case was supposed to be locked,' he said. 'You shouldn't have been able to get into it at all.'

Flick decided not to mention the way she'd forced the latches. Was Jonathan really angry? Was he going to ban her from the travel agency and say she couldn't be a Society member after all? She swallowed, feeling regret and anxiety balling up in her throat. 'I'm really sorry. I just opened it up to have a look, and I sort of fell in.'

Jonathan sighed, and went to take the kettle off the boil. Flick followed him. The kettle's underside was glowing, and Jonathan fanned his hand quickly after turning the gas off. 'You shouldn't apologise for being curious. And, in fairness, I didn't forbid you to touch. I'm glad you made it out all right. I assumed it was locked tight, and safe.' He checked his cuffs. 'Since it was supposed to be locked, it could have been dangerous.'

Flick relaxed slightly. He didn't seem overly cross or disappointed, which in turn made her feel slightly odd. 'It didn't seem dangerous, exactly. Just . . . empty. Really empty.' She swallowed. 'Dead.'

He looked at her. 'You're back, and that's all that matters.' He went over to the desk, and half-collapsed into the chair. 'However, simply because you didn't *experience* any danger doesn't mean it doesn't exist.'

Flick bit her lip. The knowledge that the cases could be dangerous was like finding a worm at the centre of a chocolate truffle. Shamefaced, she pulled the workbook, now creased from its inelegant journey back to Strangeworlds, out of her pocket. She held it out to Jonathan. 'I found this.'

'You took something from another world?'

Jonathan's eyes popped behind his glasses. 'After I distinctly—'

'It says *Daniel Mercator* on the front,' Flick said quickly, before Jonathan could build up steam.

Jonathan's mouth snapped shut like a trap. He blinked rapidly, and took the workbook out of Flick's hand. 'Where did you find this?'

'It was on a desk in a lighthouse, with a load of other papers. I didn't open it,' she added hurriedly. 'I just saw the name . . . it was the only thing I could read. The rest was all another language. Is it your dad's?'

'Yes.' Jonathan opened it. 'Yes, it's one of his notebooks. He always took one with him.' He turned a few pages. 'This is hardly used, though. A few scribbled notes, and what looks like a list.'

Flick leaned over the desk to see. 'A list?' she asked, curiously.

Jonathan showed her. 'A list of worlds. There are crosses next to some of them.'

There was a silence. And then their eyes locked at the same time.

Flick's heart quickened. 'Do you think—'

'It's possible.'

'This could be where—'

'I suppose he—'

'He could have gone to all of the worlds on that list. And got stuck in one of them. We could find him!'

'Maybe,' Jonathan whispered. 'Maybe . . .' He stared at the list, apparently lost in a world in his own head.

Flick, on the other hand, was bursting with excitement. She wanted to dive into another suitcase immediately and begin the search, but Jonathan seemed to be having some sort of crisis, so first things first. There was only one thing to do: make some more tea, and do it properly, this time.

It gave her hands something to do, but the gears of her mind took the opportunity to start grinding away twice as fast as usual. That strange, empty world. What *could* Jonathan's dad have been doing there?

When she brought the tea back through on a tray, Jonathan was staring into space, eyes glazed over. Flick cleared her throat and he jumped. He came and sat down in one of the armchairs by the hearth and Flick sat in the other.

They sat and drank their tea without saying much, and slowly the colour came back into Jonathan's cheeks. Flick watched him sit up as the sugar hit his system. She relaxed slightly, feeling the comforting hug of the case-lined walls, the stained-on black of the grate, the misty leaded windows with their fading gilt letter-work. The fear and discomfort she'd felt in the lighthouse was already fading, replaced by a sharp thrill of adventure.

'What shall we do?' she asked at last. 'Do you know where all the suitcases are for those worlds? Can we search for him?'

Jonathan had to smile. 'Anyone would think he was *your* father. Look ...' He passed Flick the notebook again. 'The list has crosses on it, here, here and here. Not in order, though. Places he went to, do you think?'

'I'd say so.' Flick nodded, happy to be consulted. 'But we don't know where he went next?'

'No, but surely *someone* must have seen him,' Jonathan insisted. 'He might have told someone where he was going.' He frowned. 'I wonder *why* these places are on his list. There doesn't seem to be any real correlation between them.'

Flick read down the list.

The City of Five Lights X
Tam's Forest X
Snowmore

The Break
Coral City X
Desert of Dreams

Flick handed the book back. 'They've got to be linked somehow, or they wouldn't be on the same list,' she said. 'Could it have been something to do with being a Custodian?'

'That seems likely. He always took his duties very seriously.' Jonathan looked up at the wall of suitcases. There was still one missing. 'It's a lead and I should follow it.'

Flick shifted on the chair. 'Just you?' she asked.

Jonathan shrugged. 'It doesn't have to be just me. In fact, I'd prefer if it wasn't.'

It was as though he was dangling the future in front of her like bait. Flick's desire for adventure – which had sat in her chest like recently kindled fire ever since she'd walked into the agency for the first time – fought against her lifetime of ice-cold cautious responsibility. That feeling of wrongness she'd felt in the lighthouse still sat in the pit of her stomach and it made her hesitate. But then she thought of the brilliance of the crystal world and the possibility of dozens of suitcases, quietly waiting for her to step into. The fiery desire for adventure burned more brightly and won.

'What do you think?' Jonathan asked softly. 'Because I really should investigate this.'

'*We* should investigate,' Flick corrected him. 'I'm not going anywhere, yet.'

CHAPTER THIRTEEN

Flick hurried home, back to the cooking and smell of baby rusk. And found herself stuck in and around the house for the next week. She tried to keep herself, and her mind, occupied, until the next time she could get back. With the chaos of moving finally over, things were back to normal in the Hudson family – that meant Flick doing the washing, going to the corner shop to put money on the gas card, trying to make meals that included something green, and tackling the mountain of summer homework that Byron Hall School had sent her through the post.

It wasn't easy; every time she had a moment to herself, she started thinking about Strangeworlds Travel Agency. The place was even invading her dreams, twisting ordinary thoughts into mysteries, colourful worlds, suitcases and travel. Whether she was taking Freddy to be weighed, or doing the ironing, sitting in the bank whilst her dad got their address changed, or riding the bus that made her teeth rattle – all the while she was thinking about the agency.

Flick had never really understood what people meant by 'itchy feet', unless it was something they'd caught from the swimming pool, but she really did *itch* to go back to Strangeworlds. It was as though someone had an invisible part of herself on a string and they'd tied one end of it to the travel agency.

She tried to be content at home. The new house was starting to look lived-in now, and there were fewer boxes around to fall over. Freddy had already learned to scale the child gate at the bottom of the stairs. Flick had suggested tethering him to a steel ring set into the ground, like a horse, but for some reason her parents hadn't gone for it.

It was rare enough for Flick's mum to get a day off during the week, and Flick had been looking forward to them 'going out', as had been promised the evening before. Only it turned out that 'going out' meant going to the Big Tesco to buy Freddy enough nappies to sink several ships. Flick being allowed to choose what was for dinner apparently constituted a treat.

They'd just unpacked the trolley, and her mother handed her baby brother over, and Flick held him aloft to keep rusk-flecked-drool off her sleeves. 'Don't forget,' her mum said, 'you've got to give him his tea tonight. Your dad's at that training course, and I'm on afters.'

Flick almost dropped her brother in surprised annoyance. 'Mu-um,' she whined.

'Oh, give over,' her mum sighed, wrestling the pushchair (which was putting up the sort of fight an octopus would be proud of) into the back of the car. 'You never know. One day you might have one of your own and think of all the practice you'll have had.'

'I am definitely *not* having one of my own.'

'You'll change your mind.' The pushchair finally gave up and collapsed into an unrecognisable pile of metal. Her mum hefted it into the car.

Flick shifted Freddy in her arms. 'If I've got to live in the same house as something small and dribbly, it's going to be a miniature sausage dog called Simon.' She glared down at her brother.

Freddy gummed happily at her coat. Flick often wondered if her brother was part-goat. He never seemed to eat real food; he preferred chewing on objects, people's clothes or car keys or chair legs.

'We've got a chap coming over to install the house alarm, tomorrow,' her mum said, when they'd finally buckled Freddy into his car seat and set off, Disney songs blasting out of the old stereo. 'You'll have to make yourself scarce.'

'Yeah, I was going to go out,' Flick said, delighted to have an excuse to run to Strangeworlds land right in her lap. 'Is Dad going to be back in time for that?'

'He says he is, yes . . .' Her mum made a rude gesture at a car that jumped the line at the roundabout. 'Make sure he gives you the code before you go out, in case. I'll be the last home.'

Flick looked out of the car window. She'd been letting herself into her home since she was about seven, when her mum had started cashing-up after hours at work. She remembered walking past all the waiting parents when she was coming out of school, head held high because she didn't need anyone to come and take her home – she could take care of herself. She was much more grown up than the other kids; she had her own key and knew how to do things like turn the gas on and use the oven timer.

But the novelty of it soon wore off, and there were

times when it was raining hard and her friends were getting into warm cars, and she had to walk back to the flat alone, arriving cold and wet. She'd sit wrapped in one of her nanna's old blankets and place her uniform on the radiators, watching as it fogged up the windows. The steam would cause damp, and her dad would have to paint the ceiling again to cover the mould spots that speckled the corners. It wasn't Flick's fault – the damp came back every winter when all the clothes were dried indoors – but she knew that if she was taken home in a warm car, the rain hitting the window instead of her head, the problem wouldn't be as bad.

'Is Freddy settled in at his new day-care, then?' Flick asked, grappling for a topic of conversation she thought her mother would be interested in.

'Yes, he seems to have.' Her mum's smile sagged a little. 'You know, when you were born, I had a year off. I would have liked to do the same for Freddy, but . . .'

Flick's chest ached with something like guilt. 'Stuff costs more now,' she said.

'That's very true. And it wasn't exactly a career, what I did before. It'll be a lot easier when Freddy starts school; he can come home with you.' Her mum pulled up at the lights. She turned and looked at Flick. 'I'm very proud of you, you know. You're so grown up.'

Flick made her mouth stretch into a smile-shape. The truth was, she hadn't always felt grown up. The first time she let herself into the old flat, she'd hidden in her room afraid of burglars. She'd rung her nanna several times, once to ask her how you knew when milk was still good to drink. She used to make up stories about what the people in the flats around her were doing in order to feel less alone.

She wasn't a grown-up person by nature.

She'd had to become one.

And until she walked into Strangeworlds, she hadn't even realised that she had been so busy trying to be responsible that she'd forgotten how to have fun.

She blinked as the car started moving again. 'I'll make sure I'm out early, tomorrow,' she said. 'Get out of everyone's hair. I'll do some stuff in the village.'

'That sounds good,' her mother said. 'What did you have planned?'

Flick looked out of the window and smiled to herself. 'Just a bit of sightseeing.'

CHAPTER FOURTEEN

When Flick got to Strangeworlds the next day, Jonathan was sprawled on the floor on his belly in front of an open suitcase.

'Good morning, close the door,' he said without turning around.

'Are you OK?' Flick asked, shutting the door behind her.

'Perfectly fine, thank you for your concern. Though some tea wouldn't go amiss, if you're heading in that direction. Ah.' Jonathan reached into the suitcase and grabbed out of it a large metal hook with three prongs. He clipped it onto the edge of the suitcase and shouted down into the swirling depths: 'All right, you've got a decent hold now. Pull yourself up.'

'Thank heavens for that,' a voice groaned. Only

he didn't say *heavens*. He said something much shorter. 'I'm getting cramp here, Mercator. And that's without mentioning the frostbite on me extremities.'

'No one wants to hear about that, thank you, Mr Golding.' Jonathan stuck a hand into the case. It came back out joined to another, which was in turn attached to a man with a huge orange moustache. 'You'll be fine, keep moving your toes.'

'Damned cloud-storms . . .'

Flick watched in amazement as a man stepped out of the case, snow clinging to his boots and trousers. His coat was damp and had several slashes on one sleeve, but he nevertheless seemed rather pleased with himself. He lifted a cracked pair of tinted goggles to reveal two tiny eyes hidden under eyebrows like twin ginger kitten tails.

The man harrumphed. 'Not exactly pleasant scaling a frozen waterfall just to have to hang about at the top because you can't see the damned suitcase. Hope that won't be a regular occurrence.'

'*Don't lose your luggage*,' Jonathan said, his voice as clipped as a privet hedge. 'Take the case with you, if you don't want to lose sight of it. You're old enough to remember that.' He sniffed disapprovingly at the melting snow dripping onto his floor.

The man opened his mouth to retort, then seemed to notice Flick for the first time. He did a small double-take that made his moustache flap. 'You're real, are you?'

Flick shrugged. 'Pretty much.'

'Hm. Fair enough. Children I can cope with. It's the adults that cause all the damned bother in this world. And the others.' Only he didn't say *damned*, either. 'That one's a good one,' he nodded at the case. 'But don't annoy the yeti. Beast's got a right temper.'

'I did tell you not to mention his haircut,' Jonathan sighed.

'Well, I got away, didn't I?' The man grinned. 'Oh, before I forget, this is for you.' He pulled a journal out of the inside of his coat. The pages were curled up on the edges, but Jonathan looked very pleased to receive it.

'Oh, excellent. Did you notice much?'

'Difficult to say, with the storm. But the landscape's the same. Didn't even need my map.'

'Thank you, Mr Golding,' Jonathan said. He nodded at Flick. 'This is Felicity, by the way. She's a new Society member.'

Flick smiled, feeling a bit sheepish.

Mr Golding, however, beamed. 'Oh, excellent. Nice to meet you. Just what this place needs, Mercator. New blood.' He slapped his hands together. 'Now, you mustn't let me keep you. I've got places to be in this world, now.' He gave Flick a nod of friendship, and blustered right out of the shop.

Flick stared at Jonathan, her eyebrows so high she thought they had probably floated right off her face.

Jonathan smirked. 'Busy day. Now, what happened to that tea?'

*

Jonathan put the snow-case back in its slot on the wall once Mr Golding had left and clapped his hands together. 'And now for you, Felicity, a trip.'

Flick nodded. A stir of excitement was beginning to fizz in her chest.

'I thought we could multitask,' he said. 'Since this is your first official trip. Somewhere that takes you somewhere truly amazing, the finest that Strangeworlds has to offer, *and* was on my dad's list.' As he spoke, he reached up to one of the higher openings and pulled out a popcorn-yellow suitcase bound in what looked like snakeskin. It had a candy-pink trim running around the edge and sparkling gold catches. 'This is somewhat of a crowd-pleaser.'

Flick came forward. 'What's inside it? Where's inside it?'

'A rather interesting take on the laws of physics.' Jonathan pushed the gold catches. They popped open and the scent of strawberry laces and sticky sugar floated out, as well as the sound of birds chirruping.

'It . . . it's a fun place?' Flick found herself smiling.

'It is. You'll see.'

*

Flick clambered out of the case and stood on the ground. Except it didn't feel much like the ground she was used to. It felt soft yet bouncy, almost like she was standing on a bouncy castle whilst it was only half-inflated. She kept her arms out to the side slightly as she shuffled forward to keep her balance.

Jonathan stepped out behind her like a tweed-wearing flamingo and took a moment to pull the case through behind him. 'Oh, nothing changes,' he said, looking up.

Flick followed his eye. In the lavender-coloured sky,

a warm sun glowed and candyfloss-pink clouds skirted overhead on the wind. In the distance, a gleaming city of polished marble, or coral, rose from behind the lush teal hills. There were towers and spires that twisted and disappeared into the clouds, and the sun lanced from every polished surface.

'Where are we?' Flick breathed in awe.

'On the outskirts of Coral City,' Jonathan said. 'We'll head into the city soon, but . . .' He rocked on his heels. 'Notice anything unusual about this place?'

'The ground is all . . . squashy.' Flick pressed firmly with her foot and felt the soft ground spring back. The grass rippled outwards from her foot. 'It's like elastic.'

'Exactly.' Jonathan's eyes glittered. 'Like a trampoline. Watch.' Jonathan put the case down. And, with an uncharacteristic look of glee on his face, he bent his knees slightly and gave an experimental sort of bob on the ground.

'What are you—'

'This!' Jonathan *bounced*. He bounced off the ground, going straight up into the air like a cork in water.

Flick gasped, ready for his inevitable crash to the ground . . . but it never came.

Jonathan's bounce peaked and then he came back

down again as though he had an invisible parachute – slowly, straight down, and with more elegance than anyone ought to have if they've leapt clean off the dirt.

'What on earth?' Flick gawped.

'*On Earth*?' he scoffed. 'We couldn't be further from it. Like I told you – an interesting take on physics. Low gravity and semi-flexible ground; for us that equals a great deal of bounce.' He grinned. 'Have a go.'

Flick examined her shoes. 'Um . . .'

'You're not embarrassed, are you?' Jonathan said. 'It's just physics.'

Flick imagined herself falling back to the ground in a tangled heap of arms and broken legs. 'Is there . . . a technique?'

'Felicity,' Jonathan sighed. 'There is no wrong way to do this. Go ahead.' He bobbed a little on the path. 'Give it a try.'

Flick rolled her eyes. This was ridiculous. She felt herself blushing and looked away from Jonathan, before giving a small, experimental jump. Her feet bounced off the squashy ground, and she went up.

And up.

'------!' she squeaked. She braced herself to plummet

back to the earth, but instead she descended slowly, like a penny dropping through gel, back down until her shoes settled neatly on the ground. 'I can fly!' Flick cried. She jumped again, bouncing off the ground and shooting up like a rocket.

'Yes.' Jonathan rolled his eyes. 'You can *almost* fly.'

Flick laughed as she reached the peak of her jump. This time, she tried a somersault, remembering how she'd tried over and over to do one on the trampolines at Skegness Pier until her time ran out and she had to get off. She was sure, with this sort of height, that she could manage it.

She turned in the air but got stuck halfway, landing softly on the ground on her back. Jonathan appeared in her vision, shaking his head.

'You need more height for that sort of thing. Come on, there's a place I think will do the trick . . .'

It was difficult to walk with dignity when the world made everything springy, but Jonathan managed it somehow, even though Flick was bouncing all over the place like a slow-motion rubber ball. Occasionally, Jonathan would give a delighted bounce, sailing up into the air before coming down gracefully, all the time trying and failing to hide a grin.

They bounced on through the countryside of deep

purple bushes and the bright green grass. The lilac stones that made up the path were large and egg-shaped, though gradually the path began to thin, the stones giving way to grass before running out entirely.

'Where are we going?' asked Flick.

'Somewhere we can fly.'

There were no people around, but she could see small grey animals, like rabbits but with six legs, watching them from large hump-like burrows in the ground. They twitched their pink noses as Flick passed them.

'What are they?'

'Animals. I don't know if they have a name; I've never thought to ask.'

'Do any people live here?' Flick asked, thinking of the city she had seen in the distance and wondering why they hadn't seen any other humans.

'Oh, yes. This is a quiet part of the countryside. We can go to the city later and meet the people.'

'It must be so fun to live here and be able to bounce around everywhere,' Flick said wistfully, taking a rather large bounce herself as she said it.

'The people who live here have evolved to deal with the gravity,' Jonathan responded. 'I remember when I came with my father. They thought I was extremely odd for bouncing all over the place. Some of them laughed at me.'

Flick watched Jonathan's careful strides. That explained why he was taking such pains to walk normally over the surface. Strange; she wouldn't have thought of him as someone who cared much about what other people thought.

They went up a small incline, the deep green grass giving way to chipped shale in a delicate lilac-silver, and stopped on the top of a hill. It crested outwards like a wave, or perhaps a generously wide diving board.

'We're going to jump off this?' Flick's eyes went wide.

'Only if you're not afraid.' Jonathan gave her a condescending look. 'We can always go home.' He patted the suitcase.

Flick edged to the lip of the hill and peered over.

Below, dropping many, many feet down, was a canyon. And within it, great globes of translucent *somethings* rolled around together, like bubbles in an enormous bathtub.

Torn between wanting to see closer and wanting to do a commando-roll away from the edge of the cliff, Flick frantically tugged at Jonathan's arm. 'What are those?'

'A sort of plant, with fruits kind of like giant grapes. They're attached to vines that grow from within the canyon,' Jonathan said. 'They're sturdier than they look – they won't pop when you land on them.' He flexed his arms a little. 'A running jump can be best, if you're nervous.'

'What makes you think I'm nervous?' Flick said, hiding her trembling hands in her pockets.

'Nothing whatsoever. I'll see you at the bottom.' Jonathan smiled. And with a spin on his heel, he tipped backwards off the edge, the suitcase still in his hand.

Flick gasped and leaned over the edge.

Jonathan was falling backwards as though he was resting on a Lilo; one hand under his head, ankles crossed, giving Flick a cheery wave with the hand that still held the suitcase.

Well. If he could do it . . .

Flick took a deep breath and, sending a silent apology to her mother, shut her eyes tight and leapt off the edge of the cliff.

She tensed horribly as she launched herself into the air, her stomach feeling as though it had chosen to stay on the top of the hill. Despite seeing Jonathan do it first, she still half-expected to plummet down like a rock.

But the wind didn't whip at her face; it caressed, and Flick opened her eyes to see the side of the cliff falling away gently, like a delicately peeled fruit.

The air was like a cushion beneath her body, plumped up under her back. But she found that, if she angled herself like *so*, with her arms and legs tight together, she could drop like an arrow. Or, as she flung out her limbs again, she could float downwards like a dream.

'Enjoying yourself?' Jonathan appeared beside her.

'You were below me!'

'Yes, but this isn't like falling. This is like swimming. See?' He pushed his arms up above his head, and brought them down firmly, rising up in the air as though pushing himself through water. 'You don't have to settle for falling. Not if you can fly.'

Flick tried to right herself, kicking her legs a little, and ended up on her side before dropping downwards again.

'Maybe next time?' Jonathan called after her.

Flick felt, rather than saw, the spheres meet her. They were, as Jonathan said, soft and squashy, and gave way under her weight. The suitcase lay on top of one. She grabbed it by the handle, and bounced her way free of the bubbles, back to more solid ground.

Above her, Jonathan was treading air, occasionally kicking his legs like a frog.

This is ridiculous, she thought. Then she grinned, propped the suitcase against one of the candy-floss trees, and started up the hill again.

This time, Flick didn't hesitate to jump.

CHAPTER FIFTEEN

Jonathan lowered the leaf he'd been fanning himself with as Flick collapsed onto the ground next to him, after completing a triple backflip on her latest jump.

'Enjoying yourself, are you?' he asked, with a knowing smirk.

Flick gazed up at the rose-tinted clouds. 'Maybe.' She was suddenly brimming with questions. 'Are the worlds other planets?'

'Other worlds can be any size whatsoever. They might contain a planet and a sun. Maybe a moon. Or they may not be what we think of as a planet, at all. There are worlds made entirely of the fires of burning rock, the edges of cut-crystal, or simply pure darkness, and the shadows that twist within. There are worlds where you can sail to the edge and right over, and then there are worlds we can't even visit because the air is toxic to us, or the entire place is underwater. Each one different, each one a miracle in its own way.'

'And can we get to each one through a suitcase?'

Jonathan shrugged. 'I don't know how many worlds there are in the multiverse. Likely I don't have access to them all at Strangeworlds. I doubt it. But I have more than enough.'

'How many cases do you have?'

'Seven-hundred and forty-three,' he said automatically. 'That, in the grand scheme of things, is not a large number at all.'

Flick thought about the cases stacked in the travel agency. There had been a lot of them, but definitely less than one hundred. *Where were the rest of them?*

Jonathan stood, and brushed off his trouser legs. 'We should head into the city now. This visit can't be all fun and games.'

*

Coral City was as twisty as its namesake. Spires of rock and stone and glimmering pearl spiralled into the sky, moving ever-so-slightly to and fro as though in a breeze. Translucent vehicles that looked like bubble-cars made of frosted glass rolled slowly on three wheels over white stone roads. The people, and there weren't as many of them as Flick would have expected in a city, looked completely unremarkable, aside from the fact a lot of them had pastel-coloured hair. One or two of them had little pets that looked like long-eared cats with six legs trotting beside them on leads. Once they were amongst the buildings, Jonathan took out his magnifying glass. He seemed satisfied with what he saw and handed the instrument to Flick, who delightedly peered through it to see swirling magic wafting through the streets and rushing between the buildings like water around rocks. There were no trees lining the paths, but there were tall jagged rocks that reminded Flick of the salt lamp in her parents' room.

'Where do you think your dad would have gone?' she asked, reluctantly giving the magnifier back.

'The confectioner's,' Jonathan said. 'He always went to a specific one whenever he came here – it's the only place in the multiverse that sells Wilson's Whirly-Wax in buzzberry flavour.'

It turned out the sweet shop was on the fifteenth floor of a building that had seemed to be made of semi-solid gel. Flick could see her footprints slowly disappearing from where she'd walked on the gummy-like floor.

The entire sky-scraper structure was filled with shops – two or three on every floor – that sold different kinds of food. There was fruit with reaching tentacle roots, oblong vegetables with skins as thick as car tyres and a shop selling bottles of pop that fizzed and bubbled in every colour of the rainbow.

The sweet shop itself wasn't large and had the look of an old-fashioned corner shop, but it was crammed full of so much confectionery that it was a wonder it hadn't fallen straight down to the floor below. There were packets of spiral gummies filled with fizzing sherbet known as Salisbury Twists (not to be sold to the under-fives, as they could cause mild levitation), small pink and blue jelly beans called 'Doctor Stobbart's Immersion-Caps' (if you ate one, you developed an insatiable urge to take a bubble bath), and great slabs of chocolate-covered honeycomb, that (for some reason) had to be sold by the customer's blood type. There were chocolates and tubes of powders, twisted paper bags of chunky toffee, bricks of cake toffees and liquids in glass bottles decorated with glitter.

Flick stuck to the sweets that came with the smaller warning labels, using a tiny golden scoop to choose.

Jonathan was reading the label of something called 'Indescribable Badger Bits' with a frown on his face.

'I wouldn't, unless you've got a spare set of teeth,' the woman behind the counter called to him. Her purple hair, the exact same shade as her nail polish and eye-makeup, was in such a large beehive that it almost brushed the ceiling. 'They use that stuff to break up the roads, you know.'

'Fair enough.' Jonathan straightened up. 'I'll stick to something I know.'

'What's in these, please?' Flick held up a tub labelled *Melting Frobisher Leaves*.

'You're not from around here, are you?' The woman raised her eyebrows.

'What gave us away?'

'You've got no idea what it is you're after.' It didn't sound as though she thought this was a bad thing.

Jonathan picked up the nearest jar and took it over to the counter. 'This isn't my first time here. It's just been a while, that's all.'

'You're from over Silver Gate way?' she asked, taking a silvery pair of tongs and starting to weigh out the confectionery onto a set of scales.

Jonathan gave a non-committal hum, as if he couldn't care less about giving the lady information.

But his fingers were tight on the suitcase. As the woman screwed the lid back onto the jar, Flick noticed Jonathan glance in her direction.

She frowned. Was he nervous about her being with him? If they needed to keep Strangeworlds a secret, she wasn't about to blow their cover.

The owner of the sweet shop bagged up Jonathan's candy and handed it over. 'That's two and a half,' she said.

Jonathan took something shiny and hexagonal from his pocket and gave it to her. 'Thank you. Do you have buzzberry Whirly-Wax, at all?'

The woman's smile fell. 'Oh, I'm afraid not. We can't get hold of buzzberries any more.'

Jonathan looked surprised. 'Really? Why not?'

'All the trouble over Mount Fission way,' the shopkeeper said. 'Nothing's been growing at all, not just fruit. Something to do with the weather, I think. Snow coming down in the midst of summer, red-hot days in winter, the whole thing isn't right.'

'Oh, what a shame,' he said lightly, but Flick could tell he was covering his shock. 'I suppose I'll just have to get a different flavour then.'

'Truth be told, you're taking it better than the last person who came in asking for them – a gentleman a couple of months ago. When I said there was none to be had he ran out of the shop.' She chuckled.

Jonathan laughed along with her, but he looked very troubled.

Flick came over with her own chosen jar. 'Is this good?'

'Oh, Cloudfloss!' The woman looked delighted. 'Lovely stuff. Just don't eat it all at once – gives you stomach-fog.'

Flick didn't know what that was, but she didn't fancy finding out either.

They paid and said goodbye. They left the shop and walked onto a balcony that leaned out over the road. Below them, shining vehicles like polished beetles trundled down the white roads. People dressed in clothes of glittering gossamer and slices of lurid plastic strolled on the paved sidewalks, and there was a busker leaning against a wall, playing an oversized guitar. If Flick gazed into the distance, she could see the wobbling of the soft landscape moving like little waves lapping at bases of the buildings. It made her feel slightly seasick.

She glanced at Jonathan. 'Think it was your dad who ran out of the shop?'

He was opening his paper bag. 'Mm. Annoying, if it was. This is the only place I know he would have come to in this world and we didn't learn anything about where he might have gone to next.' His uncertain look became a smile and Flick realised she was drifting upwards, very slowly, like a particularly sneaky balloon.

She grabbed the balcony railing and pulled herself back down again. 'At least we know he was here. Even if we don't know why. And we saw that there's plenty of magic floating around,' she added, remembering her new Society responsibilities.

'That's true. But still ... I am disappointed.' Jonathan sighed, then tore the pincer off a gummy scorpion with his teeth. 'These are not as tasty as I anticipated.'

Flick sniggered, then steadied herself as she started to float away again. 'That was only our first try, Jonathan. We'll keep looking for clues. We've got a whole list of places to try.'

'A whole travel agency, if it comes to it,' he said. 'Seven hundred suitcases, and billions of things to see in each one.'

A soft feeling, somewhere between happy and sad, grew in Flick's chest. She stared out at the strange city. This place was unfamiliar, and strange, but ... she loved it. And she might never come here again.

'I want to do it properly,' she said. 'Become a proper Society member. Pledge, badge, everything. I want to see as much as I can.'

Jonathan gazed at the mist in the distance. 'The first new Strangeworlds Society member in a long time.' He smiled warmly at her. 'Welcome, Felicity Hudson.'

*

'You've already got a copy of the guidebook,' he said when they got back. 'It's yours now, so you may write your name in it. As a Custodian, you'll have to record new places you visit, what you find out, what sort of currency they use, even what the weather is like – it's all useful. And, if you're with me, you can use a magnifying glass.'

Flick turned the pages of her guidebook, feeling the soft edges of the paper. She wanted to squeeze it, give it a hug, but thought Jonathan might raise an eyebrow at her. 'Why can't I have a magnifying glass of my own?'

'Society rules.' Jonathan folded his arms. 'Head Custodians only. To prevent misuse. Now, there are a few other rules of course. The most important being that you mustn't share the true nature of the travel agency with anyone who is not magically conscious.'

Flick frowned. 'But what if I don't know if they are or not?'

'Then don't say anything to anyone. Err on the side of caution. And that includes your parents.'

Flick hadn't even considered telling her parents. They weren't the type to believe in magic. But now she wondered about something. 'If I'm magical does that mean my parents are magical too?'

'Not necessarily. These things can skip a generation or two. Has there ever been anything . . . . interesting about your family?'

Flick thought about it. If either of her parents *were* magical, they were doing a brilliant job of hiding it. As for extended family . . . her dad was an orphan and had grown up in children's homes. Her mum's parents, Nanna and Grandad Pitchford, were special to her but they weren't exactly magical. She didn't have any aunts or uncles. 'Not really,' she said.

Jonathan pulled a sympathetic face. 'It isn't important, I don't think. Who knows? It's unpredictable – sometimes it can simply crop up out of nowhere.'

Flick couldn't help feeling slightly put out. 'This is something I'm good at. And I can't even tell anyone.'

'You can tell me.'

'You already know,' Flick said.

Jonathan shrugged. 'That's the price, I'm afraid. The price of adventure.'

Flick nodded and put the worn and battered guidebook into her bag. 'I'll be back. As soon as I can.'

'Oh, I do hope so. Now, the real work begins.'

CHAPTER SIXTEEN

Two frustrating, parent-filled days later, Flick was back in the travel agency. She had whispered about Strangeworlds to Freddy, trusting him not to blab her secrets, but otherwise had no one to talk to. How could she concentrate on mundane things like trying on school uniform or choosing between German and French when there were whole worlds that wanted her attention?

When she finally got a day to herself, she ran down the street as though she could fly.

Jonathan didn't waste any time. As soon as he saw her he took down a very battered brown case with a tree painted on the side. 'You're lucky it's been a busy few days. I nearly hopped into this one by myself.'

'The next one on your dad's list?'

'Yes. And I've got rather a soft spot for this one. My dad took me here when I was a couple of years older than you. I would have liked to be able to hop in and out every weekend, but . . .' He shrugged. 'He was very protective.'

'What's in it?' Flick asked, excited.

'A forest. An enchanted one, naturally.' Jonathan undid the catches, and the smell of pine filled the room. He left it open while he went to lock the shop door, flipping the sign to 'Closed'. He shoved the deadbolt across the door.

A thought popped into Flick's head. 'Wait – what if one of the other cases needs you?'

'There's no one scheduled to make a return today,' Jonathan said. 'It will be fine to be gone for a few hours. Time moves faster, where we are going.'

'Is it a safe place?'

'Mostly harmless. It's fine, so long as you don't wander too far into the trees.'

Flick frowned. 'Why? What's in the trees?'

'Oh, nothing too deadly,' Jonathan said. 'Spiders, bugs . . . that sort of thing.'

'I'm not a fan of anything with more than seven eyes,' said Flick, thinking of the plate-sized spiders the packing had unearthed in the old flat.

'Then stick to the open spaces.' Jonathan stepped back from the case. 'Want to go first?'

'You'll be right behind me?'

'I certainly will. Got your guidebook?'

Flick patted the back pocket of her jeans, shook out her hands, and took a deliberate step into the case. This time she didn't pause, even when it felt like there were two of her – she kept on going, walking with a less-than-graceful stumble, but then she was out, and standing . . .

. . . standing on a carpet of brown leaves and pine needles, thin bits of green grass pushing valiantly through. The sky was wide open above her, blown-glass blue with scars of clouds streaking through it. Green assaulted the corners of her vision, from above and below, and her ears were hit with *silence*.

Not the total silence of the lighthouse world. A more natural silence – one that still had the voice of the wind in it.

The sky was a dome of blue; Flick felt like a bug trapped in a glass. The sheer flat of the green and brown beneath Flick's trainers was like the piece of card slid underneath to trap her, and she realised that although this place *looked* like a vast world, there were *edges* to it.

She squinted up, trying to see the curve of the sky.

There was a horizon, but – Flick couldn't say for sure how she knew this, but she did – the world ended there. It was the same way when you're in a greenhouse, you know you're inside, even if there are clever plants and temperature controls that make you think you're somewhere tropical. Jonathan was right: some worlds were indeed very small.

Jonathan himself stepped elegantly out of the case then, dusted off his jacket, and quickly pulled the case through after him.

'This place is tiny, isn't it?' Flick asked.

'Yes, it's . . .' Jonathan frowned and peered around. 'Can you hear that?'

'No, I can't. Just how small *is* this world?'

'Felicity, shush.'

'It's got to be about the size of a shopping centre, and not even a very big—'

'Shh!'

'Don't shush me!' Flick said indignantly.

Jonathan held a hand up. 'We can discuss its size later. But right now, I'd appreciate it if you could stop prattling and concentrate on what's actually important.'

'And what's that?'

'What can you hear?'

They both listened.

'Nothing,' Flick said softly. 'It's quiet.'

'Yes.' Jonathan's grip on the case tightened. 'No birds singing. Barely any wind. No animals.'

'What does that mean?' Flick whispered, her confusion immediately crushed by a heap of nerves.

'I think it means we are being watched,' Jonathan said. 'Perhaps we should—'

But whatever Jonathan had been going to say remained a mystery. At that moment, a large woven net dropped from the trees and landed on the two travellers. It knocked them to the ground as joyous whoops of triumph filled their ears.

Flick groaned, every rib in her chest complaining in pain. She managed to turn her head in time to see what looked like a herd of small, hairy, Ewok-like beings rush out of the undergrowth, brandishing sticks and bellowing at the tops of their lungs.

'How dare you?!' Jonathan yelled at them, his face in the pine needles, glasses smeared with soil. 'Release us immediately, you absolute degenerates!'

'What's the password?' one of the beings crowed in perfect, albeit slightly snotty, English. Flick could see that the fur covering them was actually a sort of hairy onesie with a hood.

'How could you possibly expect me to know that?'

'Wrong! Wrong, wrong, wrong, wrong!' The hairy beasts started up a chant. 'Wrong, wrong, wrong, wrong—'

'What are they?' Flick yelped, trying to get to her hands and knees and failing.

'They're children.' Jonathan coughed. 'I've not seen them for . . . I don't know, years . . .'

'You've not seen us before, mister,' the apparent ringleader (for he had the biggest and most obnoxious-looking sharpened stick) shouted. 'We don't remember you one bit. No grown-ups come here by order of me.'

'I wasn't a grown-up when I was here last.' Jonathan spat out a pine needle.

'And you're not a grown-up now,' Flick said.

'Oh, that's hardly the . . . look. I used to come here when I was little. Little-er.'

'No, you never did.'

'I did.'

The leader pulled his furry hood down, revealing the face of a boy about nine years old. He had blue and black paint streaked down his face and hair that looked as though it was last washed on the day he was born. He leaned down to squint at Jonathan.

'What's your name?'

'Mercator.'

The boy straightened up. 'Oh. And what about her?'

'I'm Flick,' Flick said quickly, trying not to sound as panicky as she felt. 'I'm just – just a kid. We're not enemies.'

The boy nodded. 'Oh, all right. Set them free.'

There were disappointed groans, but the rest of the children lifted the net off the ground, and Flick crawled out, Jonathan following. They stood, rather embarrassed, covered in dirt and leaves. Flick brushed some dead grass off her sleeves, thankful for once in her life that she was the one who put the washing in, so there'd be no questions about the stains.

Jonathan rubbed his glasses against his shirt to clean them.

'You know what? I do remember you. You look . . . different,' the leader boy sniffed at Jonathan.

'Of course I do.' Jonathan replaced his glasses and glowered down at him, looking absolutely murderous. 'It's been *years* since I saw you last. Why haven't *you* grown up, Tam?'

The boy, Tam, shrugged, and pulled a face a gargoyle would be proud of. 'Don't grow up here, do we? That'd be boring.'

'No one's arguing with that,' Flick said, before she could stop herself.

Tam gave her a grin, showing teeth with a big gap at the front, before looking back at Jonathan. 'Where'd you go, anyway, Mercator?'

'I grew up,' Jonathan said.

'Did you miss us?'

'A little.'

'Not a lot, then.' There was muttering, of the sort that gets your nerves up. Even more so when it's accompanied by the clattering of sharpened branches. Flick swallowed.

Jonathan rolled his eyes. 'Tam, I only wanted to show my friend your home.'

Flick's brain tripped over the word *friend* and came to a halt. She felt unexpectedly pleased. She would have expected Jonathan to call them *acquaintances*, if anything. Friends seemed as good a label as any. She bit back a smile at the realisation that the first new friend she'd made in Little Wyverns was an eccentric teenager with a penchant for old suits and a travel agency full of magic.

Jonathan was still talking. 'I remember your home, you know, Tam. How lovely it is. And how peaceful.' He gave the boy's rudimentary spear a deliberate look.

'Peaceful is boring!' Tam yelled. The other children crowed loudly, and two of them punched each other on the side of the head.

'Well, it was peaceful the last time I came here,' Jonathan said, over the din. 'I came before I left for school, and I thought you'd all grown up, or left. It was nothing but me and the birds.'

Tam sniffed. 'Nah, we weren't gone. We didn't want to bother you. We didn't mind you coming and reading. You were too big to really play properly, so we left you alone. And after that you didn't come any more. But then, someone else started coming.'

'Who? Was it my dad?' Jonathan's eyes went wide.

Flick felt a jolt of anticipation.

'No, not him.' Tam shook his head. Jonathan's face fell, and so did Flick's hopes. 'Some other man. He had grey hair and he wore a big hat, and he was wide.' He tapped his shoulders. 'And strong-looking, he was. He looked like he could rip a tree in half.'

'And he was loud,' a girl interjected. 'Used to stomp around like a giant, he did.'

Jonathan frowned. 'And you're certain he wasn't from here?'

'He had one of *them*.' Tam pointed at the suitcase.

'A suitcase?' Flick asked. She turned to Jonathan. 'Then he must have come from Strangeworlds, mustn't he?'

Jonathan didn't answer. 'He had a shooter,' one of the other kids piped up. She had half a thorn bush in her hair, and she held her stick like a rifle, to demonstrate. 'He shooted it at the rabbits.'

'And the deers.'

'And the birds.'

'A gun?' Jonathan's eyes were wide. 'Look, this isn't a game, is it? You honestly saw this man?'

Tam nodded. 'That's why we did the net. We said we'd catch him good and proper, next time. But he stopped coming. Took the poor dead rabbits and went back into the suitcase he carried.'

'Good he did,' someone snorted, 'else we'd've done for him.'

'Him and ten like him!'

Flick's insides felt quite trembly. She didn't like this story of the man with the gun one bit. 'Jonathan,' she whispered. 'Could it have been a customer? A Society member?'

'I suppose,' Jonathan frowned. 'But Dad wouldn't have let anyone through here with a gun, I'm sure of it.'

162

'Unless he didn't know he had it. He could have hidden it. Or . . .' *Or threatened your dad*, she thought. She put a lid on that possibility. She didn't know Jonathan's dad, but the idea of anything like that happening in Strangeworlds made her feel sick.

'I'm sure there's a logical explanation.' Jonathan bit his lip, then turned back to Tam. 'If this man did come through Strangeworlds, then I do apologise.'

Tam wiped his nose with the back of his hand, which seemed to mean he accepted the apology. 'It's OK. He stopped coming.'

'All right,' Jonathan brushed at his suit and put on a falsely cheery expression. 'Well, we had better be off.'

'No.' Tam shook his head. 'You've got to come back and see the House! You've not seen it in so long – I bet you never even seen the third level!'

'Really, Tam, I don't know if—'

Tam glared.

'All right,' Jonathan said, relenting. 'We'll come and see. Just for a bit.'

The children cheered and banged their sticks together, howling at the sky as they turned to lead the way.

'Follow them, but be careful,' Jonathan hissed in Flick's ear. 'They're not what they seem. Don't eat or drink anything they give you. Don't promise them anything or say you will stay longer. And don't tell them your real name.'

'I already told them!' Flick squeaked in horror.

'No, you said "Flick". That's fine. Do not tell them your *full name*. Understood?'

'But they know your name? From before?'

'They know *a* name,' Jonathan sighed. 'Not my first name. Trust me, I'll be all right.'

They were pushed apart by a boy with bright ginger hair, who enthusiastically handed them both a stick.

Flick took it and allowed herself to be led deeper and deeper into the forest.

CHAPTER SEVENTEEN

There are several rules that must be obeyed if you are going to cavort with fae, or beings that have fae-like properties, such as Tam's gang of forever-children. If Flick had taken the time to consult the guidebook in her pocket, she would have found a page towards the back with a set of rules:

When Dealing with Fae, or Fae-like Beings

1. Eat nothing offered to you by the fae.
2. Tell them not your true name.
3. Do not sleep!
4. Do not stray from the path.
5. Remember – they can only tell the truth.

It can be difficult to be sure whether or not your hosts are members of the fae family; however, there are some signs to look out for:

1. A childishness and desire to play.
2. Agelessness.
3. A delight in songs, games and performance.
4. Untraceable Magic – for example, making objects appear out of thin air, vanishing or shape-shifting without using spells or bottled magic.

As always, treat your hosts with respect, but abide by the above terms.

Flick stepped carefully as the children led them through the woodland. The forest was not like the ones Flick was familiar with back home. The forest of scrubby trees and bracken not too far from the new house was all cut through with paths made of tarmac and brick. In Tam's forest, there were trees, and there was dusty ground to walk on, but no real path at all. If they hadn't had the children to follow, Flick knew they would be lost, and quickly. Bright toadstools, unnatural fire-engine red with white spots, grew in twos and threes at the bases of the trees. Occasionally, out of the corner of her eye, she would see something scuttle away on more legs than she felt was necessary.

'This forest has . . . *things* in it,' she said.

Jonathan nodded. 'Yes. Don't wander off.'

They were quickly herded down a small hill, where the trees spread out into a perfect circle around a clearing filled with wooden tree-houses and slides and rope-bridges and swings and hammocks.

Flick stopped walking. Of course she was probably way too old for playgrounds now, and since Freddy was born she'd had to push him on the baby swings and do nothing else, but this . . . she wanted to pelt down the hill and climb up the first ladder and never stop until she ran out of breath. 'That is like . . . it's like the best adventure playground *ever*,' she said, her mouth hanging open.

Jonathan gave her an expression that was one blink away from murder. 'Don't you dare,' he said quietly. 'I'm not leaving you here, so don't you even *start* liking this place. Don't. You absolutely mustn't take a liking to it.' There was a soft sort of desperation in his voice.

'Why?' Flick tore her gaze away from the playground.

'Because if you like it enough, then you might want to stay,' he said, hefting the suitcase from one hand to another. 'You're not too old to get yourself stuck here. And we have to leave, preferably before too long.' He pulled his sleeve down to look at his watch. The three hands were spinning in both directions (and a few new ones), so there was no way to tell the time. 'Oh, hell. Time's gone all askew. I can't tell how fast it's moving.'

Fear exploded like a grenade in Flick's stomach. 'We're not going to get home and find everyone's gotten old, are we?'

'I doubt it,' said Jonathan. 'We have a few hours before anyone would miss us, I think. Maybe a little less – this is time governed by children, remember. Enjoyable things always seem to pass very quickly, and dull moments seem to take forever, yes? Well, here, they quite literally do.' He leaned in. 'Remember what I told you – they must not know your name. Eat nothing they offer. And promise them nothing.'

They reached the bottom of the slope, the tiny warrior children all but dragging them through their playground village like prizes. More children poured out of the dens and huts to cheer and whoop and yell to one another.

It was a mash-up of every playground Flick had been to in her life. But it wasn't designed how an adult would make it – this was a playground as designed by a child. There was no soft padding on the ground, but there were hammocks and rope-swings and the bridges that stretched off into the sky. Flick grinned as she watched a small girl use one of the slides, whizzing down it so fast she must have defied several laws of physics. Ladders were nailed onto the highest sides of the buildings and there were holes in the ground here and there that led to tunnels.

In the centre of the wooden playground was a thin table, tree-stump seats lined up on its longer sides. The table itself was stacked high with food. The children thundered towards it, dragging their visitors with them.

Jonathan didn't appear to have any reservations about sitting. He swept over to the table like a dignitary and rolled one of the tree-stumps out of the way, choosing to sit on the suitcase, instead. He picked up a plate and began to fill it immediately, copying the children either side of him, who were grabbing handfuls of macaroni cheese and orange crisps and blue cake. Some of it even made it onto the plates in front of them.

Flick was shoved down onto a stool opposite Jonathan, a plate and spoon thrust into her hands.

Surprisingly, the plates and cutlery were ceramic and metal, as if from a fine china service, or a grown-up's cupboard. She stared at the mountains of junk food in front of her. Flick didn't usually like food that was neon, but something inside her was delighted at the prospect of getting to taste all these colours that didn't occur in nature and her stomach snarled in impatience.

She reached out with her spoon, and then stopped dead.

Don't eat or drink anything they give you echoed in her head.

Flick squinted at the food. Ignoring her stomach, she poked at the glistening jelly in front of her. It wobbled to and fro, making a noise like a deflating balloon. Flick sat back. Food didn't generally make the sort of noises it did in cartoons. There was something not quite right about it. Where was it cooked, for starters? Where did it come from?

Was it even real?

Around her, the children were loading their plates up, and even Jonathan was choosing things, whilst answering the occasional question from the small child next to him. While not actually eating the food, he was doing a wonderful job of spooning things up and twirling his knife and fork, and he was even being artistic about it. Flick saw that he had made a face on his plate, cutting a tomato in half to use as a nose under the spaghetti he'd arranged like hair.

Oh . . .

Flick's eyes went wide as she realised. *He's not eating, he's* playing*! He's doing things kids do with their food. So they don't notice anything!*

Flick gripped her spoon. She'd played this game herself before, when her mum would put a load of fish pie or something else disgusting in front of her and she'd sit and stir it around her plate and look busy so she wouldn't get told off for not eating. It was all a distraction.

She scooped up a huge mound of mashed potato, and began to sculpt it into a snowman, adding some grated cheese for mortar.

There was a huge BANG from one end of the table.

Flick jumped, accidentally squashing her snowman flat.

Tam was standing up on his seat, holding a cup that looked like an immense beer tankard, though it was revealed (after he waved it around too enthusiastically) to contain banana milkshake. 'Shut up, everyone!'

Everyone shut up.

'I welcome to our table the guests we captured in our net-trap.' Tam beamed. 'The girl Flick, and the Mercator, who is now a grown-up.'

There was applause, and the smash of cutlery on plates.

Jonathan smiled mildly and Flick gave a nervous wave.

'We only take kids to our Home,' Tam said, stepping into a bowl of custard. 'Usually. Grown-ups come now and again, but we don't like them to stay here, in our place. But . . .' He grinned. 'I think it's different if we knew them when they were kids, too. This is the best place for them, I think. They can stay here. And they will!'

The children nodded, as if this made perfect sense.

They will? Flick gawped at Jonathan in barely disguised horror. Jonathan's wan expression had frozen into something resembling dread.

'We wouldn't want to impose,' he said, sounding slightly strangled.

Tam took a swig from his tankard. ''S'not a bother. Always room for more. And we can show you how to play again. Maybe you'll even *be* young again!' He grinned, and the other children made a lot of noise.

Flick was glad she couldn't see her own face. She knew her teeth were showing, but it wasn't in the smile she'd put on when Tam first started speaking. She couldn't *stay* here; this was insane.

Tam was rounding off his speech with some threats. 'So don't give our guests any bother, you lot. Now, eat your dinner or you'll go straight to bed.' He sat back down. Mayhem resumed.

Flick jumped as Jonathan cleared his throat at her, and stared deliberately at her unmoving hands.

She stared at the pancake snowman. He needed sculpting again. And also some eyes. She wondered how far she would get if she abandoned Jonathan and ran for it. Probably not far enough. And besides, where would she go? Under the cover of reaching for a green pea in the centre of the table, she hissed at Jonathan, 'What are we going to *do*? I'm not stopping here!'

'We simply need to get away without causing alarm,' he murmured back, swirling tomato sauce for rosy cheeks on his plate-face. 'They never insisted I stayed before. I don't know if the rules of this place have changed, or if the man with the gun has made them nervous, but they do seem rather keen for us to stay this time.'

'*Keen?* Tam seems to think we've agreed to it already.' She scowled at her spoon. 'I know there are a lot of them, but they're small. Can we fight them off, if we have to?'

Jonathan shook his head. 'This is their world, so they will always win, no matter the opponent. And we don't want to offend them. We might need to come here again.'

'You are far too calm about this.'

'I've faced worse odds.' He shrugged. 'Getting away as part of a game would be the best option.'

'A game?'

'Hide-and-seek, perhaps?'

'But everyone's eating,' Flick pointed out, waving her spoon. A clump of rice pudding flicked off the end, smashing like a cricket ball into a boy's soup.

There was a horrible silence.

'Oi!' the boy yelled, brushing the soup stains from his front.

Flick couldn't remember how to speak. Her spoon dripped pudding onto the tablecloth. 'Um.'

The boy she'd hit was screwing up his face like he was preparing to unleash a howl of Freddy-like proportions.

Tam looked up from his slab of cake, frowning down the table. He raised a hand in the direction of his stick.

Flick didn't know what made her do it. She grabbed her spoon, scooped up what was left of her ramshackle snowman, looked once to take aim –

– and launched the potato straight at Jonathan.

It hit him between the eyes, and he fell comically backwards off the suitcase with a yell. He managed to flip his own plate in Flick's direction as he went, and the spaghetti and tomato and scrambled eggs splattered down her front and showered the girl next to her as well. The girl let out a bleat like an angry goat and flung her spoonful of chocolate ice cream so it scattered over the squealing eaters opposite.

A small boy grabbed a handful of baked beans and mashed them down the back of Flick's neck.

Flick shrieked and squirted the ketchup bottle at him, missing and catching the girl next to him in the ear, who howled and chucked her bowl of chips up into the air so it came down like confetti.

The game spread along the table like chickenpox at a soft-play centre.

Food was thrown, soup was spilled, crockery was smashed and icing was rubbed into the table-top like varnish. The screams grew louder and happier with every passing moment.

Jonathan grabbed Flick's arm and yanked her over the table. 'Come *on*!' he snarled, dragging her through what was left of the feast. Flick staggered upright, snatching up the suitcase and running like mad. The two of them ran down the length of the table, past Tam (who didn't notice them leaving as he was busy using a thick breadstick as a sword) and under one of the swinging rope-bridges where a boy was throwing popcorn like flowers down onto his play-fighting friends.

Flick ducked behind one of the smaller houses. 'Jonathan! Over here!' she hissed. Jonathan skidded around the corner and Flick unclasped the suitcase. The lid sprang open, and the familiar, warm smell of the travel agency hit them in the face. 'Let's go.'

Flick scrambled into the suitcase, still covered in food, the vertigo hitting her again as she climbed up out of this world, and back down into her own.

CHAPTER EIGHTEEN

They staggered out in a tangle. Flick caught herself on the desk as Jonathan stumbled to get his balance and almost fell into the fireplace.

The smell and feel of the travel agency wrapped itself around them like a hug, welcoming them back, though it felt rather stern – as if it was rather annoyed they had dared to venture out in the first place.

Flick caught sight of herself in the mirror that hung over the mantelpiece. 'My clothes!' she wailed, looking down at the mess of pasta, peas and pie down her front. 'And my hair.'

Jonathan beamed. 'You did excellently well there, I must say. Credit where it's due, and all that. I know I said it would be a quiet one, but adventure called, and you rose to the occasion wonderfully. Well done. Well done, indeed.' The effect of his praise was rather spoiled by the fact he had ketchup and mashed potato smeared over his glasses and down his face.

Flick tapped her chin. 'Er . . . you've got a bit of something . . .'

'Yes, we both look slightly worse for wear.' Jonathan checked himself over. 'You can have a showers upstairs if you want.'

'A comb would be a start,' she sighed. 'I don't know if there's any saving my t-shirt.' A blob of something orange slid down the front of it and plopped onto the floorboards.

'I might have something. Wait here.' Jonathan disappeared upstairs, whilst Flick started trying to pick food from her hair with a damp bit of tissue.

'Here.' Jonathan was back quickly, handing her a very fine comb with several teeth missing. 'I think it's an old nit comb. And there's this,' he held out a pink t-shirt. 'It might be a bit big. Sorry. The bathroom's all yours.'

'Thanks.' Flick took the t-shirt and went through the tiny kitchen to the stairs.

She'd never been upstairs at Strangeworlds. It felt off-limits, somehow.

The stairs were narrow – barely an adult's shoulders wide – and they rose sharply. The sides of the stairway lacked a handrail and were instead trimmed with picture frames of various ages and sizes, the inhabitants within staring out with sombre faces.

Flick stared at a couple in Victorian dress – the man had a suitcase in one hand. Then the same couple, with another man, the three of them now laughing – the photographer must have said something funny at just the right moment.

She continued climbing the stairs. The pictures drew a map of years, as the people in them aged. Sometimes they stood outside the shop, and sometimes the subjects sat in a parlour. A lot of them were the image of Jonathan. The same curly dark hair, the same white face and the same outward look of both pride and responsibility. One photo was obviously taken at a wedding, with a bride in a white dress and a beaming groom in a turban and a long embroidered shirt that went down to his knees. Flick liked him – he was obviously having the best day of his life.

Gradually, the pictures allowed colour to drip into their frames, and without warning, Flick found herself looking at Jonathan's double.

She stared at the picture, her fingertips brushing the wall to steady herself as she stood, one foot up on the next step.

A boy grinned out of the frame, his top front teeth missing, drowned in too-big school uniform. It looked a bit like the uniform for Byron Hall – tie, knee-socks, school cap and everything Flick had laughed at when the uniform brochure had arrived, right up until she saw the prices. The boy in the photo had Jonathan's curly hair, or else Jonathan had his, and although Flick had never seen Jonathan grin with such carefree happiness, she knew that if he did, he would look almost exactly like that.

She realised that the boy in the picture had to be Jonathan's dad.

'Are you all right?' Jonathan called.

'Yeah, sorry,' she called back, taking the last few steps quickly. The last picture, at the top, was of a couple (the man with Jonathan's dark curls, the woman with long brown hair and a motherly smile) looking down at a baby wrapped in a white blanket. She didn't need to ask who the baby was.

In the bathroom, she stripped off her top and filled the sink, picking off the biggest bits of muck before letting her t-shirt soak. She noted that Jonathan's organised attitude to how the travel agency should function did not extend to his bathroom, where there were empty shampoo bottles stacked next to full ones, tiny slivers of soap congregating in the dish and a razor waiting rather hazardously in the same jam-jar as his toothbrush.

She picked up one of the combs on the side of the sink, wondering why there were so many hair-products when Jonathan's hair gave the impression he was dragged backwards through a hedge on a daily basis.

Flick's hair got fluffier and more ragged with every stroke of the comb. At least the mashed potato was working its way out. She rinsed it as much as she could and rubbed a towel on her head before pulling the dry t-shirt on. It smelled old, as if it had been sat in a drawer for years, and it was a bit too big, but it was better than nothing.

Pausing on the landing, she noted a room with the door shut, which she assumed was where Jonathan slept, and another that had no door at all, but seemed to be a sort of walk-in wardrobe crossed with a jumble sale. There were clothes of all kinds hanging on racks, folded in piles, or heaped on the floor. Flick saw a massive wetsuit, some funny-looking goggles, a brightly coloured scarf that looked like something her mum would wear, and even a couple of Babygros.

She trotted down the stairs, the noise making Jonathan look up from filling the tin kettle at the sink. He'd changed his shirt and had the sleeves of the new one rolled up. 'All OK?'

'Yeah. Thanks.' She leaned against the counter-top. It felt incredibly surreal to be back in the quiet travel agency; surreal and almost . . . boring. Flick wanted to start planning their next trip immediately – her fingers itched to pull cases out of the wall in the front room. She tapped the counter-top, instead. 'So, is it always like that? Running, and escaping? Is there always adventure? Is it always . . .' she tried to think of a word that was somewhere between *dangerous* and *fun*. '. . . like that?'

Jonathan looked at her for a good half-minute. The silence was so heavy it could have turned a bus into an oven tray. But then a real smile crept onto his face and settled there, almost invisible unless you knew what you were looking for. 'Yes. It is.'

Flick grinned back.

*

An hour later, Flick's t-shirt was drying in front of the fire and she had just finished off a sticky bun.

Jonathan was writing in one of the thick books on the desk, a cold cup of tea next to him as he scribbled. Flick's own report in the guidebook had been much shorter.

'I really can't understand Tam's determination to have us stay,' Jonathan said without looking up. 'You'd think a frightening encounter with an adult would have made the lot of them keen to be rid of us. It was as though they *needed* us to stay. Very strange indeed.'

Flick hummed in agreement. She spun Jonathan's magnifying glass in her fingers and looked through it. Once again, the suitcase they had travelled through was glowing and glittering with magic, much more than the others slotted into the wall.

'Having fun?' Jonathan asked. He snapped shut the book and turned to find a place for it on the bookshelves.

'Sort of,' she smiled, wafting a hand through the clinging magic. 'Just thinking, really.' She lowered the magnifier. 'I guess the case glows because it's been used, right?'

Jonathan, still browsing the bookcase, paused.

'The suitcase we used to get to Tam's forest.' Flick pointed at it. 'It's glowing. So's the crystal forest one, and the . . . lighthouse one.' She blushed. 'It's because they've been used, right?'

Jonathan didn't reply. He was still staring at the bookcase, holding the book he'd been writing in.

Flick shook her head at him and peered through the magnifying glass again. The magic swirled, as if greeting her, and a warm feeling spread through her chest down to her fingertips. 'I love this. Seeing all this hidden stuff. Makes me feel like I really belong in The Strangeworlds Society. Like . . . this is what it's all about.'

Jonathan shoved the book in between two novels. 'Yes,' he said vaguely.

Flick lowered the magnifying glass and stroked a finger down the handle affectionately. She really didn't want to let go of it. 'You said there's always adventure,' she said. 'Jonathan, are you listening?'

Jonathan shook his head slightly as if dislodging something. 'What? Yes, I am listening.' He turned and made a focussed face. 'I'm always listening to you.'

She sighed, before softening her tone. 'I know we're meant to be looking for him, but, Jonathan, are you sure your dad *wants* to be found? Or that he's . . .' She pulled a sympathetic face.

Jonathan tapped the desk as if trying to concentrate. 'If he's out there, I shall find him. Custodians do not relinquish their duties lightly, even in the face of danger.'

'Danger?' Flick sat up.

Jonathan shrugged. He sat down in the desk chair, and absent-mindedly tapped a finger on the polished desk-surface. 'You'll never have an adventure by being overly cautious all the time. I've seen people return from their world of choice looking as though they regret coming back. Some, I think, would choose to stay.'

'Is that possible?' Flick asked, thinking of how readily her brain had rejected the idea of staying in Tam's forest. The wrongness of it had felt all-encompassing. But that didn't mean that someone else wouldn't think differently. 'Could you stay in another world? If you wanted?'

'I've never known anyone stay in another world by choice. But that's why I tell my customers not to lose their luggage. *Don't ever lose your luggage.* It's your only way back.' He adjusted his glasses.

'On the other hand, there are whole worlds for you to hide in,' Flick said. 'If you didn't want to be found.'

Jonathan straightened a few loose papers on the desk. 'It would be very difficult to live in a world you weren't born in.'

'Why?' Flick asked curiously.

Jonathan leaned forward on his elbows. 'You're born with a limited amount of life-force inside you. It's a sort of magic of your own. Living in your own world makes it tick away, day by day, year by year, until eventually you run out. It's what gives you your time in this world.'

For a moment Flick thought she could feel her life ticking away to the cacophony of clocks on the mantelpiece. She didn't like it. 'And when you're in other worlds?'

'Living in a world you don't belong to drains your life-force away. At first you simply feel tired, then ill and, eventually, it's thought that you would die long before your time. Your only hope is to return home. If the spark of your life normally burns away one match at a time, then becoming trapped in a world where you're not meant to be ... would be like lighting a bonfire.'

Flick looked at him. Without saying a word, she knew they were both thinking of Daniel Mercator.

CHAPTER
NINETEEN

I t is a truth universally acknowledged that a lie told to protect someone will inevitably do more harm than good in the long run. And that the 'long run' may come around much sooner than anticipated.

Jonathan disliked lies, as a rule. Telling them made him deeply uncomfortable, and after Felicity had gone home that afternoon, he spent the rest of the day and night feeling extremely guilty.

He'd grown up in the sort of household where lies were a garnish on conversation. His parents were well-intentioned liars, of course. Strangeworlds Travel Agency wasn't the sort of thing they wanted wee Jonathan to go blabbing to his friends about. Likewise, the truth about the contents of the suitcases was kept from him, in case he should get it into his head that climbing into one would promise him a jolly old time.

Jonathan was told from a young age that the things in the travel agency (where he was taken only when there was absolutely no one to take him elsewhere) were not for touching. Jonathan never saw anyone climb in or out of a suitcase, and the truth about the family profession remained secret until he was a teenager.

And the way he found out was not exactly the way that his parents would have wanted.

Almost four years previous to current events, a sulky fourteen-year-old Jonathan got back to the family home after school to find the front door locked.

The locked door confused him. He hadn't been given his own key because one of his parents was always home to receive him.

He tried the handle again and knocked on the windows, finally getting his phone out and calling the house, feeling embarrassed because he knew people on the street would be watching him struggle to get into his own house.

The phone rang. But there was no answer.

Annoyed, and getting cold, he tried his parents' mobiles. The calls didn't even connect, and that was when he realised where they were. That stupid old shop they ran. There was never a good signal there. Jonathan's dad always said it was because of the lead on the roof.

Cross, hungry and getting colder, he slouched off into town. Having no money for the bus, he resigned himself to the walk. He kept to the main roads, thinking that if his parents were driving home, they might see him in their car and they could pull over and pick him up. In his head, he plotted the arguments they would have, and he mentally won them all. He ignored the cold biting into his bare legs and pulled his bobble-hat down over his ears, looking down at the pavement as he walked, his shadow slowly getting longer as the cars' headlights came on, flashing over him one after the other.

By the time he got into town, Jonathan's phone battery was almost flat, and he was so irritated he didn't feel cold any more. His parents had never left him like this, and he was furious. He got to the tatty old shop and saw a lamp lit inside. So, they were in, then. His parents were religious about turning off lights that weren't being used.

The shop door was unlocked. Jonathan let himself in, breathing in the warm air from the fire in the grate, giving dirty looks to the suitcases in their neat slots.

'Mum?' he called. 'Dad?'

There was no answer.

Jonathan checked the desk for a note or some sort of clue as to where his parents were. Nothing. There was his dad's phone, though. As usual, there was no signal to speak of on the phone's display.

But . . . why hadn't his dad taken it with him, if he wasn't here?

He went upstairs, checked the rooms that were full of junk and old clothes and came back down again. He stood for a moment, trying to think logically, when the bell in the church next door clanged for seven.

It was later than he'd thought.

And they weren't here. The door was unlocked. None of this made any sense.

Something cold and slimy coiled under Jonathan's skin, replacing his annoyance with a desire to stop existing, just for a minute. He placed both hands flat on the desk to feel the grain, thinking it might ground him and stop the sick feeling.

He stayed there for several minutes.

Then he went to make a cup of tea on the old stove, knowing his parents would be angry at him for using the gas on his own. Somehow, it was comforting to know they would be angry. If they were angry, they'd be there, with him.

He made three cups, brewing them slowly, adding the sugar in carefully measured spoonfuls, the milk in scientific drips. He brought them through one at a time, telling himself lies. Giving the universe silent challenges.

They'll be back by the time the kettle has boiled. They'll be back by the time I've added the milk. They'll be back by the time I've carried the third cup through.

They were not back.

Jonathan wrapped his hands around one of the cups, sat on the ancient swivel chair behind the desk, and waited.

Outside, the sun had long since gone down.

The shadows cast by the amber streetlamps were extremely long, reaching along the pavement like fingers, heading to the shop door.

Jonathan put down his cold tea and locked and bolted the door. He turned on the desk lamp and closed the blinds halfway, leaving them open enough so that the light inside would still be visible from the high-street, in case someone came back and knocked on the door. In case his dad, called out on an urgent errand, remembered he'd forgotten his phone, and came back for it.

191

No one came.

The fire in the grate burned out, a wisp of grey smoke escaping from the chimney and curling through the shop like a snake. Jonathan realised he'd been sitting still for a long time. He stretched blood back into his limbs and went upstairs to the small bedroom, where there were a few old blankets and brought some down, along with a cushion.

He curled up in one of the armchairs beside the dead fire with the blankets over his legs, the chill of the lonely shop soaking into his body as he fought sleep, until eventually, around midnight, he dropped off against his will.

*

He was woken, several hours later, by the sound of a scream.

Jonathan started, sitting bolt upright. Before his eyes, the impossible was happening – someone was climbing out of one of the old suitcases like it was a trap-door.

'Dad?' Jonathan whispered, stunned. In the lamplight, Jonathan could see that his dad's face was bleeding. At the sight of Jonathan, his dad let out a horrible, moaning gasp.

The suitcase lid fell down and slammed shut.

Jonathan's dad stared at his son as if he might not be real.

Jonathan had a million and one questions.

But only one made it to his lips.

'Where's Mum?'

His dad's face crumpled.

And nothing was ever the same, after that.

CHAPTER TWENTY

Flick examined the battered and fraying patch Jonathan had given her. A golden magnifying glass, with a jagged lightning bolt in the circular part, representing a schism, she assumed. She'd recited the pledge, standing holding her *Study of Particulars* like a holy book in the middle of the room whilst Jonathan mouthed the words along with her like an over-eager parent at a school play. After that, he'd handed her the red patch to pin onto the sleeve of her choice.

'I'm sorry it's pre-used,' Jonathan said. 'You don't have to sew it on right this minute, but if you're going to be a Society member, you get the goody bag. Badge, access to books, and your name in the ledger.'

'And a magnifying glass?' Flick asked, chancing it.

Jonathan didn't look up from where he was writing her name, *Felicity Esme Hudson*, in a big ledger. 'No, I'm afraid not,' he said. 'There's only one here, and that stays with me.'

Flick couldn't help feeling rather put out. She liked the magnifying glass and being able to see magic. Travelling to magical worlds was one thing, but to know that there was magic in her own world as well . . . it was truly delicious, and she wanted to taste it again.

She adjusted her backpack. At Jonathan's request, she had come this time with a bag packed with overnight things, a change of clothes and some snacks. 'A longer visit,' he had suggested, pacing around like he might burst if he stood still. 'That's a proper Strangeworlds Society adventure, not simply hopping in and out of cases like changing your socks. And . . .' he produced a pink and gold suitcase with a flourish, 'if we're going to track down my father any place, it will be here.'

An excited jolt shot through Flick. 'Why?'

'Because this place is the City of Five Lights,' he beamed. 'Multiversal hub and home to a Strangeworlds Society outpost.'

Flick made a clueless face. 'In English, please?'

Jonathan put the suitcase down on the floor. 'Imagine a place where the barriers between worlds are all extremely thin.'

Flick dutifully imagined. 'Is that different to a schism?'

'Yes, although there *are* a lot of schisms there. This is somewhere so utterly soaked in transference energy that it has become a sort of intersection. There are also many suitcases that lead to it – this is only one of them.'

Flick pointed at the case on the floor. 'That's not out of the wall, is it?'

'No. This is from the Back Room.'

'The Back Room?'

'There are seven hundred-odd suitcases, Felicity,' Jonathan said. 'Quite obviously, they're not all in the room with us. Where would they fit? This is a travel agency, not a TARDIS. The suitcases you need you keep in the travel agency. Everything else, you store safely.' He picked up the City of Five Lights guidebook and leafed through it. 'Five Lights really is a fascinating city. It been theorised that the place is actually a *product* of condensed magical energy – it came into being *because* of the schisms.' He handed the book to Flick.

Flick skimmed to where Jonathan's finger tapped at a paragraph.

... though it is entirely possible (and indeed recommended) for travel agents to use Suitcase #76 when travelling to the City of Five Lights. It is important to bear in mind that the city itself is constructed – perhaps held together – by the existence of schisms and as a result is extremely fragile. If the schism balance were to shift, the result could be catastrophic. The city is a hub of trade and magic* and there are often people on the street with seemingly magical abilities.

*Five Lights is one of the places where condensed magical energy may be obtained – see currency notes.

Flick frowned. 'The balance in this place is fragile?'

'Yes, and that's probably why my father went there. He might have been concerned about it. Because magic is used so frequently as an energy source, like fuel, it needs replenishing. Usually, the amount of people and travellers seems to do the trick.'

'Seems to,' Flick repeated, not feeling entirely convinced. 'Do they use magic to do spells?'

'And as currency. This place doesn't deal in money,' Jonathan said. 'They deal in valuables. So ...' he took out a small cloth bag from his pocket and tipped several items out into his hand. 'I've got a badge from when I was ten' – he held up a pink Happy Birthday badge – 'a thimble from my collection and some shells from the beach from when I was little.' He put the objects back, and tightened the bag's drawstring. 'Not terribly valuable, but enough for a souvenir or two. Hopefully somewhere to stay.'

'So it's the sentimental value that makes the items worth something?' Flick asked. She thought of her slice of agate and wondered how much that was worth.

'The importance and significance it has to a living person.' Jonathan nodded. 'That is magical. It can be used to trade for all sorts of things. You can even bottle magic and save it up until you have enough for what you need to do or make. It's simply a form of energy.'

Flick patted her empty pockets. It didn't feel fair that Jonathan was going to be the only one giving things away. 'You should have asked me to bring something.'

'I don't want you to lose anything you value,' Jonathan said, moving the case into the centre of the room.

Flick read the Five Lights guidebook again. 'The city exists because of the schisms, then? Is that right?'

'It's a theory,' Jonathan said, taking the book back. 'But some people believe that it might be possible for a world to come into existence if there is enough concentrated magic.'

Flick frowned as a thought came into her head. 'Does that mean someone could create a world? A new one? If they had enough magic?'

Jonathan paused. 'I suppose they could. But I doubt it would exist for very long.'

'Why?'

'Worlds don't create magic of their own; they're just supported by it. It's life that creates magic. People, animals, plants, even bacteria. Living things are responsible for looking after the existence of their world, whether they are aware of it or not. A created world would be little more than an empty room. And even if someone tried to stay in it . . . you remember what I told you about living in a world that isn't your own?'

Flick nodded uneasily. 'You burn up.'

'And the hungry world would burn with you.' Jonathan's eyes unfocussed for a moment behind his glasses. Then he blinked and shrugged. 'On that cheery note, let our next trip begin! And the City of Five Lights is also home to one special place in particular.'

'What's that?'

Jonathan's smile morphed into one much more genuine. 'Quickspark's Travel Emporium. Another travel agency, and off-world outpost of The Strangeworlds Society.'

*

The City of Five Lights was seated in a sort of universal crease – if there was a map of all the known worlds and their links, the City of Five Lights would have been the centre spread. Due to its abundance of schisms, it was very much used to what other worlds might call the strange or unusual. The place was consistently dealing with magic and weirdness. Even the geography of the place rearranged itself now and again.

So no one batted an eyelid when a pink suitcase appeared in the town square and two young people proceeded to climb out of it, pulling the case inside out somehow, before standing and brushing themselves off.

Travellers, thought the general public.

Customers, thought the salespeople.

Victims, thought the Thieves.

*

Flick watched Jonathan yank the suitcase through, and she tried to get her bearings as the world bustled around them.

The funny thing about visiting a new place is that one immediately tries to liken it to an old, familiar place. Or even somewhere you've seen on television, or in a picture on the wall of a stranger's house, to try and make it feel friendlier.

It's a rather funny thing, memory. It doesn't work in straight lines.

So, although Flick had never been to Spain, looking around at the City of Five Lights somehow reminded her of a Spanish city. The city was split into several quads, or squares (though they were all circular, so perhaps they should have been called *rounds*), and each one had a fountain. You could, she thought, if you knew what you were doing, navigate through the city using the fountains, as each one was carved with different birds, or fish, or plants. Fireworking out from the fountains were coral-pink stone walkways bordered with pink and white cobbles. Tall iron gas-lamps stood here and there, dozing in the day before their nightshift. Walking along the pathways with carts on wheels or trays hung around their necks, were people selling everything from tiny glass beads to bunches of blue and purple fruit to immense rolls of fabric. Lining the town's squares were shops, packed tight, practically elbowing one another out of the way for prominence on the sprawling streets.

Flick let her feet start walking, as feet tend to want to do when they're surrounded by others doing the same, Jonathan following a step behind. She read the signs in the windows and over the shop doors. They said things like: *Cat Skulls: Various Sizes Available* and *High-quality Lightning – Buy Two Bolts, Get One Free*. There was even a very grotty-looking shop with nothing but threadbare black curtains hanging in the window and a sign that simply said: *Enquire Within*.

There were dozens upon dozens of people bustling to and fro. At first glance, some of them looked like people Flick might have seen walking down a street in Little Wyverns, but a closer look made Flick realise they were not from her own world at all. There were people with complex gold and silver rings pinned through their pointed ears and others wearing gloves that were made for six fingers instead of five. Flick saw a man with ice-blue skin who had an array of droplet-shaped glass bottles slung on a belt of loops around his hips. He was trying to catch the eye of passers-by, some of whom slowed down to look at his wares. There was a woman a few yards to his left, who looked a little like one of Flick's teachers at her old primary school, aside from the fact she was covered from the neck down in vibrant floral tattoos that actually moved on her skin as if the wind was blowing them. She almost blended in with the flowers and plants she was selling from a small cart on wheels.

'Look.' Jonathan tapped Flick's arm and pointed towards the centre of the square.

There were a couple of girls who had made a space for themselves close by the fountain. One was putting a hat down on the ground and the other was mounting something like a unicycle, except that it had a translucent ball in place of a wheel. A crowd began to gather.

'Are they acrobats?' Flick asked, excitement and delight making her hop from foot to foot as she tried to see over people's heads.

'Performers. They'll do their act and people will donate some trinkets, if they like it.'

The girl on the bubble-cycle was pedalling to and fro, faster and faster, until the unicycle rose into the air like a helium balloon.

Flick gasped.

The girl on the ground, her sparkly leotard glittering in the sunlight, beamed as several tokens landed in the hat on the ground. She did a backwards somersault as if to say thanks. Above her, the girl on the bubble-cycle had spread her arms out to the sides and was pedalling like mad to stay aloft. She reached down and took the hand of her partner, and it wasn't long before the two of them were on the cycle together, the first girl still pedalling, the other standing on her shoulders, both enjoying the applause.

'Can we give them something?' Flick asked.

'I don't see why not.' Jonathan fished in his pocket and pulled out his trinkets, perusing them carefully, before choosing the birthday badge. He flicked it into the hat. 'Pink was never really me, anyway.'

Flick watched the girls give Jonathan a nod of thanks. 'Why did you get a pink badge, then?'

'Because the person who gave it to me thought I was a girl. Now, come on. Lots to see.'

They didn't rush as they walked through the City of Five Lights. You couldn't rush – the place was far too busy for that. There was no distinction between pavement and road, so tricycles and scooters and strange little open cars with shuddering and banging motors swerved through the crowds, which parted grudgingly to let them through. There were sellers all over the place, touting and competing for attention.

'High-flying kites, right here, ladies and gents. Get a high-flying kite for the kiddies, only needs a breath of wind to stay up all day. Only a small trinket needed, good people . . .'

'Never feel the wet again! Genuine merrow-skin, fresh off the boats. Waterproof guaranteed . . .'

'Lowest commission in the City of Five Lights. We bottle what others won't. Yes, madam, even from a knick-knack! We'll only skim off what's honest, and you'll soon be back again for more. Best bottling in Five Lights, ask anyone here today . . .'

This last stallholder had a display on his cart that was made entirely of bottles of various sizes, including some of the droplet-shaped ones Flick had seen earlier hanging from the man's belt at the fountain.

Flick poked Jonathan. 'What's bottling? What are those?'

Jonathan rolled his eyes. 'Check your guidebook.'

They paused against a wall while Flick took out the guidebook for the City of Five Lights.

'There,' Jonathan pointed. 'Bottling.'

ON THE BOTTLING
OF MAGICAL ENERGY

In some worlds, it can be essential to carry magic with you. There are numerous places where it is possible to obtain bottled magical energy, and the most convenient is the City of Five Lights.

Bottled magic is generated from a distilling process, whereby the energy an object contains is taken from it and stored for later use. Bottling destroys the object itself, and the distillers often take some of the object's magic for themselves as payment.

To use the bottled magic, the glass must be smashed and destroyed, releasing the energy stored inside it.

Bottled magical energy has the following uses:

1. Currency.
2. Social Status.
3. Use in magical acts, such as temporarily 'vanishing' a small object.
4. Travel via schism to and from the City of Five Lights (See: *Schisms*).

Flick looked up. 'You said no one should travel through a schism,' she said accusingly.

'You shouldn't. Because the schism would take the magic keeping you alive. But if you have some spare, such as a bottle or three . . .'

'Oh. So, it's like having a battery, then?' Flick mused.

'A little. And the amount needed would depend on the person. People born in Five Lights are already very magical. We, on the other hand, are not.'

Flick felt rather disheartened at the news that other people were substantially more magical than she was. 'So, we'd need a lot of extra magic to use a schism?'

'More than you could imagine. I can't even fathom what we might trade for that amount of magic. And remember, we are supposed to maintain a balance of magic and schism – the last thing this place needs is us trying to hoard magic like specialised dragons. We don't need to, anyway. We have the suitcase.' He held it up. 'And that is the safest and most elegant way to travel. Now, I don't know about you, but I'm starving. Lunch? There's a delightful place called the Marigold not too far from here.'

CHAPTER TWENTY-ONE

Across the square, a man with white-blond hair and a red coat watched the travellers with unblinking interest. He took a small lined notebook from his pocket and penned a short note. The ink shone for a moment, before vanishing into the paper like snow melting into a pond.

The man, a professional Thief, stood and cricked his neck. He flapped his scarlet coat out before fastening the single gold button at his waist. There was no need for a Thief to blend in. A decent Thief could wear the brightest red and still not be troubled as he did his job. Going unnoticed was for amateurs. And thieving in Five Lights was especially profitable – the value of a stolen item was much higher than one freely given, after all.

The Thief watched the travellers enter the food

district. He mentally assessed the two of them. Young. Inexperienced. And most importantly, carrying a suitcase. That was what he'd been waiting for.

Months he'd been sitting, watching for a Strangeworlds Society member coming into Five Lights. Months of anxiety, of fear that he and his employers had missed out on their only chance.

The notebook in his pocket stirred, and he took it out to read the response. Then he smiled.

The Thief moved through the busy quad and down a slender alleyway leading to a quiet, stone-lined street. He roughly dragged his hand over the biting stonework, drawing blood. Feeling where the sharp metal seal of the Thieves was hammered into the wall, he pressed his bleeding palm onto it. The toll paid, the metal seal trembled beneath his touch, and the entire wall shifted. The brickwork slid sideways, like a screen door, allowing the man to slip into a narrow stone walkway and listen as the door that shouldn't have been there closed quietly behind him.

He took a moment to press a cotton handkerchief to his bleeding hand before starting down the passage. There was no light, and if he wanted any he would have to buy it himself. He tolerated the darkness the way one might tolerate an unpleasant visitor – by knowing that, eventually, he would be far away from it.

It was how all the First Class Thieves endured the city.

The man came to the door at the end of the passage and lifted the iron knocker hung in the shape of a crown, beaten flat.

A bored woman's voice invited him in.

The Thief went into a room that, although small, had enough darkness at the edges to make it appear large. The woman who had asked him in ignored his entrance. She sat at a desk the width and breadth of a double bed, the chair behind it the sort with wings, though not for flying. The book of maps she was reading was browning and hand-bound and probably should have been handled by someone wearing gloves. She licked a finger and turned the page.

The man cleared his throat. 'A member of The Strangeworlds Society is here.'

The woman looked up from the book with an uninterested expression. 'Yes, I got your message, Hid.' She tapped a notepad on the desk. 'A child, though. Not the man?'

'Well, he is almost a man, this one. But he is Daniel

Mercator's child, Overseer. He is the spit of him.' Hid mimed spitting, for emphasis.

The Overseer rested her chin on her hand. 'I see.'

'He has a suitcase with him,' Hid said. 'A schism contained in a box.'

The Overseer said nothing. The two Thieves stared at each other, their lives before Five Lights hanging over them like a dark cloud. Some things were better never spoken of. And, in some instances, buried.

'You did say it would only be a matter of time before Five Lights was at risk, Glean. Madam Overseer,' Hid said, carefully correcting his manners.

'The Unseen could already be here, and we would know nothing of them,' Glean sighed. Then she stood and cracked her knuckles. 'The Mercator boy will head for The Strangeworlds Society outpost – Quickspark's. It will be interesting to see how he reacts to what he finds.'

'His suitcase, though. It could be a way out. *Our* way out.'

Glean slowly steepled her fingers, two of them meeting at a time. 'It doubtless leads back to his own world. Tempting. Though it would involve having to deal with other Strangeworlds Society members who might come to try and defend the place. The boy might be threatened into providing something else, of course.'

A crafty expression came over Hid's face. 'He has another child with him.'

Glean frowned. 'Another Mercator? I wasn't aware the Head Custodian had more than one child.'

'I don't know who she is. But she could be valuable.'

'You mean as leverage. Take the girl, and have him trade a suitcase for her safe return?'

Hid nodded. 'Better to negotiate for a world we truly *want* than thieving for scraps, Overseer.'

A smile slowly crept over Glean's face. 'Then take her. When you can.'

*

Flick felt her jacket move. She looked down to see a hand retreating out of her pocket. 'Hey!'

Jonathan turned around.

'Are you picking my pocket?' Flick grabbed the wrist of a girl in a red coat.

'Ow,' the girl winced. Her tight dark curls were cut very short. She seemed to be about the same age as Flick. 'You've got open pockets, haven't you? Fair game.'

'Fair game?' Flick's eyebrows shot up in outrage.

'I've got a licence.' The girl extracted a small card

from her sleeve with her free hand. 'See?'

Jonathan took it.

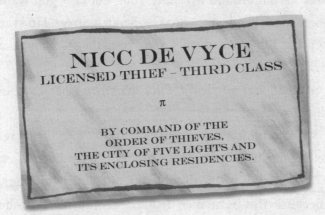

NICC DE VYCE
LICENSED THIEF – THIRD CLASS

π

BY COMMAND OF THE
ORDER OF THIEVES,
THE CITY OF FIVE LIGHTS AND
ITS ENCLOSING RESIDENCIES.

'This seems to check out.' He handed it to Flick. 'Apologies, Miss de Vyce.'

'Out of towners, are you?' The Thief rubbed her wrist as Flick let go.

'You could say that.'

'Well, watch yourselves. Thieves got a new quota, today, so there's lots of us on the ground.' She sniffed and glanced about. 'Did I hear you say you're going to the Marigold Inn?'

Flick scowled, not wanting to tell this Thief anything. 'We might have been.'

'You'll struggle. It's not been around for a while, that place.'

'What do you mean?' asked Flick.

Nicc de Vyce blinked at her. 'Wow. You really *aren't* from around here, are you? Look, if you want some food, head west onto Cat-Scratch Street. Find the Wilting Lily. Tell them I sent you, they'll do you a deal.'

'What sort of deal?' Flick narrowed her eyes in distrust.

Jonathan looked suspicious too. 'Why are you telling us this?'

Nicc held up a thimble. It was very familiar. 'Because this is a nice trinket. Don't worry,' she grinned, as Jonathan checked his pockets. 'I left you a receipt. Catch you later, out-of-towners.' And she stepped backwards and melted into the bustling crowd.

Jonathan took a piece of paper from his pocket. 'Receipt of Theft,' he read. 'One thimble. Well, that's that, then.'

'We should tell the police,' Flick said, as they started walking again. She felt incredibly annoyed by Nicc's brazen thievery and kept her hands stuffed into her pockets as she walked.

'There'd be no point in reporting it,' Jonathan sighed. 'Thieves have a licence to practise here. It's as much a job as being a plumber or engineer.'

'And they leave receipts?' Flick stepped back to let a herd of very small brown sheep amble down the road. They were like cuddly toys. A shepherd was driving them, a dark stick in his hand.

'I suppose it makes the whole process official. I dread to imagine what they think of anyone operating freelance. Still. The tip about the inn wasn't bad.'

'You think we should trust her?'

'Well, why not? Would we trust a baker, or a florist? Probably. Well, why not a Thief? Remember: this isn't our world. We shouldn't impose our rules or expectations on it.'

Cat-Scratch Street was easy enough to find, and they didn't have to go far before they found the Wilting Lily. A large, green-white painted inn, it had a swinging sign with a dying white flower on it. There were a lot of tables and chairs outside, and several of the tables were occupied by couples and groups drinking wine and eating olives.

Jonathan led the way inside, and Flick sighed in pleasure at the coolness of the air – she hadn't realised how warm the City of Five Lights was.

'Table for two, is it?' An older gentleman with a beard in two fine plaits came forward to greet them.

He caught sight of the suitcase. 'Or are you looking for a room?'

'Both, if possible,' Jonathan said.

'Someone called de Vyce sent us,' Flick added.

The man beamed. 'Niccy! Ah, she's a good honest girl.'

'Isn't she a Thief?' Flick asked incredulously.

'Absolutely! She'll be one of the best one day, you mark my words. A room and a table for Niccy's friends. No charge!'

'We shall certainly pay,' Jonathan said.

'Then let us meet halfway. You pay for your food, I give you the room for the night gratis.' The man spread his hands out, showing he had nothing to hide. 'You won't find a better offer than that.'

'Thank you,' Flick smiled. 'What's your name?'

'Jesper, my friends call me,' he said. 'And my enemies call me a stubborn old man who knows too much for his own good. Now – a table. The patio has lovely shade. Follow me, please?'

Jesper took them out to the back of the inn, where a patio shaded by lush green trees waited for them. Jesper put a jug of what tasted like lemonade on the table and handed Flick a menu, before leaving.

'This is nice.' Flick opened the menu. 'Is this as nice as the place you wanted to go?'

'Hm?' He looked up, as if he didn't know what she meant.

'You want to go somewhere else. The . . . Marzipan?'

'The Marigold,' he corrected her. 'This place is nicer, actually. We've fallen rather lucky. Almost worth the theft of the thimble, though we don't have much left to trade. We shall have to be very careful from here on in.'

'Why's that?' A red-coated figure helped herself to one of the spare seats and they looked up, startled. 'Oh, don't mind me,' Nicc said as she filled her empty glass with the drink from the jug.

'I don't believe we arranged to share our lunch,' Jonathan managed, as he watched Nicc take a sip of the drink.

'I don't make plans,' Nicc grinned. Her eyes sparkled with humour, and the freckles over her nose made her look cute, rather than sneaky. 'I never know when I might get a better offer.'

'Not above stealing your food as well, then?' Flick asked cuttingly. The attempted rifling through her pockets still stung.

'Above?' Nicc put her glass down. 'What do you mean?'

'Well . . . stealing,' Flick said. 'You don't have to steal. You could buy things.'

'With what?' Nicc cast a hand around. 'I don't have the talent or skill to make anything. I can't perform, save for going unseen. And I don't come from a rich family. Thieving is a respectable job. I take what I need, and I pay my way with it.'

'But you're stealing things that belong to other people,' Flick insisted.

Nicc leaned an elbow on the table. 'What's your name, out-of-towner?'

'Flick.'

'Flick? Well, Miss Flick, I don't know where you've dropped in from, but Thieving is not the same as stealing. Stealing is done by folks who want more than they need. Taking for the sake of taking or taking to deprive someone. Thieving is a skill. An art-form. It is going unseen, noticing what the owner is not guarding and Thieving it into your ownership. Using that to trade for what you need. I'm not taking things to keep or to hoard. I'm taking them to survive. It's what the Order does.'

'So . . .' Flick frowned. 'It's a skill? That you learn?'

'Yes,' Nicc nodded excitedly. 'You go to the school, learn the tricks and when you get your licence, you go out and thieve. The Order takes a cut to keep the school running and that's that. Look,' Nicc pointed at one of the large buildings that loomed past the gardens. 'See that red-brick building? That's the Order of Thieves.'

'Right in the middle of the city,' Jonathan mused.

Flick tapped the menu in front of her. 'What do you do with the things you thieve? Do you bottle them into magic?'

'Sometimes,' Nicc said, nodding. 'The Order doesn't like us to store too much magic, though. Prefers if we deal in items.'

'Why?'

'Well . . .' Nicc stopped. Then she frowned. 'I'm not sure.'

'Balance,' Jonathan said, as if it was a suggestion, but Flick thought it was probably more an explanation for her sake. 'Too much stored magic can't be a good thing.'

Nicc sniffed. 'I don't know about that. I don't like magic. Don't trust it. I know there's a rumour some of the higher-ups like to get a lot of magic and schism-jump. You'd never catch me doing something like that. I know where I belong and it's here. Going to other worlds? I like the one I'm in, thank you.' She glanced down at the suitcase. Then lowered her voice. 'You're with The Strangeworlds Society, aren't you?'

Flick felt her muscles contract as if preparing to run, and Jonathan went slightly red.

'That obvious, is it?' he asked, aiming for bravado and landing on nervousness.

Nicc smiled, and Flick felt some of her fright give way. 'Don't worry, I'm not about to broadcast the fact you're here.'

'You've heard of us, then?'

'Never met one of you in person, but heard of, yeah. Heard you were all gone, actually.'

Jonathan's expression shut down. His face was as readable as a blank slate. 'And where did you hear that?'

'The Thieves. I heard you'd not been around for a long time. Not properly. Just a skeleton crew, is that right?'

Flick thought about the great emptiness of the travel agency and how alone Jonathan had been in it. Even now she was with him, the place wasn't exactly packed out with Custodians.

Nicc took a swig of her drink and shrugged at the awkward silence. 'None of my business, I'm sure. But be careful. This place isn't what it used to be.'

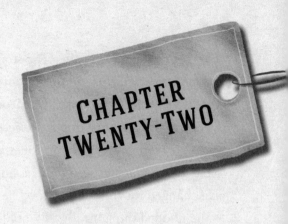

CHAPTER TWENTY-TWO

'Why did you say we should come here instead of the Marigold?' Flick asked.

Nicc clicked her tongue before she spoke. 'Because the Marigold is gone. And it's not the only thing. Five Lights really has changed. There's always been the odd time a building disappeared or one of the fountains started running backwards, but now it's happening all the time. Whole streets are vanishing. Stalls, shops . . . people.'

'People,' Jonathan repeated.

Flick's heart gave what felt like a sharp nudge.

I'm the last Mercator . . .

She gave a quick glance at Jonathan, whose face was grey.

Nicc nodded. 'Something's happening here.' She

looked at the suitcase again. 'The stories said that The Strangeworlds Society used to look after us when things like this happened. They'd send someone to investigate.'

Flick felt as if a heap of puzzle pieces had fallen into place. She trod deliberately on Jonathan's foot.

He glanced at her and gave a single nod. 'Things have changed for the Society, too,' he said to Nicc.

She nodded thoughtfully. 'I wouldn't linger around here, if I was you. Something's going wrong. And I wouldn't want you to get caught up in it.'

Flick didn't know what to say. She really needed to talk to Jonathan, alone.

Nicc de Vyce didn't stay to eat with them. She greeted Jesper merrily when he brought their food, and Flick noticed her take a bottle opener from his belt without him feeling it, before she vanished out of the inn.

Flick counted silently to one hundred before broaching the question. 'This was the last place your dad travelled to, wasn't it? Why didn't we just come here first?'

Jonathan put his cutlery down. 'When I arrived at the travel agency, after I heard he was missing, the suitcase to Five Lights – the one we always kept in the wall of cases – was gone. He travelled here. I followed him, through this spare case,' he tapped it beneath the table. 'I tried asking around for him. People were kind, but not especially helpful. Or else downright hostile when I tried to get any scrap of information I thought might help. Nothing anyone said gave me a clue. I didn't stay long. Went back to Strangeworlds, tried to make sense of *why* he would have . . . gone. And that was a couple of months ago.'

Flick tapped the table as she thought. 'Do you think he knew about what Nicc told us, then? The disappearing streets, buildings vanishing and so on?'

'He must have,' Jonathan said. 'He always took his Head Custodian duties very seriously. He would have come here to investigate.'

Flick paused, not sure she wanted to know the answer to her next question. 'What do you think he found out?'

Jonathan didn't answer.

The space between them could have frosted over.

Flick pushed her plate away. 'Could someone have kidnapped him? The Thieves?'

Jonathan pulled a sceptical face. 'I doubt it. Even they have rules and a code of conduct. People, for instance, shouldn't be stolen.'

'People?' Flick coughed.

'Yes.' Jonathan fished out the Five Lights guidebook for her to see. 'Apparently, there's an agreement with the City Guards. People are strictly off-limits. Inanimate objects only.'

Flick scanned the page.

In accordance with orders from the Five Lights City Guards, theft is restricted to objects that are not alive. This includes a ban on thieving both animals and people. Incidents of kidnap should be reported to the Guards, who will assist you.

'I don't know what to say,' Flick said. And she didn't. Everything pointed to Daniel Mercator having come here and then . . . vanishing. Either he was dead, or he'd deliberately run away, or someone held him hostage. None of the outcomes were comforting.

Jonathan gave a sad sort of shrug.

Sympathy settled over Flick like a blanket. 'So . . . What made you come back now? After all this time?'

Jonathan looked up at her. 'You.'

A shiver crept over Flick, like spiders' steps over her skin. For some reason, it didn't feel entirely welcome to have been part of Jonathan's decision to come back.

When they had eaten, Jesper showed them to their

room. Jonathan assured Flick that, even if they slept overnight at the City of Five Lights, only a few hours would pass in their own world. The room was split into separate compartments with sliding doors separating the two beds. The beds themselves were on the floor and were rounded at both ends, like used bars of soap. They were padded on the inside and a snug mattress filled the bottom, along with a pile of blankets and pillows. Flick was reminded of cocoons.

Jonathan pushed back the third screen and made a delighted sound at the bathtub and sinks. 'This is delightfully rustic. I'm sure we could have done worse.'

Flick pressed the bed's mattress with a hand. It felt the perfect mixture of firm and soft. 'I can't wait to sleep in it.'

'You don't want to *sleep* yet,' Jonathan said, going over to the window. 'The sun is going down. And night-time is when this place really comes alive.'

*

Jonathan wasn't wrong. As the sun dropped below the horizon, the City of Five Lights lived up to its name. The fountains central to the quads each had five frosted glass lamps atop them, and as the darkness crept in, the lamps lit up in a bright blue-white light. Tiny fairy lights were strung between the surrounding buildings and the fountains, creating a cobweb of twinkling lights over the heads of the tourists and shoppers below. Each stall and cart followed suit, their wheels and displays sparkling with colourful lights that glowed and glimmered, competing to be the most noticeable.

Flick watched from their window as a magician took to the square, smashing two bottles of magic beneath his boots before catching the mists of the escaping magic and changing it from magical energy into light energy. It was as though he was holding two tiny suns in his hands. He gave them a twist, and again, until he had three smaller balls in each hand. And then, he began to juggle them. The balls of light didn't act like the juggling balls Flick knew. They drifted slowly through the air, leaving glowing, ribbon-like trails in their wake, and as the juggler turned on the spot, he became surrounded by a waterfall of light. Flick laughed, her earlier unease almost forgotten.

Flick and Jonathan went out into the evening. Jonathan still had the case in his hand; he was too nervous to leave it behind. The evening air was warm, and there was a smell of roasting garlic and herbs coming from the kitchen of the Wilting Lily. Outside, stallholders were glazing nuts in sugar, turning meat on wooden sticks, frying battered hoops that looked a little like onion rings and stuffing thin, pita-like breads full of spiced vegetables and rice.

Flick's stomach growled. She nudged Jonathan and pointed to the stall with the stuffed pitas. 'Can we?'

He rolled his eyes but followed her over.

'Lovely evening!' The woman making the food beamed at them. 'Best street food in Five Lights. You've chosen wisely. What can I get for you?'

'What's in these?' Flick asked politely.

'Spiced yellow peas, rice and rough-cut peppers.' The woman showed her the frying pan, where more of the mixture was cooking. Flick leaned forward and sniffed appreciatively at the fragrant steam. 'And jumping crickers, of course.'

Flick froze, her mouth drying up like the Sahara. 'Jumping what?'

'Crickers.' The woman spooned up something brown that Flick had taken to be a vegetable; only now she could see it had legs. Several of them. 'Very nice. Filling and not too spicy. You want two?'

Flick gawped in silent horror at the insect on the spoon.

Jonathan was shaking with suppressed mirth as he

patted Flick on the shoulder. 'As much as my friend here enjoys eating invertebrates,' he said, grinning wickedly, 'I am a vegetarian. Do you have anything without wing-cases?'

'Of course. One for each of you?'

Jonathan parted with two seashells for the food, as Flick recovered enough to thank the stallholder, and they then both walked over to the fountain to eat their snack. The pitas were doughy and squishy and warm, with a subtle hint of what tasted like coconut in the bread. The rice and vegetables inside were delicious, and Flick sat in happy silence as she chewed.

Flick beamed. She was in another world. A world she had never known existed before today! The warm evening air was like a welcoming hug, and the lights and music around her were like magic. And there was even *real* magic! She beamed, mouth full, as she watched a girl spin a glass hoop filled with tiny twinkling light up her arms, over her head and down her body to her feet, before freeing one of her feet and gracefully balancing on one leg, the hoop still spinning merrily on the other. The hoop then dissolved into a flurry of pink-white blossoms, which swirled through the busy square before vanishing completely.

'This is the best day I've ever had,' she said, once

she'd swallowed.

Jonathan blinked at her. His face seemed stuck somewhere between surprised and sympathetic. 'R-really?'

'I don't mean that I'm not worried about . . .' she gestured at Jonathan, who gave a sort of *I don't mind* shrug. 'Sorry. It's not fair that I'm enjoying this.'

'I don't want you to not enjoy yourself,' Jonathan said. 'It's fine, really. You don't need to apologise.'

She gazed back at the mingling crowds of people and sighed. 'I've wanted to travel places my whole life. But we've never been able to afford to go anywhere. I've never even been abroad in *our* world. And now I'm here! In another world, where there's magic and fun, and people to meet, and new things to learn. And no one else knows about it. It's like . . . it's ours.' She looked down at the suitcase. 'And we've got to look after it, right? We've got to find out what's going on here.'

'That's right.' Jonathan's expression was thoughtful.

Flick gave a cheerful swing of her legs. 'Tell me about this Quickspark place.'

Jonathan swallowed the last bite of his pita and balled up his paper bag. 'Quickspark's is a Strangeworlds outpost, a place where people trusted by the Society could be contacted in the event of anything going wrong. We have outposts in a few different worlds, but Quickspark's is especially important. Five Lights is more than just another world we visit,' he said. 'It is thought to be the very hub of the multiverse. To lose contact with it would be extremely undesirable.'

Flick turned. 'Does the outpost here have suitcases?'

'A few. But, more importantly, it has Custodians.'

'People like you?'

'They might aspire to be like me, certainly,' Jonathan said, smirking.

Flick rolled her eyes. 'And you want to go see them? All right.' She looked back at the crowds of people, some of whom were wearing glowing jewellery. The crowd was like a mass of fireflies, moving gently through the gathering darkness. 'As long as you know what you're doing.'

'We have plenty of time.' Jonathan showed her his watch, which was still keeping Earth time. 'Besides, there's nothing too dangerous here.'

CHAPTER TWENTY-THREE

'Quickspark's Travel Emporium isn't too much of a walk from here,' Jonathan said as they left the Wilting Lily the next morning. The sun was already beating down onto the city, which seemed subdued and sleepy after its long night. There were a few scattered carts selling breakfasts and teas, but none of the trinkets or toys or performers from before. Flick felt rather out of place as they walked over the square, as though she was seeing a part of the City of Five Lights that was supposed to remain private.

'What's the point in keeping suitcases in other worlds?' Flick asked as they turned down a side-street. 'Sounds a bit of a security risk, to me.'

Jonathan smiled. 'Don't keep all your suitcases in one basket, I say. Think of them as back doors – if there's a wolf prowling on the Strangeworlds front porch, you'll go out through the back. It hardly makes sense for there to only be one point of entry and exit to other worlds. Plus, what if you needed to visit somewhere without anyone else knowing about it?'

'Why would you need to keep it a secret anyway?' Flick frowned. 'Anyone who saw would be part of the Society, wouldn't they?'

'After one hundred and forty-seven years of travel, I would be very surprised if no one ever visited another world or three in secret.'

'I don't get why you'd want to keep secrets from an already secret society,' Flick said shrewdly. 'Do you know secrets that I don't?'

'I know everything my father told me, and I've answered all of your questions,' Jonathan said.

Except that one, Flick thought to herself.

They went down one of the smaller alleyways where the gloom clung to the walls like burnt-on chimney smoke. There were no signs outside the shops they passed, and the flagstones were somewhat sunken, misshapen from centuries of footsteps.

'It should be here,' Jonathan said, examining his guidebook. 'At the end of Spectral Lane.' He looked up at the building to his right.

And then went very, very still.

'What's wrong ...' Flick followed his gaze and trailed off.

A dusty window stared back at them. Above the window, there was a pale oblong of stone where a sign should have been. Inside, the shop was completely empty.

Flick stepped forward. Her footsteps sounded very loud. 'Is this it?'

'It should have been here.' Jonathan closed his book. 'It *was* here.' He put a hand to the window.

Flick stepped up to the shop front. There was grime on the window and thick spider-webs over the cracks between the bricks. It felt empty, even on the outside.

Jonathan stepped back, as if expecting the view to change. 'It was here when I last came. It's always been here.' He had gone very pale. 'I don't understand.'

Flick went to the door, which was a heavy wooden one, and pushed it. 'It's not locked,' she said, as it creaked open. Flick pushed the door further and went inside.

The room was icy cold. Wallpaper – a handsome design of trees and rivers that had faded to skeleton lines – was half-torn from the walls. There was a fireplace, like the one in Strangeworlds, in the centre of the wall. The mirror over the fireplace was smashed and there were shards of glass on the floor. There were two chairs overturned on the rug, and a desk with scattered papers littered over it.

The wide floorboards were dull with a thin layer of dust.

Flick stepped further in. 'There's nothing here.' Her voice was loud in the eerie empty space. 'What happened?'

Jonathan followed her in. He dragged a finger over a shelf and wrinkled his nose at the dust. 'Not been left too long.' He'd gone paler than ever, his eyes like saucers, gleaming in the dim light. His usual swagger had completely evaporated, his shoulders up and tense, and he was gripping the suitcase so hard his knuckles were white.

The cold feeling under Flick's skin grew as she watched the lost movements of her companion. He looked out of his depth. Drowning in disbelief.

A suspicion began to form in Flick's mind, like a snake uncoiling in the shadows. She gripped the ends of her sleeves tight. 'You knew your dad came here,' she said. 'Why did you bring *me* here?'

Jonathan shook his head like he was in a trance.

'Jonathan,' she snapped, louder, startling him out of wherever his mind was. 'What's going on? Why are we *here*?'

He didn't answer.

The suspicion struck a hard punch to Flick's brain. And then dread, like a slow-motion drip of poison to her stomach, began to gather. 'You . . . you didn't just come here to show me the outpost, did you?'

Jonathan shook his head. He looked utterly lost.

Flick pressed her fingers to her temples as if she could slow down her thoughts, which were beginning to race. 'You said you came here before looking for your dad. But you couldn't find him. So . . .' she blinked rapidly, 'what's changed? Why have you come back *now*?'

Jonathan gave a very forced laugh. 'You think that's what's important, right now? We simply have nothing else pressing to think about, after all. It's not as though an entire Society building has been – been *ransacked*!'

Flick ignored the snappish sarcasm. 'What's going on, Jonathan?' she asked, her heart thudding in her ears.

'An outstanding question,' he replied, not really answering. He paused, his foot scuffing against something close to one of the overturned chairs.

'What's that?' Flick frowned as he bent down and extracted a thin piece of paper. He shook it out and read it.

'Oh.' Jonathan's face went from fearful to disgusted and back to fearful like someone was flicking through a series of increasingly unflattering filters. 'Oh, they wouldn't . . .'

'What *is* it?' Flick reached over and grabbed the paper.

RECEIPT OF THEFT

CONDUCTED BY THE THIEVES
OF FIVE LIGHTS
AT
QUICKSPARK'S TRAVEL EMPORIUM
FOR THE SUM TOTAL OF
ALL GOODS

RE-PURCHASE BY ARRANGEMENT ONLY.

Flick turned the note over. It had a stamp on the reverse side – a hand clutching a drawstring purse. 'Someone took it all?' The growing acceptance she'd been feeling about Thieves was immediately replaced by a raging sense of injustice.

'It's all gone,' Jonathan said flatly. 'Everything here is gone. The suitcases. The people. The . . . everything. That's it, then. A dead end. It's over. Everything I did . . . bringing you here . . . it was all pointless.'

'What do you mean, *bringing me here*? Jonathan, you're freaking me out.'

Jonathan went over to the window-seat and sat down. 'It means that coming here was a complete waste of time. I've got no one to ask, no suitcases to take back, and I can't even check if they were used lately . . .' He went to brush at his eyes, but the suitcase swung from his wrist and hit him hard in the chest. 'Ouch . . . for god's sake!' He thumped the wooden seat.

Flick waited until his jaw had unclenched. Jonathan seemed to her like a frightened animal with teeth and claws – he wasn't like Flick had ever seen him. 'Jonathan . . . ask about what? Why did you bring me here?'

He gave another bitter laugh. 'I might as well tell you . . . we didn't come here just to update the guidebooks, or to show you the pretty lights. I wanted to come here to trace my father.'

Flick's mouth dropped open. 'But I thought you said you'd already asked the people here? They couldn't help you?'

Jonathan was looking anywhere except at her. 'That's what I thought. Until you walked into Strangeworlds.'

'What do you mean?'

A twist of utter misery crossed his face. 'When I look through a magnifying glass,' he said, 'do you know what I see? A soft golden glow. A blurred light moving to and fro.'

The tension in Flick's chest began to wind tighter.

'I don't see sparkles,' Jonathan said. 'I don't see glitter; I don't see which suitcases have been used. And I certainly do not see schisms. Because *no one* is supposed to be able to do that.'

Flick's clockwork tension strained against her ribcage. 'I don't understand.'

He sighed. 'The only person who was ever able to see schisms was my great-great-great-grandmother, Elara Mercator. And no one since.'

'You can't see schisms?' Flick realised she couldn't feel her legs. The tension in her chest had gone but now she was numb.

Jonathan shook his head. 'No one can. Except you.'

CHAPTER TWENTY-FOUR

lick felt as if she ought to gasp.

But all she felt was empty. It was as though something had burst inside her, and all the joy and happiness and excitement she'd ever felt about Strangeworlds was being dragged into an abyss.

'Why didn't you tell me?' she asked.

'If you'd seen the look on your face when you realised you could see magic . . .'

'No,' she stepped forward. 'Why didn't you *tell* me?'

'Because I wanted it to be me, all right?' he yelled, standing up quickly and dropping the suitcase to the ground. 'This is *my* family's business. It's my history. *My* great-great-great-grandmother who invented the suitcases, who founded The Strangeworlds Society. No one else could do what she did. And then . . .' He shook his head bitterly, 'And then you wander in, off the street, a nobody . . . and you could see all of it. It was like you'd snatched it away from me.'

'I didn't take anything from you,' Flick said. She looked around at the ransacked and ruined emporium. 'What did you even want me to do?'

Jonathan's anger vanished like flicking a switch. 'You were supposed to find him.'

'Find your dad?'

He nodded. 'You can see schisms. You can tell which suitcases have been used and maybe even in what order. I knew he came to Five Lights and it must have been to use this agency. He was going somewhere in one of their suitcases. You could have helped me to find where he went next. Even if we couldn't follow him all the way, we could have—'

'We?' Flick gawped. 'Jonathan, you didn't even tell me only I could do those things! And I thought you could see schisms too! I . . .' She looked at her hands, remembering how the sparks of magic had caressed her skin. It was as if the magic in the air had known she was special, too.

No, not special.

A freak.

'I don't want to do this,' she said quietly.

'You have to!' Jonathan exploded.

'You lied to me,' Flick snapped, her throat tightening as she fought off tears. 'You lied to me so you could use me like – like a tool!'

Jonathan gave a laugh that Flick wanted to slap clean off his face. 'You're an outsider! You're just a girl with a bit of magic and you were actually going to walk away from all this! I had to keep you coming, don't you understand? You've got a gift, and you don't even know how to use it. God only knows what else you can do. You need me.'

'No,' Flick shook her head. 'You need *me*. You were using me.'

'I never intended you to feel like that,' he said.

'Oh, apology accepted,' Flick snapped. 'You've been stringing me along with nice trips and sweets, and . . . oh god, why couldn't you tell me I'm like this?' Flick shook her head. Her jaw was aching from clenching her teeth. She'd never felt so angry in her whole life. Or so lost. She didn't know what she was capable of, or even what it truly meant. 'I don't want to do this.'

'See? I knew you would refuse to help me—'

She pointed at him. 'You lied to me. If you want

someone's help, Jonathan, you don't manipulate them. You ask, and you hope they say yes. And if you took one look at me and thought I wouldn't help you . . .' Flick shook her head. 'You don't know me at all. And I don't want you to.' She stamped towards the door.

'So that's it?' Jonathan called. 'You're marching off into a world you don't know, with no way of getting back, because you're angry?'

'I'm going for a think.' Flick grabbed the door handle. 'I'm not your tool, Jonathan. You can't twist me to work how you want. If I decide to help you, it's my decision. You don't get to force me into it.'

She let the door slam.

CHAPTER TWENTY-FIVE

Flick stormed angrily through the streets. It was busier now. The roads and sidewalks were crowded again, and Flick only worked out where she was from the tall central fountain in the middle of the quadrangle.

How dare *Jonathan lie to me like that?* Her mind buzzed like it was filled with angry bees. *Why didn't he tell me I was special for seeing schisms the first time I did it? He just wanted to use me.*

She pushed through a group of chattering children and caught sight of the Wilting Lily up ahead. She didn't know why she was marching back there. She needed to get away from all of this. Everything.

'Whatchit.' Someone grabbed her arm.

Flick turned, fist raised.

Nicc let her go and held her hands up. 'Whoa. Take it easy, short stuff. Where are you running to?'

Flick dropped her arm. 'Back to the inn.'

'Right . . .' Nicc frowned. 'Where's your friend?'

'He isn't my friend.'

Nicc raised her eyebrows. 'Oh. Well, where's your associate, then?'

'Back on Spectre Street.'

'Huh. Used to be a nice street, back in the day . . .' She put her hands in her pockets. 'You've had a fall-out?'

'Something like that.'

Nicc sighed. 'How are you going to get home?'

Flick opened her mouth to explain about the suitcases, then quickly realised it was back with Jonathan. She didn't actually have a way to get home without him. The idea of relying on him made her want to scream.

Nicc took in her expression and seemed to understand. 'I'll take you back to the Lily. He can find you there. He'll come back for you. Or else he'll have me to answer to.' Nicc jerked her head. 'Come on, Flick. This way.'

*

'Maybe he was worried you wouldn't want to help him if you knew. Didn't want to scare you off?' Nicc said, half an hour later. They were in the Wilting Lily, mugs of soup between them.

'I would have helped,' Flick said indignantly, stirring her lunch with a very long metal spoon. 'Now I feel like I don't even know who I am any more. I can do things that even he can't, and . . .' She looked again at her hands, imagining the magic washing over them. She wished more than ever she had a magnifying glass of her own. Just to see the swirling glitter again would make her feel better – to know it was real and try to make peace with the fact that only she could see it.

'He must have had a good reason.'

Flick let go of her spoon. 'But who keeps something like that from their friend?'

Nicc raised her eyebrows at her.

Flick pushed her mug away. 'I don't trust liars. If he wants to find his dad, he can do it on his own.' But even as she spoke, she felt rotten. It wasn't Daniel Mercator's fault his son was the prince of deception.

'What happened to his father?' Nicc asked.

'I don't know,' Flick said. 'He came here and then disappeared. We don't know what happened. He could even be dead.'

Nicc sat back and sighed. 'Grief does funny things to people.'

Flick blinked.

'Makes you forget what's important.' The Thief scratched at her hair. 'I don't think Jonathan did any of this on purpose. I think he was just really sad. That can make you not yourself.'

'That's not an excuse!' Flick said.

'I'm not saying it is. I'm saying maybe it explains his behaviour, a bit. You don't have to think it was OK, but— hello?' Nicc looked up.

Flick followed her gaze, as two shadows fell across the table.

'On your way, de Vyce,' the owner of one of the shadows growled. It was a hooded man with a Thief's red cloak and a curtain of lank hair.

'Says who?' Nicc didn't move from her seat.

'We don't explain ourselves to the lower classes, you filthy little pickpocket. On your way.'

'Every Thief was a pickpocket once. Hid, isn't it?' She tried to see inside the red hood. 'I've done nothing wrong, you can ask anyone. I've flashed my licence.'

The second figure – a woman – pushed her own hood back. She was very short, with cropped hair. 'We are not here for you, de Vyce.'

Flick froze.

Nicc glanced at her, then back at her Thief colleagues. 'What's the kid got to do with anything, Pinch?'

'You're both kids, de Vyce. Listen to your elders and be on your way. This does not concern you.'

'I haven't done anything,' Flick said, panicking.

'We have orders to bring you in.' Pinch smiled, and she smiled like a cold knife. 'De Vyce, if you don't plan on assisting us, be on your way.'

Nicc ignored her. 'Orders? From who?'

Hid's smile joined Pinch's. And his was even colder. 'The Overseer.'

Pinch clamped a hand down on Flick's shoulder. 'Stand up without fussing, child. Come with us.'

'I'm not going anywhere.' Flick tried to brush off the woman's hand, but it was like a vice.

'Then we shall *take* you.'

'You can't steal people,' Flick said. 'You can't.'

Pinch beamed, simply delighted. 'Oh, heard that rumour, have you?'

Then, before Flick could blink, she was hauled to her feet, her arms pinned behind her back.

'Hid, the mask,' Pinch demanded.

'Get *off* her!' Nicc punched at Hid's arm, making him pause for an instant, long enough for Nicc to pull a handful of dusty glitter from inside her cloak. She blew it straight into the man's eyes.

Hid howled, clawing at his face.

Pinch tightened her grip on Flick's arms. She yanked Flick backwards. Flick yelled and she kicked out, trying to throw her weight to the floor, to escape.

Hid, still blinking glitter out of his eyes, swiped with an arm. He caught hold of Nicc's wrist as she came at him with nothing but her hands. He threw her backwards into her chair, then pulled a black hood from inside his cloak and tossed it at Pinch.

Flick screamed as Pinch grabbed the hood and yanked it down over her head.

And then everything went black.

CHAPTER TWENTY-SIX

Jonathan let Felicity go, annoyance burning through him like wildfire. At least, he told himself that the sick and twisty feeling running through his insides was annoyance.

A not-so-small part of him suspected it was actually guilt.

Yes, he'd lied. No, not *lied*, as such. Avoided the truth.

He'd had to lie, anyway. Avoid the truth, rather. People were all so selfish. Felicity could have easily decided that her powers meant she should be in charge. There was no reason to think she would have helped him.

And yet, you never gave her the chance to offer, a soft voice nudged the back of his mind.

He ignored it and lifted the suitcase. He should go after her. There was enough at stake now, without losing someone else. She'd been gone for a while. It didn't look as though she was coming back. She would have gone back to the inn.

Jonathan exited the shop and gave a quick glance up and down the alleyway. There was no sign of Felicity – she had marched out of sight.

'Silly girl,' he muttered.

'She certainly is.'

Jonathan jumped at the voice, which was far, far too close. 'Where in the *blazes* did you come from?'

A woman pushed a burnished scarlet hood back from her head. She had short brown hair and a pair of spectacles that sat flush against her face like goggles. She also had a smile on her face that might have been called *beguiling*, but to Jonathan it merely looked hungry. 'You got our note, I see?' Her eyes flicked to the paper in Jonathan's hand.

Jonathan made himself stand up straight. '*Your* note?'

'Yes, our note,' she sighed. 'I've come with a message from the Overseer.'

'And who might that be?'

The Thief raised her eyebrows. 'I thought everyone knew Overseer Glean.'

'Glean. How very imaginative,' Jonathan drawled. 'What is your message?'

The Thief gave a quick glance over Jonathan's suit. He forced himself to keep staring at her face, as much as he now wanted to check his pockets. 'I'm Lute. You're Mercator's child.'

Jonathan couldn't help it. 'You know my father?'

She smiled. 'You have a famous name.'

'I'll thank you to judge me on my own terms, not my surname, if it's all the same to you.'

'Except that it isn't all the same to me.' Lute stepped even closer, into Jonathan's personal space. His lip twitched as he tried not to curl it in distaste. 'Strangeworlders have much to answer for, around here.'

'The message?'

She took a battered book from her inside pocket. 'Would you like to see your friend again?'

Jonathan recognised the guidebook immediately. 'Felicity? Where is she?'

'Safe. For now. Although the clock is ticking, Mercator. We want to arrange an exchange.'

'An exchange? For what?'

'We want a way out of this world,' Lute said. 'A suitcase.'

Jonathan laughed. 'You want me to trade a suitcase – something so valuable its worth couldn't be measured – for a girl I barely know?'

'She's your friend.'

'She's really not,' he said slowly.

Lute's face fell, uncertain, for the first time. 'We will allow you to purchase her back,' she said.

Jonathan gestured at the shop behind him. 'Did you not get what you wanted from the people here?'

Lute blushed. 'We have reason to believe the Custodians here were tipped off about the likelihood of a raid. When we came to the emporium, there were no cases to be found. It seems they had secreted the suitcases away.'

Jonathan blinked, then his face cracked into a grin. 'Ha. The Society was one step ahead, wasn't it? And anyway,' he asked, 'what would be the point in your taking a suitcase? You can't survive in a world that isn't your own. Your life-magic would drain out of you.'

Lute's expression didn't shift. 'Magic certainly is the key to life but as Thieves we can always obtain more. First Class Thieves are skilled bottlers. We know how to weave magic and to take it from any source.'

A sort of sharp horror ran through Jonathan's veins. 'Any source?'

'Any.'

'From people?'

'Why not?' She shrugged.

Jonathan fought off the urge to push her away. 'You'd suck the energy out of a new world to survive?'

'Why not? It isn't as though this is the only world we have.'

Jonathan shook his head. 'No.'

'No? What do you mean *no*?'

'I mean: No, as Head Custodian I can't allow you to do that.'

Her eyes flicked to the suitcase in his hand. 'The Overseer is being very generous. You may return to Strangeworlds and select a suitcase for us, allowing you to choose which world we move to. I could just as easily take that case from your hand.'

Jonathan tried not to flinch. 'You would have to take my hand as well.'

Lute gave a sinister smile. 'That would be just fine.'

Jonathan suppressed a shudder. Suitcases were two-way doors. If Thieves were twisted enough to drain magic out of *anything*, giving them access to Strangeworlds would mean putting his entire world at risk. His world, and the hundreds of others linked to Earth.

'You honestly expect me to exchange a suitcase for Felicity? You think I value *anyone* enough to do that?' he scoffed.

'I do.'

'She is nothing to me,' he half-laughed. 'She wouldn't even help me when I . . . She's useless. Hardly much of a bargaining chip.'

'I certainly hope you are lying, for your sake.' Lute pressed Felicity's guidebook into Jonathan's grip. 'The Overseer will give you until the lanterns are lit to present yourself. Tick-tock, little Mercator. Choose a world for us to feast upon, or your Felicity may end up devoured herself.'

Jonathan watched her sweep around the corner, before he exhaled and leaned against the wall. Then stood up again, sharply, a question coming to him abruptly. 'But . . .' he shook his head, 'why on earth would they want to leave Five Lights so badly?'

CHAPTER TWENTY-SEVEN

The Thieves didn't hurt Flick as they pulled her through the streets. But they held her tight and steered her this way and that, so she had no hope of being able to remember where she was being taken. She concentrated on trying to listen to anything that might help her, but the hood over her face made it almost impossible. She tried, anyway. Concentrating helped take her mind off what might happen to her once she got to wherever she was being taken.

And why did they have her, anyway? She wasn't important. And Thieves weren't meant to take people. This was all wrong.

Everything Jonathan had told her was wrong . . .

She felt a sudden surge of anger and her muscles

bunched up, making the Thieves tighten their hold on her arms.

The temperature dropped and the ground went into a downwards slope. Flick's trainers skidded on the damp surface she was walking on, and she thought about sewers and tunnels and caves. But Nicc said the Thieves had a grand building. Why was she being taken *down*?

And then the hood was removed, and the strong hands held her shoulders steady as she caught her balance.

'Get *off* me.' She pushed the hands away. 'Where am I? What is this?'

'You are in my private office,' a soft voice came from across the room. 'Welcome.'

Flick turned towards the voice.

The room was not large – about the size of her living room – and every surface had been covered with soft rugs and carpets. There were even carpets on the walls and the ceiling. It made the room feel small and close, like there wasn't enough air in it. There were a great many crystal-fronted cabinets around the walls, full of shining glass objects. The room was lit by two enormous chandeliers hanging from the carpeted ceiling, light dripping off their dangling crystals. And occupying a space on the far wall, between two cabinets that were full to bursting of those shimmering glass bottles, was a desk as wide as a man was tall and as deep as a sofa.

A woman sat behind it, watching Flick with an expression of soft amusement. She wore the lush scarlet of the Thieves, but as a waistcoat rather than a cloak. Red bands of velvet encircled her biceps and wrists, and as she stood, Flick saw a flash of scarlet trim running down the outside of each trouser leg. The woman was not tall – about Flick's height – but she moved like someone with a great deal of physical strength. She came around the desk and walked over to Flick, her hands behind her back.

'Good morning,' she smiled. She tucked some of her blonde hair behind one ear. 'I do hope my Order members didn't harm you.'

Flick shook her head, fear battling with curiosity. 'Who are you?'

The woman's smile didn't move. It was as if she had learned to smile by studying a picture of someone else doing it; her mouth was the right shape, but her eyes were all wrong. They belonged to someone who was thinking about where to bury you. 'I am the Overseer.'

'I don't know what that is,' Flick said. 'I don't know why I'm here – please let me go. I haven't done anything wrong. This is a mistake.'

The Overseer's disconcerting smile did not change. 'It is not a mistake, child. We have Thieved you for a purpose. You came here with the Mercator boy, didn't you?'

'Jonathan?' Flick asked, then felt like kicking herself.

'Quite. We require something from him, and you are suitable leverage.'

'What do you . . .' Flick's mind helpfully answered her own half-formed question: *A suitcase. That's the only valuable thing he's got.*

'I can see you understand. This is not personal. We simply require what he has. We will exchange your freedom for one of the boy's suitcases. Simple.'

'But why do you need a suitcase?' Flick glanced at the piles of magic-filled bottles. Surely there was enough magic stored inside them for any number of trips through a schism. 'Where do you want to go?'

'Anywhere,' Pinch supplied from behind her. 'Away from here.'

'Silence.' The Overseer glared, her false smile falling clean off her face.

Flick looked between them. 'But what's wrong with here? You can steal anything you like, apparently, and there's magic and it's fun . . .' She trailed off as the Overseer gaped at her in astonishment.

'You travel between worlds,' she said, 'and yet you are ignorant of the plight of this one?'

'Plight?' Flick said. 'You mean the streets disappearing? What's wrong with this place?'

The Thieves exchanged looks.

The Overseer rolled her eyes. 'Save me from the ignorance of children. I *told* you to take the older Mercator when he arrived weeks ago!'

'He was too quick, ma'am,' Pinch said. 'By the time we got word that Daniel Mercator was in Five Lights, he'd gone.'

Flick stared. 'You know about Jonathan's dad?'

'Shut up.' The Overseer turned back to her Thieves. 'It does not matter how much these children do or do not know. Lute has gone to the Mercator boy. The wheels are in motion. Continue as planned. Jonathan Mercator has until the lanterns are lit to bring us what we need.'

Pinch put a hand on Flick's shoulder again. 'And the girl?'

'Put her in the Waiting Room. And call a meeting of the First Class. Everyone must be prepared to leave.'

'What are you talking about?' Flick tried to get out of Pinch's gripping fingers, but it was like trying to escape a bear trap. 'What's *happening* in this world?'

The Overseer looked at her. 'This world, child, is doomed. And we do not intend to be here when the end comes.'

'The end? What do you mean *doomed*?'

The Overseer beckoned to Pinch. 'Hood her, Pinch. Take her to the Waiting Room. And call the others.'

'No! Don't – wait – I—' Flick's cries were cut short as the dark hood fell over her eyes again, and this time, the blackness erased even the feel of the ground beneath her feet.

CHAPTER TWENTY-EIGHT

Jonathan let himself back into Quickspark's, too nervous to stay in the street. He checked the coast was clear before climbing into his suitcase and quickly pulling it through behind him.

He tumbled back into the travel agency and slammed the suitcase lid shut. He puffed out a breath. He was home. He was safe!

But the emptiness and quietness of Strangeworlds felt strangely wrong.

The clocks ticked their weird ticks, and there was the occasional *glug* from the ancient water-pipes. But the atmosphere of the place was changed.

Felicity wasn't there.

Jonathan sat on the floor of Strangeworlds, feeling

extremely alone. The walls of the travel agency seemed to loom over him in disapproval. He'd never intended for any of this to happen. He'd only wanted his father back.

Jonathan pressed the heels of his hands to his eye sockets as the misery of his situation washed over him. He'd been utterly selfish, there was no point denying it, and now he was faced with this stupid, *impossible* decision. It was all his own fault. If he'd simply been honest with Felicity in the first place, if they had stayed together instead of fighting, she would not have been taken.

And they expected him to give up an entire world to get her back?

With a sick feeling of shame, Jonathan acknowledged that, if the Thieves had asked for a suitcase in return for his father, Jonathan would have handed one over without question.

What sort of person did that make him?

Jonathan lowered his hands and looked around the travel agency. All he could see were the cases, each containing an entire world. He could choose one. He could. Any one of the suitcases he had could be handed over to the Thieves in exchange for Felicity.

Tentatively, he reached for one and pulled it down.

It was a case he knew. It led to a world of knights, villages, farmers and witches. It was quiet and fairly peaceful, and Jonathan had learned to horse-ride there when he was fifteen.

He could give it to the Thieves. Give it to them and get Felicity back. Apologise to her.

Was she worth giving up an entire world for? Not just giving up, but dooming to world-collapse, destruction and nothingness?

Was anyone?

No.

He pushed the case away and dragged himself to his feet.

If he gave the Thieves this source of magical energy, he wouldn't simply be giving up a suitcase. He'd be sacrificing an entire unique world, and all the living beings within it. He'd have to live with the knowledge that he had enabled the Thieves to drain every speck of magic from a world in their efforts to stay alive.

He wouldn't be – couldn't be – that person.

Felicity was his friend. A real friend, right up until he ruined it. The first real friend he'd had for a long time.

Jonathan wanted his friend back. He wanted his father back. But there was no way he could give up a suitcase. Not now, not ever. He was the last Head Custodian of The Strangeworlds Society. And he would not hand over a world to Thieves to be used and emptied.

He would have to get Felicity back another way.

And he would.

*

Flick sat up sharply.

It took her eyes a moment to catch up. And when they did, she was tempted to shut them again, and try and restart her brain because this couldn't be right . . .

She was sitting on the floor in a place that was rather like her dentist's waiting room. The floor was covered in threadbare carpet tiles. Metal and foam chairs were arranged in a semi-circle around a coffee table topped with books and magazines in a language Flick didn't recognise. One of the chairs was covered with broken toys, including a sad teddy bear with only one leg. It reminded her of a lot of Freddy's toys, which regularly went through amputations when her brother's teeth punctured the stuffing. The sudden thought of Freddy and her parents made Flick press a hand to her chest to try and shift the dragging ache that started.

There were two other people in the waiting area with her, an elderly couple who were watching her curiously, books in their hands. There was also a woman behind a desk that separated the waiting area from the small reception area at the front of the room.

Flick ignored the couple and stood. Her legs felt steady despite being dragged all over the city. She remembered being under the hood ... she could still smell the strange weave of it, and then ... she was here. There was no memory of anything in between.

It was as though someone had changed the channel in her head.

She went over to the woman behind the desk. 'Excuse me. What's going on? How did I get here?'

The woman at the desk sighed. She had sharp slices of blonde hair and an expression to match. Some people are born to work in certain professions, and the Receptionist was one of them. She disliked almost everyone, except for herself and her cat, Mr Plimsol. And, as Flick was neither of these, the Receptionist gave Flick a curled lip that wouldn't have been out of place if someone wafted a plate of rotting prawns under her chin.

She pointed at her name badge, which was only a

piece of lined paper folded over her blazer lapel with 'Receptionist' scrawled on it. 'Does this say, "Ask Me Anything"?'

'No,' Felicity said. 'It says "Receptionist". Which must be an anagram for *unhelpful pain in the—*'

There was a sudden fit of coughing from behind Flick as the old man in one of the chairs interrupted her. 'She's a lot of things,' he managed to croak, 'but what she is most is a gaoler.' He grinned.

The Receptionist closed her false-lashed eyes with a practised expression of purest scorn. 'Sir,' she managed when she had prised her lids open again, 'I am not a gaoler. I am the Receptionist. When you're collected, I'll call you through.'

'What do you mean, "collected"?' Flick asked, in no mood for bewilderment.

'I mean, when you are picked up. Collected. Claimed.' She studied Flick with the same expression she might have worn if someone asked her to examine something freshly pulled from the sewer. Then sniffed. 'Someone will be along directly to collect you.'

Flick sat back down. But moments later her leg started bouncing up and down with pent-up nervous energy. She stayed sat down for less than a minute before she got straight up again. 'Why are you both just sitting here?' she asked the older couple, making them jump. 'Why aren't you trying to get out?'

'Try, if you like,' said the man who'd spoken before. He had a reddish nose, watery eyes and hands that curled in like claws, but he had a kind face, like someone's grandad. 'Vault over the desk, give old smacked-bum-face a good shove and make for the door, but you won't get out.'

'Why not?'

'Locked,' he said. 'We've tried to open it many a time, but it won't give. And if you tick her off,' he nodded at the Receptionist, 'she can turn very nasty. Once she didn't turn the heating on for two days and let us freeze. All because Darilyn threw a book at her.'

'Worth it,' Darilyn said, under her breath. 'It was a hardback.' She checked to see if the Receptionist was looking, then stuck her tongue out at her.

Flick smiled, but it didn't last long. 'So you both got kidnapped? Same as me?'

'Same as you. I'm Greysen.' The man held a hand out and Flick shook it, though it was shaking a little by itself.

'Flick Hudson.'

'Not from Five Lights with those clothes, are you?'

'I came with . . . a friend. Sort of.'

'Oh? What did you come here for?'

'We came to—' She stopped, the wound of Jonathan's betrayal still raw. 'It doesn't matter. I got kidnapped. The Thieves want to trade me for something valuable.'

'That's usually their way. Gone are the days when Thieves were honourable. As soon as Glean took control as Overseer, things went downhill fast.' Greysen closed his book. 'You came with a friend, you said? To Five Lights?'

Flick nodded. 'He knows about – about magic, and stuff.'

The old man smiled, showing brown teeth. 'I expect he'll soon have you out of here, Flick. You only need to worry if you don't have anyone who wants you back.'

'What do you mean?'

Darilyn gave her a sad look. 'We're stuck here, aren't we? If no one comes looking, eventually . . . we'll disappear.'

'Disappear?' Flick stepped back from the woman in horror.

'Don't ask me how.' Darilyn shook her head. 'But there were more of us here, at the start, not only Greysen and me. And one day, we woke up . . . and there was just us.'

Flick looked behind her at all the empty chairs and the one stacked full of toys. Who had they been for? She felt sick. The Receptionist smirked, her red lips slicing into her face. Anger quickly took over from Flick's sick feeling and made her glare. 'What are you smirking at, lady?'

The Receptionist blinked in surprise at being spoken to so insolently. 'How dare you—'

'Did you stand there and watch those people . . . watch whatever happens to them?'

The Receptionist blushed, red spreading across her cheeks like ketchup wiped across a plate.

'Calm down, Flick.' Greysen sat up. 'She's a mean old crow, but I don't know if she'd actually sit and watch people be hurt if she could do anything about it. At least, I don't like to think so.'

'You said she kept you in the cold!'

'Yes, but she could have done worse.' He shrugged.

Flick gawped. 'Just because she could do worse doesn't mean what she does is all right!'

Darilyn shushed her gently. 'We know, we know. But don't make life difficult for us.'

Flick paused. 'If I get angry at her will she get angry at you?' she asked in a lowered voice.

'There's every chance, yes.'

Flick peered back at the Receptionist, who was twirling a pencil in her fingers, then nodded and sat back in her chair, exhausted by the hurricane of feelings inside her.

Greysen went back to his book. 'I wouldn't worry. You'll be out of here before you know it.'

Flick swallowed. She was worlds away from home, stranded without a suitcase and stuck in a tiny room with no hope of escape. She had never felt less convinced of anything in all her life.

CHAPTER TWENTY-NINE

As a rule, Jonathan Mercator hated asking for help from anyone who wasn't either a medical professional or simply taller and better equipped to reach the biscuits that were on the top shelf. But times were pressing, and he knew that as bitter as his own pride tasted, he was going to have to swallow it. He picked up his guidebook and leafed through it quickly. He needed the List.

A Comprehensive List of Strangeworlds Society Outposts (correct as of 1987)

Strangeworlds Travel Agency – flagship base, Earth. A Custodian is available at all times. Strangeworlds is home to the largest number

of suitcases of any posting. Established by Elara Mercator in 1873.
Contact: the Mercator family.

Quickspark's Travel Emporium – secondary base, the City of Five Lights. Custodians can be contacted at all times. Home to a small number of suitcases. Established by Elara Mercator in 1880.
Contact: the Quickspark family.

Phaeton's Trading Post – secondary base, Mount Snowmore. Custodians are family in nearby village. A handful of suitcases and supplies available. Established by Nicolas Mercator, 1965.
Contact: Maskelyne.

The Laughing Dog Travel Station – emergency base, Palomar. Custodians may not be available and discretion is advised. Established by Margaret Mercator, 1952.
Contact: lost.

Thatcher's Apothecary – no Custodians on site. Established by Anna-May Thatcher, 1985.
Contact: none.

The House on the Horizon – emergency base, Desert of Dreams. One Custodian. Established by Elara Mercator, 1895.
Contact: lost.

The City of Five Lights hadn't been chosen on a whim to be an outpost – it had been chosen because of its nature. Five Lights was a place of transference and travel and it was somewhere you could get to via multiple suitcases. Jonathan himself knew of three suitcases that all led to Five Lights. Two of them were at the agency – one being the pink and gold suitcase sitting next to him. The second was filed away in the travel agency's Back Room. The third, he was sure, was with his father.

Jonathan needed to get back to Five Lights; that was essential. He was not about to abandon Felicity there. But he could not afford to use the pink and gold suitcase he had used with Felicity, in case it was stolen.

He would have to get back to Five Lights without leaving from Strangeworlds. But where from? And what would he do about returning to Strangeworlds after?

He badly wanted to ask another Custodian what to do. He was an adult, technically, but right now he needed a better adult. An adultier-adult. Except there wasn't one here. He would have to travel to find one, to find any help at all.

The trouble was, where to start?

'This,' he said to the empty travel agency, 'was not how I intended to spend my summer.'

There was no reply, of course, but Jonathan closed his eyes and nodded anyway, listening to his own thoughts.

Not only did he have to find a way to Five Lights without travelling from Strangeworlds, he also needed a suitcase to bribe the Thieves with, in exchange for Felicity. Jonathan tapped his chin as he thought. Could the Thieves be tricked? They were certainly single-mindedly focussed on escaping Five Lights. Jonathan suspected they might not examine a suitcase handed over to them too carefully. He was banking on that.

But what are they trying to get away from? he wondered again. What was wrong with Five Lights?

He pushed the thought aside, for now – there were more pressing matters at hand. He went over to the large metal trunk that sat in the wall, opposite the fireplace, and dragged it out. The metal edges dug into his hands and his legs complained about the exercise, but he ignored it all, dragging the trunk over the floorboards until it was far enough out from the wall to open the lid.

A blast of cold air hit Jonathan in the face as he lifted the curved top. There was a *smell* of cold, too, the sort that bites at the inside of your nose before snow begins.

Unlike with the suitcases, Jonathan did not simply clamber in. Instead, he swung his legs over the edge carefully, feeling for the rungs of a ladder which he knew was propped against the lining of the trunk. Once he had his balance, he descended the ladder, down into the darkness of the trunk, until his shoes met stone and he let go. He took out his keys and twisted a small, bullet-like item on the keyring. Light shone from the tiny torch, spreading ahead of him in the gloom.

The view ahead was almost entirely suitcases. Endless shelves of them. Case after case after case after case, all sitting quietly on wooden shelves that had, once, been painted white. Now they were a sort of rusty green-brown that had started to creep, like an organism, over some of the suitcases on the lower shelves.

Jonathan held his torch up and started walking.

This was the Back Room. It was a cave of darkness, used by the Society for storage.

Human beings needed very specific conditions to be able to spend any amount of time in a world other than their own. They needed a particular temperature range, the right cocktail of chemicals in the air to breathe and gravity that wasn't either too strong or too weak. As a result, the number of suitcases that were off-limits greatly outnumbered those that were suitable for travelling. Any schism that wasn't suitable to be kept in the warmth of the travel agency was locked into the Back Room.

Other types of suitcases were locked into the Back Room as well. Duplicates. Secrets not even Jonathan had been told about. And suitcases that led to The Strangeworlds Society outposts.

He walked carefully over the stone floor, torchlight shining onto the shelves.

Many of the suitcases had scraps of card and paper with names and descriptions of where they led carefully pinned onto the handles or pasted onto the sides. Jonathan felt a little rush of gratitude to whoever had attempted this curation. There was a large pile of cases heaped together on a shelf simply labelled 'Water'. Others had tags with a deep red cross marked on them.

There was one case – a white leather affair with swirling silver locks – that had a crude skull-and-crossbones drawn onto the lid.

Jonathan carefully but quickly read each description that he came across. He found a desert, a warzone, three different jungles, a coffee-shop and a prison, but nothing that told him it was one of the Society outposts he was looking for. It was taking more time than he would have liked. Time moved differently in different worlds and it was already early evening here . . .

Frustration seized hold of him, and he kicked the closest case across the floor. Feeling reckless, he grabbed an unmarked case and pushed hard at the catches, but they stayed shut.

'Locked, then,' he said, sounding calmer than he felt. He fished a permanent marker from his inside pocket and wrote 'LOCKED' on the suitcase lid. He knew he should note the suitcase description down in his guidebook, but there was little time.

Besides, he told himself, he knew all there was to know about locked worlds.

And they were not important.

ON THE SUBJECT
OF LOCKED WORLDS

Much in the way that a conventional suitcase may be put under lock and key, a suitcase containing a schism may also be locked.

World-locking is a skill that must be taught. Not everyone in possession of magical sight can master the art, in the same way that not everyone can become a competent cartographer. The method is difficult to master, as the schism within the suitcase still exists, but access to it is denied. Given enough time, and without a source of magic, it is assumed that the schism within will shrink and disappear. Only the one who locked access to a world may unlock it, though even they do not have the ability to close or erase a schism entirely.

To date, no member of The Strangeworlds Society, not even our founder, has been able to close an airborne schism completely. It is doubtful that such a thing is possible, due to schisms' hunger for magic. Even those schisms that eventually heal over and close up take many decades to do so. Starving a schism of magic by locking it away for many years may be the only way to guarantee removing it from the multiverse.

CHAPTER THIRTY

It had taken longer than he wanted, but Jonathan finally hauled two suitcases up and out of the trunk and back into the relative warmth of the travel agency. He'd finally found the suitcases that were listed as being outposts for The Strangeworlds Society and had taken the cleanest-looking ones. Even if the outposts didn't have a case that led to Five Lights, he could ask someone there for help. The Society wouldn't let him down.

Ever since his dad's disappearance, Jonathan had tried to look like he knew what he was doing. He had wanted to be good at running Strangeworlds. He'd never been much good at anything that wasn't reading or drawing. But he was more alone than he had let himself really admit.

Even when his dad was around, Strangeworlds Travel Agency had never felt like somewhere he belonged. Not really. It had first been too secret and then too full of bad memories. His dad had done his best, Jonathan knew that. But Daniel was a grieving man, trying to teach his child about the very thing that had taken his wife from him.

Jonathan had thought he knew everything, but he was beginning to suspect he had only been told about the very tip of the Strangeworlds iceberg. He hadn't even been told exactly where the outpost cases were stored.

Rather than making him feel sad, the thought stewed under Jonathan's skin. Felicity was the first person he'd spoken to in years who didn't make him feel as though he was strange and weird. She was happy, brave and clever, and he'd had no right to keep information from . . . to *lie* to her.

He'd been a terrible person.

When he got her back, he promised himself, things would be different. And if she chose to leave and never come back . . .

Well. He'd only brought that on himself.

He pulled the first case over. The label read:

Phaeton's Trading Post
Snow and Ice.
Cleats recommended.
Large settlement,
good hot chocolate,
wrap up warm.
TSS Custodian Contact: Maskelyne

The lure of a named contact had made Jonathan choose the case. He would find the Custodian, ask them if they had a suitcase that led to Five Lights, and make his next move from there.

He pushed the catches and lifted the suitcase lid quickly.

Icy air hit him in the face. Slow flurries spat out into the shop's warm air, falling to the floor as rain. Wherever this suitcase led, it was not the warm indoors of a Strangeworlds Society outpost. This was outdoors. Very outdoors, judging by the drop in temperature.

Jonathan leaned over the case to try and get a better look. All he could see was mist and snow. He briefly thought about going to get a hat and gloves . . . then his hand slipped on the slick case edge.

He tried to stop himself, but he was grabbing at thin air. The gravity inside the suitcase pulled him forward. He toppled headlong into the case and plummeted down. At the last moment, Jonathan's hand found the case handle, and he dragged it through with him.

For a second, there was only empty, frozen air.

Then, stone rushed up to meet him.

Jonathan raised his arms to catch himself a fraction of a second too late. His top half smacked into a jutting rock and he fell hard, rolling over on the frozen surface. Blood slicked from his palms onto the ice as he ended up face-down on stone and snow.

He stayed still for a moment. Common sense and a blurry memory of something he'd once read about first aid told him that trying to get straight up wasn't the best course of action. His vision was slightly off-kilter, and he panicked for a second before he realised it was because one of his glasses lenses was cracked. He gently flexed his fingers and toes. To his relief, they all moved. But then pain started to blossom under his ribs. It was bearable, though.

Slowly, Jonathan got to his feet. His legs were shaking with shock, and he couldn't get his balance. He ended up leaning against the rock face, his unsuitable brogues skidding on the frost. The ledge he had landed on was little wider than his desk at the travel agency. And then he saw the suitcase. He had dropped it in his fall and now it teetered on the cliff-edge. The gale made it rock to and fro.

One false move, or one sharp gust of wind, was all it would take.

Jonathan wiped his nose, wincing at the line of snotty blood that painted his sleeve. Carefully, he knelt back down and inched across the ledge towards the suitcase. He didn't know where the Strangeworlds outpost in this world was, or why the suitcase had brought him out onto a barren mountainside, but he wasn't in any condition to start exploring this wilderness. He would have to go back to the agency and try another case. But as he reached for the handle, the ground beneath him gave a rumble.

The mountainside swayed violently. There was a noise like a thunderstorm crashing into a marching band.

Masses of ice and chunks of snow landed around him. Jonathan threw himself forward and grabbed for the suitcase.

Then the shelf of stone beneath him fell clean away.

He didn't scream. There was no time.

Jonathan dropped through the air like Icarus. The suitcase fell as well. He reached in a blind panic, grabbed for the handle . . . and missed.

He fell *down*, tumbling through the frozen air. The wind raged around him, blowing the suitcase against his knuckles. The ground was rushing to meet him at an alarming rate. His entire body screamed at him to act; he grabbed for the suitcase again, this time getting a hold and wrenching it open. He shoved one hand inside and scrabbled on the smooth floor of the travel agency, searching, reaching for something, anything . . .

He grasped a chair leg.

Jonathan would never know quite how he did it. With a great deal of effort, he dragged himself into the suitcase, the heavy chair acting like an anchor as he pulled his torso back into Strangeworlds, the wind of the icy world still whipping at the lower half of his body as the sudden stop promised by the jagged ground came closer and—

Jonathan landed hard, chin-first on the travel agency floor. One hand had hold of the chair leg, the other was tight on the suitcase, which he had towed through with him – along with a flurry of snow. He lay on his face on the floorboards, starfished in shock.

After a moment, Jonathan rolled over on the floorboards and stared at the ceiling. 'Oh . . . fudge,' he almost said.

CHAPTER THIRTY-ONE

Flick gave the front door of the Waiting Room a shove with her shoulder. Then she grabbed the handle and pulled, bracing her feet on the doorframe and yanking with all her might. The Receptionist had agreed to let her try to open the door, to prove she wasn't being lied to.

'It won't get you anywhere, little girl,' the Receptionist sighed. 'You can't break out of this world. It's impossible. Now do you believe me?'

Flick let go of the door handle. When she pressed close to look through the pane of glass set in the door, all she could see was a heavy sort of darkness that seemed closer than the dark she was used to. She shivered. 'This isn't *right*.'

'I can't let you out,' the Receptionist said. 'Until you're collected. I *can't*.'

Exasperation made Flick want to scream. 'Then what good are you? How are people collected from here?'

'I won't tell you that.'

'Won't?' Flick's eyes narrowed. 'Or *can't*? Do you even know? Have you ever seen anyone be collected? How long have you been here?'

'That's none of your—'

Flick raised a hand to stop her, an idea starting to grow in her mind. 'Is Receptionist actually your job? Because you don't seem to know very much.' She paused and then continued, in a softer voice. 'Were you left here?'

There was a horrible pause.

Darilyn nudged her husband and they watched the Receptionist turn a worrying shade of maroon.

'You *were* left here, weren't you?' Flick said. 'Maybe you were with some other people at first, but eventually it was only you, on your own. And you thought – say, there's no one behind that desk. I should sit there. And you gave yourself a job and a title and when they brought new people you told them you were in charge, didn't you?'

The Receptionist's eyes were now rather glossy.

'And you liked being in charge, didn't you?' Flick said, not unkindly. 'I bet you did a good job of keeping the place running, but it was never supposed to be your job in the first place. You couldn't do anything else, could you? You're stuck here. Like us.'

The Receptionist sat down. She looked thoroughly miserable.

Flick went over to the desk. 'I'm right, aren't I?'

The woman nodded.

Flick felt rather guilty. 'I'm sorry. Who was meant to come for you?'

The woman sniffed. 'I don't know. Someone.'

'You've been here a long time?'

'It feels like years and years and years. But time moves differently here. I had to do something to make it feel like I had some sort of purpose.' She gave a sad laugh. 'They even brought me things. The Thieves. To keep me happy.' She gestured at her desk. 'They must have thought I was so stupid.'

'I don't think you're stupid,' Flick said. 'Just lonely.'

The Receptionist looked at her.

Flick took a deep breath. 'So, how are people brought here?'

The woman sighed and wiped her eye with a cat-patterned tissue. 'I don't know. I'm telling you the truth about that. People are brought in by the Thieves. I don't see it. No one sees it. It's a blank bit of memory.' She frowned at Flick. 'What do they even want with you? You're only a child.'

Flick felt too deflated to lie. 'They want to trade me. For a suitcase.' It sounded ridiculous.

But Greysen sat up sharply. 'A suitcase? You mean – you're not a Strangeworlder, are you?'

Flick started in surprise. 'Yes?'

Greysen collapsed back in his chair. He looked as if he'd seen a ghost.

'What is it?'

'A bit of hope,' he said breathlessly. 'We're Darilyn and Greysen Quickspark.'

Quickspark. Flick stared, her eyes going wide.

'We ran the travel emporium on Spectre Street,' Greysen said.

'But we went there and all the suitcases were gone,' said Flick.

'Ah.' Greysen tapped his nose. 'We had a tip-off. The Thieves aren't as united as they'd like to think they are. One of them sent us a letter telling us to expect a raid. We hid the cases and waited for the Thieves to come.'

'And they did,' Darilyn added bitterly.

Flick felt a rush of relief. The suitcases were safe. 'Where did you hide them?'

'That would be telling.'

'You can trust me,' she said. 'Jonathan's my . . .' she paused.

Darilyn and Greysen exchanged looks.

'Jonathan Mercator?' Greysen asked.

She nodded.

He hummed ruefully. 'That boy . . . called in recently, asking after his dad. Nothing we could tell him of course. I can remember when he first came into the emporium. Eyes like dinner-plates, asking questions left and right. He didn't know whether to be afraid or excited.'

'He'd not long lost his mum, I remember,' Darilyn added. 'Poor lad. His dad was showing him the ropes. How suitcases worked. The history of The Strangeworlds Society. He wanted him to know all about it, but . . .'

'But?' Flick asked.

Greysen folded his hands together. 'You have to remember, my girl, that grief isn't a straight road. It twists and winds. Sometimes Daniel Mercator would be an attentive father and a good teacher. Other times, he'd be a ghost. I've got no doubt he tried to teach his son as best as he could, but he wasn't a well man. He tried to protect his son by only telling him what he needed to know. I don't doubt he would have finished his training properly if he hadn't . . . disappeared.'

'You knew about him disappearing before Jonathan came looking for him?' Flick said.

'Guesswork, I'm afraid. He asked to use the emporium for a few hours, alone. When we came back, the place was empty, and the key was sitting neatly on the desk. Nothing missing, nothing stolen. We assumed he'd gone back home. It was only later, when Jonathan came searching for him that we realised something more sinister might have occurred.'

Flick rolled the information over in her head. 'Did Jonathan's dad say anything to you? Before he left?'

Darilyn shook her head. 'Nothing unusual. He seemed rather excited, but . . . that's regular behaviour for a Society member.'

Flick tried to think. 'The Thieves . . . they said Five Lights was in danger. They want to get away from the city. Did Daniel know about that?'

Darilyn nodded. 'Oh, yes. It was Greysen and I who first contacted him about it. He'd been investigating the streets disappearing and so on for some time. I don't think he ever got to the bottom of it though.'

'Wait, he did say something,' Greysen said, suddenly remembering. 'He said something about a lighthouse.'

A freezing-cold chill ran over Flick's skin. 'A lighthouse?'

'Yes. I don't know why that's just come back to me. He said he had to go somewhere – to tell someone about it. Don't ask me who, though.'

Flick sat in silence, remembering the dreadful emptiness of the lighthouse on the cliff. The lack of life. The quiet stillness that had crept under her skin. The photographs. The missing baby.

He had to tell someone about it?

Jonathan had said the Lighthouse suitcase was supposed to be locked. It had been so empty, and so dead.

Coral City was struggling to keep its plant-life alive. But the place looked almost over-saturated with magic in amongst the city's buildings.

Tam's forest was scarier and darker than Jonathan remembered it, and the rules of the place had changed.

Daniel knew about the plight of Five Lights. And he had left his notes behind in a locked suitcase . . .

Somehow, this all had to be connected.

'I can't stay here,' Flick got to her feet. 'I need to get out. Now.'

'There is no *out*, Flick. You've tried the door for yourself. If there was a way out, we would have found it by now.'

'We got in,' Flick said. 'So there has to be a way to get out.'

'I don't think this place works like that,' Darilyn said gently. 'This isn't like stepping into a suitcase. This is a prison. Rescue is your best hope. If Jonathan is your friend, perhaps he'll come for you.'

Flick's heart sank. 'I don't know what he is. Aside from a liar.'

'A liar?' Greysen frowned. 'What did he lie to you about?'

*

Jonathan's nose had more or less stopped bleeding as he dragged over the next suitcase. It was a heavy leather affair, hard and brown and dusty, with tarnished brass catches and a handle that was flaking away, revealing spun fabric beneath it.

'Thatcher's Apothecary's Shop,' Jonathan read from his guidebook. 'Strangeworlds Society outpost. Second time lucky.' It was somewhere else he'd never been before, but the clock was ticking. He didn't waste time in opening the suitcase and quickly stepping inside.

A strong smell of disinfectant and herbs assaulted his senses before his vision caught up. He made out an array of bottles and jars lining the walls and windows.

A man with long grey-black hair, and wearing a brown apron, looked up in complete shock at the suitcase and the young man who clambered out of it.

'Excuse me,' Jonathan said, straightening his bow tie. 'But I understand you are familiar with The Strangeworlds Society? I do hate to bother you like this, but ...' He sighed. 'My name is Jonathan Mercator. And I need your help.'

CHAPTER THIRTY-TWO

'He lied to me about almost everything,' Flick sighed, having explained to Greysen and Darilyn the whole business about Jonathan keeping her abilities a secret. 'He kept something special about me a secret from myself. And then expected me to help him! Who does that?'

Greysen and Darilyn exchanged a glance.

'Perhaps,' Darilyn said carefully, 'someone who has had to look after themselves for a long time.'

'I've had to look after myself, too,' Flick said.

'Your parents aren't . . .?'

'Oh, they're alive,' Flick said. 'Just . . . busy. All the time. They work a lot, and I've got a little brother . . .' She stopped, the thought of Freddy's damp shiny face like a punch to the heart. 'Sometimes they don't come home until late and I have to do things . . .'

'And they are otherwise . . . absent?'

'No,' Flick admitted. 'No, they're around me too much a lot of the time.'

Darilyn gave a small smile. 'It sounds to me as though you have the sort of home that Jonathan would very much like to have.'

Flick opened her mouth to retort, but found she didn't have anything to say.

'I'm sure I don't know your circumstances,' Darilyn said, 'but what do you think your family would do, if you were stuck here?'

The question hurt. 'They won't know where I've gone. They'll never know what happened to me.'

'As Jonathan Mercator never knew what happened to his father,' Darilyn said. 'Grief affects everyone differently. And whether or not Daniel Mercator is alive, his son is mourning him. Grief makes kind men into monsters. But they can change back.'

Flick frowned. 'OK. But he should have told me the truth, shouldn't he?'

'Yes,' Greysen said. 'He should have. But the young man you've described to me isn't the Jonathan I knew.'

'People can change. You said so.'

'They can.' He nodded. 'But let me finish. The young

man you described to me doesn't sound like Jonathan – it sounds like his father.'

'His father?'

'Indeed. When Daniel Mercator first lost his wife, he became much like the person you're describing. Secretive. Telling half-truths. Evasive. Self-serving, to an extent. He got over it, in time, of course. But when it first happened . . . it was as though she had taken all the good side of his personality with her.'

Flick thought about this. It was understandable. She didn't *want* to understand it, but she did. 'What happened to her? Jonathan never said.'

'A freak accident, from what Daniel told us,' Darilyn said. 'They were exploring a world they'd been to a dozen times before. Then there was a stampede of wild animals. They ran, holding tight to one another, but in the chaos their hands broke contact and Jodie was . . .' She winced. 'Seeing that happen to someone you love would break you.'

Flick bit her lip. 'That's horrible.'

'I'm not saying you need to forgive Jonathan right away,' Darilyn said. 'But after a loss like that, and then losing your father as well . . . it could be easy to assume there's no good left in the world.'

Flick looked at the locked door to the Waiting

Room. Everything Darilyn said made sense. But if Jonathan hadn't thought she would help him . . .

What were the chances of him trying to help her?

*

'I have to say, I didn't think I'd be seeing you today, or any other day. You Strangeworlders never change, do you?' The apothecary put a cup of herbal tea down in front of Jonathan.

'I don't want any tea,' Jonathan said. 'Unless it comes with milk and two sugars.'

'You're in shock. And there's blood on your face.'

Jonathan brushed at his upper lip. 'I need your help. Mr . . .Thatcher?'

'That's right. Though you can call me Tristyan. Jonathan . . .' He paused. 'I knew your grandfather.'

'And my father?'

'I'm afraid I never had that honour.'

Jonathan silently cursed. He picked up the cup and sipped the warm liquid. It tasted like wet paper but cooled the hot throb in his nose straight away. He put the cup down. 'Look, I'll be blunt. I need to get to the City of Five Lights. Quickly. I've wasted enough time as it is, and I only have a few hours of their time left. It

297

says in my guidebook that this place belongs to a Custodian. I need to know what suitcases you have.'

'This place *did* belong to a Custodian,' Tristyan said. 'But that is no longer the case.'

Jonathan slumped down in his chair.

'However, I do still have the suitcase you mention.' Tristyan got to his feet. He was very tall. 'I thought your travel agency had a great many suitcases, though?'

'We do. But look, it's complicated. I need to get a certain person out of a certain situation. And fast.'

Tristyan raised an eyebrow. 'Out of Five Lights? The city?'

'Yes.'

Tristyan's eyes unfocussed for a moment. Has – has the worst happened, then?'

'The worst?' Jonathan frowned. 'What do you mean?'

'You do know, don't you?' Tristyan stared. 'About what is happening to the City of Five Lights?'

'I don't know anything,' Jonathan said, wincing at how very true that statement was. 'What's wrong? What's happening to Five Lights?'

Tristyan paused. Then sat back down at the table, facing Jonathan. 'Five Lights,' he said carefully, 'is a place of schisms and magic, correct?'

'I know that. It always has been.'

'Yes. And it has been able to exist with schisms coming and going, opening and closing. The place is so rich in magic that it simply heals itself over and over. It is a wonderful world.'

Jonathan said nothing. He could feel a dull coil of dread beginning in his stomach.

'However, there is a . . . a danger. Something new. Magic is *leaking* out of Five Lights. Like water through a sieve. And it is leaking too fast for it to be replaced.'

Jonathan's mouth dropped open. 'But how? Schisms are small. They close up by themselves if left alone and with all the magic in Five Lights they should close up easily.'

'If they *are* small, yes,' Tristyan said. 'But what if there was a large schism? A very large schism?'

'How large?' asked Jonathan, the dread twisting and untwisting inside him.

Tristyan shook his head. 'No one knows. But the rate those streets have been disappearing and the way the climate and spin of the world has been changing . . .'

'The streets have been vanishing,' Jonathan repeated. 'The Thieves said they needed to escape the world. They know.'

'The Thieves of Five Lights deal in magic,' Tristyan said, nodding. 'They will be aware of what is happening.' He traced a finger around the rim of his cup. 'Five Lights is crumbling, Jonathan Mercator. It is not merely your friend who is in danger.'

'But what *caused* such a schism?' Jonathan asked. 'How could such a thing happen?'

Tristyan looked at him and seemed to be wondering if he could be trusted. 'Tell me, how did you come to run Strangeworlds Travel Agency?'

'I, er, inherited it. There was no one else left.'

Tristyan's face fell.

Jonathan was quiet for a moment. 'My mother died when I was only fourteen. And I ... I was so *angry* about the idea of the travel agency after she died ...' He sniffed. 'I felt as though the place had taken her away from me.'

Tristyan put his head to one side in sympathy.

Jonathan glanced away. His throat was aching. 'My father tried to teach me about it afterwards, but the fact it had taken my mother ... it was always hanging over us both.' He picked at a thread on his sleeve. 'And now he's ... not around. I can't ask him anything about it. I feel like I wasted the time we had together.'

Tristyan reached across the table and touched Jonathan on the arm. His carefully blank expression had softened into something like sorrow. 'The time we have with loved ones is never wasted. I know that better than most.'

Jonathan pulled his mouth into a flat sort of smile. 'You lost someone . . . because of The Strangeworlds Society?'

'Yes,' Tristyan took his hand back. 'I did.'

'I'm so sorry.'

Tristyan glanced at a picture-frame on the counter. The glass was facing away from Jonathan. 'It was a long time ago. And right now, you have a task to do. I have one single suitcase. The others were taken back to your world many years ago. I'll be quite honest with you, I don't know where it leads. It may not be anywhere useful. I think it was only left here as a gesture.' He got up abruptly and disappeared through the doorway. He was gone for only a few minutes and came back in holding an extremely dusty and faded suitcase.

He put it down on the table with a *thump*. His grey-black hair fell from behind one pointed ear.

Jonathan ran a hand over the leather, the dust gathering under his fingers like grey clouds. 'So,' he said to the suitcase, 'where do you go?'

CHAPTER THIRTY-THREE

'Y ou're quite certain this will work?' Tristyan asked, as Jonathan climbed out of a suitcase into the apothecary's shop for the second time that day, this time holding a book in one hand and a backpack in the other. 'It's very old,' Tristyan continued. 'I don't recall anyone ever using it.'

'I'm not certain of anything,' Jonathan said. 'But I need to try. They've got my friend, and it's my fault.' He dropped the enormous book he had fetched from Strangeworlds onto the floor and began to turn the pages.

'What is that?' Tristyan stepped back from the flurry of activity.

'A map-book. An old one.' Jonathan hummed as he turned to the right page. 'The last thing I want is to jump in there without knowing what's on the other side. All right. This is you.' He pointed at a labelled oval on the page. 'And that old suitcase you have leads . . .' He turned the book on its side to read a scribbled note, before flipping through the pages. He found the right page and squinted at more tightly packed writing. 'The Station. That's a Strangeworlds Society outpost.' A small spark of hope ignited in his chest. 'And from there . . .' He turned more pages in the map-book, 'There are several options, at that point. Assuming the suitcases haven't been moved.'

'Can you travel from the Station to the City of Five Lights?'

'Not directly,' Jonathan said. 'Not according to the map. But there are other cases there I can go through. My idea is to find a suitcase that will take me back to Five Lights. One that doesn't come from Strangeworlds,' he added.

Tristyan bit his lip. 'What if there isn't one to hand? You could be going in and out of suitcases over and over again. How will you carry them all with you?'

'I won't be pulling any of them through with me.' Jonathan adjusted his backpack straps. 'I'm going to jump through empty-handed. The only suitcase I'll be carrying in my hand is the one I want the Thieves to take from me.'

'But you'll be stranded. How will you get back?'

'One problem at a time, please.' Jonathan closed the book of maps and shoved it into his backpack. 'Besides, there *was* a Strangeworlds Society outpost at Five Lights – Quickspark's. It was robbed but the cases must still be in the city, somewhere. I'll find a way out.'

Tristyan stepped back. 'Can I do anything to help?'

'Keep this suitcase close by,' Jonathan said. 'Please.'

'I shall,' Tristyan said. Then he smiled. 'It almost seems foolhardy to admit that I miss this. The visits and watching you all have your adventures, I mean.'

Jonathan paused. 'You never travelled, then?'

'No, no.' The apothecary shook his head. 'Not for the likes of me. Someone has to stay at home.' A heavy expression crossed his face and he shook his head, as if to clear it. 'Until next time, Jonathan Mercator. I hope to see you again very soon.'

'Thank you,' Jonathan put a hand out. 'For the help.'

'Not at all.' Tristyan shook it.

Jonathan squared his shoulders. 'All right. Here goes nothing . . .' The old case, hidden by the apothecary for years, lay open before him. He stepped into it and vanished.

*

Jonathan wouldn't come for her.

Flick didn't want to think about it, but the miserable thought kept creeping into her mind like fog under a door.

His 'friendship' had all been a ruse to get her to help him. Why would he try and save her?

And if he didn't, what if no one ever did?

*

Jonathan clambered carefully out of the case.

Immediately a screaming noise blared close by, making his ears throb, and he froze in fear before realising it was a train whistle.

'The Station . . .' he whispered under his breath, his muscles slowly unbunching. 'Of course.' He turned to the suitcase that led back to Tristyan's apothecary's shop. He took hold of the handle on the outside and steeled himself to do something incredibly unnatural. He pushed the handle *inwards*, pressing the suitcase back on itself, back into the apothecary' shop. Doing it felt awfully wrong – like missing a step walking down the stairs. The suitcase popped out of his grip and vanished. Jonathan shuddered. He'd only done that once before, and his dad had come straight back for him, afterwards. This time, he was on his own. He shook off the feeling and hopped down from the luggage-rack the suitcase was stored on. He seemed to be in some sort of train station storage room. There was a lot of luggage around, most of it modern and on wheels. He crept across the small, gloomy room to peer out of the frosted glass window in the door. There was a cobweb over the doorway. Good. That meant no one regularly came in. He had time.

The screaming whistle came again, like an elbow into his brain, reminding him that time was running out.

Jonathan took out the map. According to it, there were five cases hidden here at the Station. There were descriptions of what each suitcase looked like, but not a lot of detail. He needed to find them. Fast.

He went over to the oldest-looking suitcases on the racks and started to open them, one by one.

*

Fear condensed in Flick's stomach like sour milk, turning into a hard ball of pain that pushed at her insides and made her feel faint.

As much as she complained and griped and moaned about her own family, she was also terrified – deathly terrified – at the prospect of never seeing them again. What if by the time she finally escaped this place her parents were old and didn't remember her? Or what if – and she could barely stand to think it – what if by the time she got back they were gone forever?

She remembered last year, when her mum was working late all the time and was getting only a few hours of sleep every night. But her mum had still turned up to Parents' Evening and had told Flick she was proud of her as they walked home in the driving rain. And her dad had sat bolt upright at her last keyboard recital, though he'd fallen asleep on the bus on the way home and Flick had to shake him so they wouldn't miss their stop.

And the last time she was sick, her mum and dad took it in turns to stay with her when she felt hot and cold and shaky, and there had always been someone next to her bed when she'd needed a hand to hold. And even Freddy had crawled in, and had given her hand a sympathetic chew before he was taken away . . .

She was going to see them again. No Thieves were going to stop her.

She curled her hands into fists and felt her skin tingle. Some sort of electricity or power was running through her bones, catching at her breath, making her joints ache and her muscles twitch with a drive she couldn't ignore.

Resolve can be a powerful weapon. And resolve, when wrapped in righteous ferocity and fear, can cut through the impossible. It makes mothers lift cars off their babies, it makes athletes break world records and it was about to make Felicity Hudson change the nature of magic forever.

CHAPTER THIRTY-FOUR

Jonathan felt as if he had spent days lifting suitcase lids before finding a Strangeworlds one he could use. It was lime green and lifted easily from the rack, dragging a lot of cobwebs and spider-corpses with it.

Jonathan had also found the *other* suitcase he was looking for. This one was iron-grey, trimmed in white. He put it to one side, to take with him. The idea he'd had in the apothecary's shop was growing.

He undid the latches of the green case and stepped inside. He kept a tight hold of the grey case as he stepped out again, blinking quickly to get his bearings.

And then, he froze.

He was in an opulent room dripping with lush furnishings, gold and diamonds. There was a U-shaped table in the centre, heaped up with exotic-looking fruits and other foods, and candles glowed here and there amongst the treats. And the occupants of the room – two dozen very tall, very beautiful people with blue-green faces – were turned towards Jonathan in surprise. The fae.

There was a *smash* as someone dropped something.

Jonathan gave a very nervous smile that was more teeth than anything else. 'Ah, do excuse me,' he said. 'Apologies for the interruption . . .'

One of the fae-people stood up, looking from Jonathan to her companions as though wondering if she was seeing things.

Jonathan ploughed on, 'I'm not planning on hanging around, don't mind me. I'm merely looking for another suitcase?' He lifted the one he held. 'I believe there will be one somewhere . . . around . . . here . . .'

The faces continued to stare.

'I'm from The Strangeworlds Society?' he tried. 'My name . . .' He paused, uneasy about handing over his name to beings he wasn't entirely sure meant well.

One of the beings turned and muttered something to another. Another moved his hand lazily towards his golden cutlery.

There was nothing for it.

'My name's Mercator,' Jonathan said, giving away his name like a gift. 'Please. I need your help.'

Faces lit up in recognition, and several of the pointy-eared fae chattered excitedly. The one who was standing said something, and Jonathan caught the word 'luggage'.

'Luggage? Do you have a suitcase?' Jonathan asked. He stepped forward, pleading. 'I am trying to get back to the City of Five Lights. My friend is in danger.'

The standing fae-woman walked over. 'We can show you. We owe your family a favour.' She opened a door to the outside, leading the way into a dark garden. 'And then our bargain is complete.' She strode out and Jonathan jogged after her. The night air was cool, and she walked quickly over the grass between great ornamental flower beds.

'You owe us a favour? Who gave you the case?' Jonathan panted as he struggled to keep up.

The fae-woman looked at him. 'The one who gave us custody of the luggage was a woman of your species named Elara Mercator. She gave us an escape route.'

Jonathan stopped dead on the path. 'Escape?'

The woman nodded.

We want a way out of this world . . . Lute's words swam around Jonathan's mind. He glanced down at the grey suitcase in his hand. 'Is this world in danger?' he asked.

The woman seemed unsurprised at his question. 'All worlds are in danger, young one. The balance of schism and magic is perilous. The Strangeworlders have always known this.' She did not smile.

'Balance,' Jonathan repeated. He thought of the vanishing streets in Five Lights. The disappeared settlement from the mountainside. The struggle to grow plants in Coral City. The changing attitude of Tam and his tribe of children.

And he thought of Flick. Her magic. Her powers. Her skill.

Something had changed in the multiverse.

Something huge.

Was the answer to it all at Five Lights? Was Tristyan right? Was there really a massive schism? And could it have caused all of these bizarre happenings?

The fae-woman stopped at what looked like a summerhouse and opened the door. Inside was a veritable mountain of shining objects, clothes, swords and – in the midst of it – a battered cream-and-brown suitcase.

'Thank you.' Jonathan's knees almost buckled in relief. 'Oh, thank you.' He picked up the case and felt like hugging it tight.

'Do you know where it leads?' she asked him.

He nodded. 'If my map is correct, it leads to Five Lights.'

The woman shook her head. 'That place is treacherous. You must value your friend a great deal.'

Jonathan tightened his grip on the suitcase in his arms. 'I . . . suppose I do.'

'I wish you luck, young Mercator. Five Lights is a world wounded. It will need healing, if it is not too late.'

Jonathan put the suitcase down. 'All roads lead to the city,' he said to himself. He lifted the lid. 'I am coming for you, Felicity.'

*

The ball of fear inside Flick seemed to grow spines of anger. This was unfair. It was

So.

MASSIVELY.

Unfair.

She didn't deserve this. She had never done anything so bad as to deserve this.

Stay here, forever?

That . . . that was *wrong*.

Flick gritted her teeth. She stood, without really thinking about it, her limbs starting to shake with the furious unfairness and anger at it all. Her blood vessels felt like they were charged with electricity, every blood-cell fizzing with energy, anger and enough fear to make tears start to run down her face.

'I . . .' Flick forced out between her teeth, 'I . . . am not . . . staying . . . here.'

Her vision blurred, and the whole room seemed to shift around her. It was as though the air darkened, and her own body started to emit a light of its own.

She gasped, anger and fear boiling under her skin.

I am not staying here.

She punched at the wall.

The wall should have battered the skin from her knuckles.

Instead, it *moved*.

In an instant, the wall was no longer there – not in Flick's mind, anyway. There was only the fierce burn inside her, the light she could barely contain battering against her skin. Her hands splayed out against where the wall had been, her pink and purple chipped nail polish glittering like sparks in the darkness.

It wasn't fair.

I am not staying here.

Her anger was stronger than her prison. Her resolve was unstoppable. It pressed against the walls, pushing them outwards, bending them, contorting them, until –

The world around her shattered like glass. Her sight cracked as though she'd punched a mirror. Cracks and shards of the world bit into Flick's mind and she staggered. A hurricane of magic swirled around her. She raised her head again, fighting her way through the flying bits of matter like she was walking through a flock of silently screaming birds. Pain ached in every joint of her body, and each breath seemed to take an age. The cutting shards of the world splintered away into nothingness, but there was something coming forward like an ocean, rushing up to catch her, though too fast, much too fast.

Hitting water at speed, Flick had once read, was like hitting tarmac.

She threw a hand out.

And the very threads of the multiverse parted for her like blades of grass.

CHAPTER THIRTY-FIVE

The multiverse lurched around Flick. She thrust her arm out further, trying to hold onto it. The broken shards of magic sliced against her skin, though they didn't hurt her body – they hurt something deeper, something hidden away and unknown. Something that Flick hadn't even known existed until it threatened to make her fold up in pain.

She felt a dark swell of energy, like adrenaline without the nausea, begin to surge in her chest. It ran through her blood vessels, powering something inside her she hadn't known existed, like an internal machine she had started up and had no idea how to turn off.

She could only try to steer it.

Schisms are bridges between worlds. And these bridges cross over an unseen space of pure nothingness. To attempt to go into this dead space, to break into the emptiness, would lead to the hungry darkness eating every single drop of magic from your life.

If you were to try to step through it, the schism would help itself to every single drop of magic from you . . .

No one can step from one world to another without using a suitcase or bottled magic.

No one ever had.

Not before now.

A curl of dark energy, like the fingertip of her own shadow, reached out from inside Flick, and brushed against another world.

And then gripped, tight.

Flick felt a wrenching around her belly like she'd been lassoed. She almost let go of the shadow-hold she had on the world ahead of her, but something told her not to. Flick shut her eyes in terror. If she'd kept them open, she would have experienced something similar to what the suitcases went through when they were pulled through after their travellers.

And then . . .

The Waiting Room folded like an origami sculpture. It collapsed at the edges, the walls of the space falling inwards into nothing, vanishing as though someone had pressed 'delete'. The centre of the space bulged and swelled, curving outwards as it scrunched up like discarded paper. The tiny world gave a last heave, pushing out its occupants like toothpaste from a tube.

And a schism – a brand-new, shining, terrible schism – tore open in the City of Five Lights.

Flick opened her eyes to see the pavement racing up to meet her and caught herself just short of face-planting. The other occupants of the room tumbled after her, including the Receptionist, who was letting out a very impressive stream of swear-words as she tried to simultaneously keep her hair in place and avoid cracking her head open on the cobblestones.

Flick stumbled upright, her vision swimming and her arms and legs feeling cold – as though there was no blood in them. Pins and needles started up her calves, and she stamped her feet, trying to get them working again.

She turned and looked behind her.

There was nothing there.

Even though Flick couldn't see schisms without one of Jonathan's lenses, she somehow knew there was nothing to see. The schism she had created and escaped through, was gone. Closed up, healed by magical energy. Flick supposed it must have taken it from the collapsing Waiting Room.

She'd created a schism.

Now who's not particularly magical, eh? she thought, seconds before a colossal headache clocked into her temple. A cramp started in her right foot, and she flexed her toes quickly, limping over to where Darilyn and Greysen were lying on the ground.

A faint shimmering, silver glow surrounded the two Quicksparks. They were staring in shock at one another as their wrinkles disappeared, their skin smoothed out and their hair ran through with colour, erasing the grey. Fifty years disappeared, and they became a young couple again.

Flick shook her head in disbelief. 'What's happening to you?'

'We weren't old, when we went in there.' Darilyn raised her hands and watched the backs of them smoothing out, the dark spots vanishing. 'That place took life from us, to keep itself going.'

Living in a world you don't belong to drains your life-force away. At first you simply feel tired, but then ill and, eventually, it's thought that you would die long before your time.

Darilyn looked at her hands again and then back up to Flick. 'What did you do?'

Flick shook her head. 'I don't know. I . . . broke out. I think.'

'But you *can't*,' Darilyn said. 'What *are* you?'

Flick didn't know what to say. The frightening feeling of not knowing who or what she was came rushing back, stealing her breath and making her knees suddenly give way. She sat down hard on the pavement, looking at her hands, the feeling of what she had done like a dark echo on her skin.

*

Half a mile away, at the same moment Felicity re-entered the world, Jonathan toppled into the big square in Five Lights. He had his map-book under his arm, the spare small, grey suitcase from the Station in his hand, and he was so pale he might have been mistaken for a sheet of paper, puffed up and with a smudge of a face drawn on.

'Oh, I'm here.' He smiled in faint delight at the sight of the place. 'It worked. That's good.' Ignoring the queasy feeling it gave him, he pushed the suitcase from the fae world back where it came from. Then sat back a moment, his head swimming, his vision blurring into a soup of red and black spots that told him in no circumstances was he to stand up again for the next few minutes.

*

Greysen and Darilyn wanted to go straight back to their emporium, to see what was left of it. Flick elected to go with them, thinking there was a small hope at least that Jonathan would still be there. The Custodians walked unsteadily, holding tight to each other's hands. Darilyn kept touching her husband's dark hair as if worried it might turn white again.

The Receptionist walked alongside Flick, looking dazed and confused, as though Five Lights was completely alien to her. It seemed she had nowhere to go.

'Will you be all right?' Flick asked kindly.

The Receptionist gave a sad smile. 'I suppose I'll have to see if I still have a home. What about you?'

Flick groaned. 'I need to find Jonathan. The boy I came here with. Hopefully he'll still be at the emporium. Or close by.'

The unsteady caravan of people wove across one of the city squares and down an unfamiliar street. Flick was about to ask if they were going the right way, when Darilyn pushed a leaning bit of fencing to one side and stepped out onto Spectre Street. Right beside Quickspark's Travel Emporium.

Flick followed them inside, but quickly stopped when she saw the shop was empty. 'He's not here.'

'Don't fret yet,' Greysen said, his youthful face still looking like it belonged to someone else. 'He might be in the back.'

'I hope so.' Flick swallowed nervously. 'If he's not, I'm stuck. He's got the suitcase with him—'

'Ah, suitcase. Yes, you *are* that girl.' A voice the colour of a coffin lining came from behind Flick.

She turned around and looked up, up at two Thieves sweeping out from the back of the emporium, their red cloaks swirling.

The Receptionist gasped and darted backwards out of the open door. Greysen and Darilyn stepped quickly forward to Flick's defence. The two Thieves swept in front of them with all the menace of a raised sword.

Flick met Darilyn's eyes.

Flick shook her head. She didn't need anyone getting hurt on her behalf.

She took a step backwards.

'Don't even think about running, child,' the taller Thief said. He looked from the Quicksparks to their companion. 'I'll deal with these two. You go ahead to the Overseer with the girl. She will be *very* surprised to know we found her here.'

'Yes, Hid.' The Thief in front of Flick gave a smirk. 'I do hope I don't have to drag you, little girl.'

'You're not taking me anywhere,' Flick said, wishing her voice wasn't so quivery.

Hid looked over his shoulder, and grinned. 'My colleague Swype is not opposed to violence, Strangeworlder, so I would cooperate to avoid giving them the opportunity to practise on you.' Hid looked back at Greysen and Darilyn. 'Now then, you two. We can have a pleasant little chat, and you can tell me where you've hidden the rest of your suitcases.'

Flick daren't look back at the two Custodians being marched into the back of their empty shop. She peered up into the dark red hood of the Thief in front of her.

Swype pushed their hood back to reveal white-grey hair and a smirking, pointed face. 'Why don't you save me some trouble, and follow me?'

CHAPTER THIRTY-SIX

The Thief didn't touch her, but they didn't have to. Swype directed Flick through the streets with the smallest words and sounds from the back of their throat as the two of them walked into one of the busier areas of Five Lights. The other shoppers gave them a wide berth.

Flick's emotions swung from exhausted to frustrated like a pendulum. She'd escaped from one place only to be kidnapped again almost instantly. She balled her hands into fists in her pockets and tried to think of how to get away from this Thief.

She risked glancing up at Swype. They were one of the palest people she had ever seen, as though they were on the verge of disappearing altogether. Their eyes looked as though someone had washed all the pigment away from a once-brown iris. They gave the impression they were older than they seemed, although their face was fairly free of lines and wrinkles. It was more like they *felt* old, like something over-used and worn-out.

'Stop here,' Swype said, halting in front of a blank stretch of brick.

The only thing that broke up the flatness of the wall was a metal rectangle with a sort of shelf jutting out from it. It was about the size of a paperback book. The metal was carved with a horrible image of a face grimacing in pain.

'Where are you taking me?' Flick asked, her voice sounding as small as she felt.

Swype sneered at her, as if imagining how a lack of tongue might improve her likeability. Silently, they turned back to the shelf and fished a tiny ceramic egg painted in cheerful colours from their pocket. They placed it in the metal scoop and stepped back.

The egg glowed red and yellow-hot for a moment and then it . . . died. It dried, browned and cracked, as if all the moisture had been sucked from it, somehow mummifying the ceramic.

Then the bricks swung open. Each brick rotated as if on an axle, turning on its side and twisting away out of sight as the other around it did the same. A door-sized entrance grew from the shifting brickwork, cutting itself out of the wall and opening up into a dark archway.

Flick blinked as she realised – the little egg had been payment, somehow.

Swype didn't have to tell her to walk inside, didn't have to push. They merely adjusted their body-language so Flick understood that to try to run or to refuse to move forward would be not only foolish, but also the last thing she ever did.

'Jonathan will find me,' Flick said, as she stepped into the darkness.

'I do hope so,' Swype said.

The doorway twisted closed behind them.

*

The lamps of Five Lights were lit by now, the golden light keeping the night at bay for a little while.

Jonathan had to walk half a mile before he reached the grand building of the Order of Thieves. It looked even more majestic up close, like a cathedral. There was stained glass in the windows of the lower floor, showing the emblem of the Thieves – a hand grasping a bag of coins. There was also a stained-glass scene – a pale blue bottle in front of a ragged silver lightning bolt. It was eerily similar to the Strangeworlds Society badge and made Jonathan pause for a moment.

But there was little time to stand about.

He pushed open the large wooden doors and sauntered over to the desk, where a Thief looked up in surprise.

'May I help you, sir?'

'I'm here to see the Overseer.' Jonathan straightened his tie. 'I'm expected.'

'Yes, you are.'

Jonathan turned to see a young woman holding a door open behind him. 'Good,' he said, 'I do so hate to be left hanging around in waiting rooms.'

The Thief smiled, as if Jonathan had said something incredibly amusing. 'My name is Pinch. I'll thank you to accompany me.'

'Pinch,' Jonathan repeated, with eye-rolling dislike. 'You're all so desperately imaginative with your aliases.'

Pinch gave a tiny smile. 'They grow on you.'

'Yes,' he said, 'like a fungus.'

Pinch kept up the same wan smile. There was a clink of metal as she adjusted her stance. 'Do you intend to stand there all day?' she asked.

Jonathan wished his head wasn't hurting quite so much. Tristyan's warm drink had worn off and over-frequent travelling by suitcase made you tired and sick even if you were at your best, which Jonathan decidedly was not. He found he was almost waiting for instructions, like a lost little boy. 'No, no.' He walked over to her, holding the iron-grey suitcase tight. 'I'm as anxious to get this over with as you are.'

Pinch put a hand to his back to steer him and the two of them went through the door, and onwards towards the Overseer's office.

CHAPTER THIRTY-SEVEN

Flick and Swype walked down a long winding corridor bordered by glowing blue stones that ignited as they passed and then faded into darkness again.

'This is the entrance used for visiting dignitaries and lords,' the Thief said. 'Think yourself privileged.'

'The ceilings are a bit low for my liking,' Flick said, trying to sound brave.

Swype glared down at her. 'Your silence would cost me extremely little, girl. The Overseer does not need you to be able to speak. Or stand.'

Flick clamped her mouth shut, smothering a bubble of fear that she half-thought might come out as a scream.

The corridor came to an abrupt end, and Swype pushed a door open, gesturing for Flick to enter. Flick brushed past them, hating the Thief's closeness, and into a corridor. There were several Thieves placing objects onto scales and shelves, others writing in ledgers. None of them gave Flick a second glance.

Except one.

Flick caught sight of a familiar face, with wide shocked eyes – *Nicc*! – as she was propelled through another door and shut into the room beyond.

She realised she was back in the Overseer's office. Only now, with fewer lamps lit, it felt smaller and more secretive. Flick could see a huge tapestry on the farthest wall, showing an outline of a hand grasping a bag with three coins inside it. It was the same picture as had been on the back of the receipt left at Quickspark's Emporium.

A door behind Flick opened and she turned to see the Overseer walking into the room, a frown on her face. 'Why is she here? Jonathan Mercator has not arrived yet.'

Flick blinked in confusion. 'You want Jonathan?'

'Indeed I do,' the Overseer said.

'Overseer,' Swype said, 'Pinch has gone to collect the Mercator boy. She's bringing him here.'

'Well, he's had long enough to provide us with what we asked. The lamps are lit, and his time is up.' The

Overseer gave Flick a stare, and Flick felt horribly exposed for a moment. 'Still, since we have a moment to chat ... What is your relationship to Jonathan Mercator, little girl? And what do you know of The Strangeworlds Society?'

'I am a member of The Strangeworlds Society,' Flick said quickly. She could imagine what the Thieves did with people they didn't think had any value, and she wanted to make herself seem as important as possible.

'Then you will know that I am Overseer Glean,' the Thief said. 'And that this is our city.'

'If it's your city, why are you hiding down here?' Flick said, before she could stop herself.

Swype stepped forward with intent.

Glean shook her head. 'No need for violence ...' She trailed off, as if she was adding the word *yet* in her head. Then she smiled happily at Flick. 'And as for why we "hide", as you put it, you may direct your attentions to the city itself. In your world, you disapprove of people taking things. And once, so did ours.'

Flick's mouth opened in surprise.

Glean went on: 'Keeping below ground and out of sight was an old arrangement between the city and its

Thieves. It was meant to keep so-called *crime* to acceptable levels. But as our powers grew, we turned from being relegated to the shadows to holding dominion over the city.'

'You're in charge?' Flick's question was interrupted by the door to the chamber opening, and Hid stepping in. He gave a short bow to Glean and shot Flick a malicious grin.

Fire burned under Flick's skin. 'What did you do to Greysen and Darilyn?'

'What I always do to people who can't tell me what I need to know,' he grinned.

Flick felt sick. 'You . . .'

'Now, Hid,' Glean raised a hand. 'Don't goad the girl. She isn't important.'

For some reason, those words made Flick want to scream. Instead, she glared hard at Glean, who shrugged in a way that was utterly infuriating.

'We are one of several city orders and societies who govern Five Lights,' Glean said. 'We have turned Theft from something dreadful into a mere inconvenience. We even allow customers to purchase back their wares, at a reasonable rate. We are not the villains you wish us to be, little girl. Didn't you make friends with one of our lower-classes? The de Vyce girl?'

Flick fidgeted, thinking of Nicc's shocked face out in the corridor. 'I still don't see why you have to take things. And you kidnapped me!'

'We did, but only to arrange an exchange. We meant no real malice. We merely need a way to leave this city.'

'But why?' Flick asked, confused. 'If you're in charge here why do you want to leave?'

The Overseer's expression twitched. 'Because of the schism.'

'What schism?' Flick took a look at the assembled Thieves, who all looked very uncomfortable. 'Do you mean a schism in a suitcase?'

Glean stared at her for a long time before speaking. 'You must know that Five Lights is an intensely magical city?'

'Jonathan said it was a – a hub. The centre of magic?'

'I don't know whether that is strictly true,' Glean said. 'However, it is very magical. There have always been schisms here. Not that anyone can *see* a schism, of course, but those of us who own magnifying glasses have seen magical phosphorescence drifting in one direction for some time. It is leaving this world, to feed a schism. And at such a rate that changes are seen here almost daily.'

'You've seen magic?' Flick asked. 'You've got magnifying glasses?'

Glean took a magnifying glass of silver and polished wood from her inside cloak pocket. Flick's stomach dropped. To see something she associated with Strangeworlds in the hand of a Thief made her want to snatch it out of her grasp.

Glean, as if reading her mind, chuckled. 'These lenses are very, very precious. I would say this is the most valuable object I have ever held. We know of a mere handful, and they are used only by my highly select First Class division. At that level, thieving is important, but secondary. What they concentrate on is gathering magical energy.'

Flick noted the cabinets. They seemed to pulse and glow with an eerie white light. So much magic in such a small space felt wrong. 'It's magic, those bottles?'

'Correct.'

'Why are you storing so much of it?'

Hid leaned forward. 'Madam Overseer, might I advise caution? This child asks a lot of questions. She may be a spy.'

Glean raised an eyebrow. 'Are you a spy, child? You do ask a lot of questions. And you claim to be ignorant about a great deal of things. What has become of The Strangeworlds Society if you know so little?' Her eyes narrowed. 'Does the Society still exist?'

Flick swallowed. 'If it didn't exist, how could I get here?'

'I suppose that's true. Even if it does now appear to be staffed by children.' She went over to the table, perching on the surface so she could look down at Flick. She still wore that empty smile. 'Five Lights is doomed. It is a city riveted with scars and wounds, but it has always healed itself. Until a schism, so large it could never be closed, tore its way through our sky.'

Flick imagined a great glowing tear – like the one she had seen outside Strangeworlds, only stretched across the sky like lightning, ripping through the blue above Five Lights. Unseen, it would be out of mind, not troubling anyone, until it was too late. Helplessness took hold of her and she badly wanted to grab Glean's magnifying glass, run outside and aim it up at the sky – just to see whether this woman was right or wrong. Flick didn't know which outcome she would prefer.

Glean stood straight. 'Magic is leaking out of this world faster than anyone can replace it. Which will only lead to one thing. The end of Five Lights.'

CHAPTER THIRTY-EIGHT

'I t can't be,' Flick choked out. 'Schisms can heal themselves and close, if they're left alone. Why can't this one?'

'The sheer size,' Glean sighed. 'To close up, it would need to take Five Lights with it. And it will. It has already begun. Whole streets are vanishing off the map. Magic is more difficult to bottle. Even people are disappearing.'

Like Jonathan's dad, Flick thought. She could all too easily imagine someone who looked like an older version of Jonathan being sucked into a crack in the sky and vanishing forever. The sick feeling bubbled up in her throat.

'We don't intend to stay here and let the same thing happen to us,' Glean said. 'We will leave this place and start again. We have done it before.'

'Before? But . . .' Flick remembered Jonathan's words. 'You can't survive in a world that isn't your own.'

'Oh,' Glean's smile sickened into something more genuine, and more frightening. 'There are ways to work magic that even The Strangeworlds Society does not know.'

At that moment, as if she had been waiting behind the door for a good moment to enter, Pinch walked in, propelling a swaying Jonathan in front of her.

Flick's mouth dropped open in both relief and shock.

Jonathan's hair was matted and sticking up in all directions. There was a smear of dirt on his jaw, and there was blood on his top lip. His glasses were askew.

And he had a suitcase in his hand. Flick's relief changed to a feeling of utter betrayal.

You brought them one! Flick thought, in outrage. *You actually brought them a suitcase . . . what are you thinking?*

'Jonathan . . .' she forced out through gritted teeth.

His gaze landed on her, and Flick saw that one lens of his glasses was smashed. 'Ah. There you are. Have they been treating you all right? Decent food, and so on? I can't imagine anyone knows how to make an acceptable cup of tea around here.'

Flick didn't know if he was joking or not. Her mouth flapped silently, torn between screeching in anger and wailing in despair.

'I must say, I don't think much of the décor,' he said, looking around. 'It looks like a carpet shop threw up in here.'

The Overseer bristled. 'We did not bring you here to comment on our lodgings, Mercator.'

'Yes, that ship has clearly . . . well, certainly the ship has been towed away for scrap if not actually *sailed*,' he said. 'Have you come to your senses, Overseer?'

Glean looked pointedly at the suitcase in his hand. 'You have nothing we want save for that suitcase.'

'Oh, this one?' Jonathan lifted it. 'I am afraid you're mistaken. This suitcase isn't for you. It leads back to Strangeworlds. This is for me to take Felicity home.'

Flick blinked. She looked at the suitcase again. Something nudged her in the back of the brain, but she couldn't focus on what it was.

A vein throbbed in Glean's temple. 'You *dare* come here without anything to bargain with?'

'Leaving Five Lights is not the answer for you,' Jonathan said.

Glean laughed for a moment, her eyes flashing. 'As if you have any authority to tell us what to do! If you do not hand one of your suitcases over, you cannot have the girl.' She raised her head. 'If the girl has no value to you, the magic keeping her alive shall be of use to us.'

Flick gasped. 'You can't!' She imagined herself falling to the ground, like a puppet with its strings cut as her magic was pulled out of her body and put into one of those glowing bottles.

'Pinch,' Glean pointed, 'fetch a bottle.'

The Thief moved towards one of the cabinets.

'No!'

'Stop,' Jonathan stepped forward. 'You don't have to threaten me, or Felicity. We can negotiate. This world is not lost.'

'Yet,' Glean added.

'Schisms can heal,' Jonathan said. 'They have to. It is one of the facts of the multiverse.'

'And yet, this one does not.'

'It could, if you helped it.'

'How?'

Jonathan put his shoulders back. 'How much magic would you say you have bottled in these walls?'

Glean leapt off the table-top and marched over, enraged. 'You expect us to give up our magic? We *earned* it. We took it from this world, as is our right, and we look after it.'

'You control it,' Jonathan said. 'But it isn't yours. It's a resource that should be available to everyone here. And look what's happening because it isn't allowed to flow!'

'You are honestly blaming *us* for this?' Glean leaned forward, her dark eyes fixed on Jonathan's face. 'The schisms in the fabric of the multiverse – this unstoppable schism in *my* world . . . don't you know where they came from?' Jonathan's face went from stubborn to bewildered. 'Don't you know what they will unleash?'

Something wintry and horrible frosted over inside Flick. This was an ice-cold secret, old and edged in silence. She could feel it.

Jonathan stayed silent.

A spark of delight hit Glean's eyes and she leaned forward. 'Oh! Oh, so you *don't* know. You really are a child, aren't you? Running in the dark. You travel around in your suitcases, visiting worlds like a conqueror and yet you have no idea what the true stakes are.'

Jonathan clicked his tongue. 'Are you going to tell me? Or is the suspense simply too delicious for you to spit it out?'

Glean smirked. 'Tell me: why was The Strangeworlds Society formed in the first place, little Mercator?'

'To maintain the balance of schism and magic, of course,' he said, frowning. 'To protect the worlds.'

'Protect them, Mercator? Oh, yes, well done. But from what? From whom?'

Jonathan's face fell.

Flick put a hand to her mouth. *Protect them from what? From . . . whom?*

Glean shook her head. 'If you knew what we were up against – what we were *all* up against – you would destroy those cases in a heartbeat.'

'The schisms in the cases cannot be destroyed,' Jonathan said. He looked as if he was trying to hold onto something that was slipping rapidly through his hands. 'They neither use magic nor expel it. They are safe. It is my – our – job to keep them safe.'

Glean straightened up and laughed. 'Safe? We have never been safe, not for one single moment. The multiverse is in more danger than you realise.'

Flick looked at the suitcase in Jonathan's hand. She thought about the stacks and stacks of cases back at

Strangeworlds. The multiverse was in danger? All of it? Did that include Earth? Pain bloomed in the palms of her hands, and she realised she'd anxiously clenched her fists so tightly her nails were digging into the soft skin.

Not my world, she thought to herself, the anxiety inside her balling up and lodging in her chest.

Jonathan seemed shaken, too. 'Even if that is true, you are preventing your world from being able to heal itself because of your greed,' he said plainly, though his voice was trembling. 'You cannot have wealth *and* an uninjured world. Which is it you value the most?'

Glean glared at him.

Then she drew back a hand and slapped him. Hard.

Jonathan folded up like a Slinky hitting the bottom step.

Flick rushed forward. Swype caught her by the arms. 'Stay back,' they snarled.

'Is it not for you to say whether or not we *value* things!' Glean screeched at Jonathan. 'We fled to this world to escape persecution, and you think we do not care for it?'

'You've got a funny way of showing it.' He sat up, hand to his face. 'You're tearing it into pieces instead of sharing it, and then acting surprised when the place doesn't work any more. You could solve this. You don't *need* to take yourselves somewhere else.'

'And yet, we will. We have already mastered magic in ways you could not imagine. We have even created worlds of our own.'

Jonathan's eyes went wide. 'You . . . made a . . .'

'Yes,' Glean smirked. 'Ask your little friend. She was there. We *made* a world.'

Flick pulled her arms free of Swype's grip, and stepped forward. 'There isn't a world,' she said, her voice trembling. 'Not any more.'

Glean scoffed incredulously. 'What do you mean by that?'

'There might have been one once.' Flick balled her fingers into fists. 'But there isn't any more. Because it's gone. I made it disappear.'

Glean shook her head. 'You're lying. Swype and Pinch brought you from there—'

'We did not take her from the Waiting Room, Overseer.' Swype spoke up quickly. 'She was outside Quickspark's.'

There was a silence, like the suspended quiet you hear just before a glass hits the ground and shatters.

CHAPTER THIRTY-NINE

Glean walked forward. She kept her eyes fixed on Flick, as if there was no one else in the room. The shadows seemed to creep along with her.

'You broke out of *my* world?' she asked. 'You destroyed it? How? It was *locked.*'

Flick tried to look brave. 'I wanted to get back to my family. That was all.'

'Don't get sentimental on me,' Glean spat, her eyes flashing. 'Locked worlds can only be opened by the one who sealed them.' She leaned down, her nose merely inches from Flick's. 'What *are* you?'

Flick tried not to flinch, remembering the fear in Darilyn's eyes as she asked the same question. 'I'm – I'm not anything.'

'You're either a liar or you don't yet know what you are ...' Her eyes roamed over Flick's face, searching for facts. 'Tell me how you did it. I can make you speak, if you refuse.'

'She's just a traveller,' Jonathan interrupted hastily. 'I wouldn't bring anyone here who—'

Glean rounded on him and pointed her finger like a weapon. 'Your family are liars and betrayers. The last thing we need is more input from you.' She looked back to Flick. 'I want a way out of this world and not simply whatever poor choice The Strangeworlds Society might offer me. I want a world full of magic. And you, my talented girl, are going to give it to me. Find one for me. Find me a world rich in magic. Break into it and let me through.'

'No,' Flick said, her voice sounding very small.

Glean laughed. Laughed right into her face. And her Thieves joined in.

Anger fizzed under Flick's skin. Her hands prickled.

'You are in no position to refuse,' Glean said. 'You will simply do as you are told.' Her eyes glittered. 'Break into a world for me.'

Flick shook her head. 'No. I don't even know how.'

'Clearly you do. You have done so already.'

'I won't.'

Glean rolled her eyes. 'Swype, please make her see reason.'

The pale Thief's milky eyes shone, and they lunged forward.

Flick darted out of their reach, moving quickly, trying to avoid getting trapped against the wall.

Swype shook their head as they stalked after her, crossing the centre of the room. 'There's nowhere you can run, not in here . . .' They side-stepped and darted towards Flick like a fencer.

Jonathan swung the suitcase, cracking the Thief hard on the back. The noise echoed around the room like a tree breaking in half. Swype sprawled onto the floor. They lay there groaning, as Jonathan went to hit them again.

'Someone restrain that boy,' Glean snapped.

Pinch came forward and pulled Jonathan back by his collar like he weighed nothing.

Swype spat as they got up and grabbed for Flick again, but Flick shoved her hand upwards, aiming for their nose, fighting as only a twelve-year-old can. Swype shouted as Flick hit their face.

The Thief snarled and tried to get a hold of Flick's arms, but Flick had grown up watching the older kids from the flats brawl in the playground and knew that in a real fight no one awarded you points for effort. You just had to hurt the other person, in any way you could, before they could hurt you. She scrabbled at Swype's face and made contact with their eyes, scratching them. The Thief yelled and dropped her.

'Enough,' Glean shouted. Her voice thundered through the room and made everyone freeze, as if she controlled the air. 'This is absurd. A First Class Thief not even capable of restraining a little girl.' She marched across the room and snatched the suitcase from Jonathan. She turned to face Flick. 'Now. Either you open a world for us or we go through to your precious Strangeworlds and take what we want. From wherever we want. Choose.'

Flick glared back at Glean. 'You can't go through to my world.'

Glean smirked. 'It wouldn't only be your world. All those suitcases,' she said. 'All those doorways for us to use. So. Many. Worlds.' Flick could see her yellowing teeth. 'If you don't break into a world for me, you are giving me all that. All of it. It will be *your* fault.'

Flick's vision swam. 'I – I can't – I don't know how!'

'Try.'

'I can't!'

'TRY!' Glean roared. 'Try, you useless *child* or I will drain every drop of magic in your world and let it crumble to dust!'

Flick sobbed in terror and raised her hands, remembering the punching feeling of before. That shattering of reality, the rush of magic over her skin and down her bones. It was like a memory just out of reach.

And she realised, with a quiet swell of fear that –

she *could* do it.

It wasn't quite like riding a bike – she was sure she wouldn't get it right – but the recollection of how to do it was there. It was at the back of her mind. She was sure that if she really concentrated, if she tried hard enough, she could remember how she had broken out of that horrible, tiny world.

Maybe she could find another world. Break into it for Glean. It might even be *easy* . . .

She could do it.

But she didn't want to. She could decide *not* to do what Glean was demanding. It all, really, came down to her choice. Every world was full of people like her. People like her mum and dad, little babies like Freddy. Living, loving people, who didn't deserve to have their fate taken out of their hands.

How could she hand over a world she'd never seen to these people?

But how could she not?

With a sick jolt, she realised that refusing to do as the Thief wanted might mean she never saw her family again. Everything she had been terrified of losing – her parents, Freddy, her life back on Earth – would be gone.

The angry fear she had felt in the Waiting Room swelled again. It was a hot feeling of injustice wrapped around such a profound feeling of loss that she felt it like a pit in her heart. Tears welled in Flick's eyes. Her throat ached, and she felt as if she could sink onto the floor and straight through the carpet. She could save the whole of Strangeworlds, the whole of her own world, if she did as they asked . . .

She caught Jonathan's eye.

Behind his broken glasses, one of his eyelids flickered. Very slightly, he inclined his head toward the grey suitcase in Glean's hand.

The case was dusty. Metallic iron-grey. It had dirty, rusted, off-white catches.

Realisation came softly, like the dawn breaking in Flick's mind. She cast her eyes down at the floor to hide her expression.

The suitcase in Glean's hand wasn't the suitcase Flick and Jonathan had come through.

The suitcase they had arrived through had been pearly-pink, with gold accents.

Flick looked back up at Jonathan's face. It was blank. Guarded. Was he trying to tell her something? Had he switched it?

Flick's hands were shaking. Her mind was racing. She had no time to *think*.

'I am *waiting*,' Glean snapped. 'You are wasting my time, and I do not take kindly to that.'

Either Flick trusted Jonathan, despite everything that had happened, or she didn't. She had to choose.

Glean stepped closer. 'What have you decided?'

Flick looked at Jonathan again. And made her choice.

She clenched her teeth. She screwed up her eyes and flexed her fingers, as if she was trying hard.

Glean's face lit up in desire, in hope, in greed.

Flick's arms shook. The fiery emotions inside her were still there, begging to be noticed and used, but she ignored them. She breathed slowly, feeling her arms and legs tingle, the way they do after you've run a race. And, after a minute, the tension inside her melted away.

She puffed out a breath and lowered her hands. 'I can't do it!'

Glean shook her head. 'Whatever you are, you've used up all your luck.' She thumped the case down on the floor. 'You did this, girl. We shall go to Strangeworlds Travel Agency and it shall all be ours. And you will stay here and rot.'

Jonathan made to snatch the case back from her, his eyes panicked, and for a moment Flick was terrified that she had done the wrong thing. Thief Hid grabbed his arms and held them behind his back. Jonathan twisted in his grip, gritting his teeth. 'Don't,' he said. 'Please. Trust me on this, you shouldn't . . .'

Flick looked at the dusty suitcase in Glean's hands as the Overseer ran her hands over it. It was a trick. It had to be. Or else Flick had lost everything.

Glean touched at the catches. 'This is everything we could ever need.'

'You mustn't do this,' Jonathan said. 'Five Lights can be saved. Please listen to me. I can help you!'

Glean laughed and the others smirked. 'You think you can educate us? We have forgotten more than you know. We have lived in hiding, long beyond our natural life-spans, running from one world to the next until we could run no further. This was a good world.' She gazed up, fondly. 'It was a profitable world. But it is no longer safe. And you have handed me the keys to all the worlds in the multiverse, for as long as I live.'

'Wait.' Jonathan wrestled against Hid's grip, and got loose. 'Wait – you said the schisms in the multiverse came from somewhere. You said they would unleash something. If nothing else then please, tell me what you know!'

Glean laughed. Then she stepped close and lowered her voice, so that only Jonathan and Flick could hear her. 'If you want to know what we're up against, find out where Elara Mercator came from. What her life was before she started up that pathetic travel agency. And what scared her so much that she never spoke of it to anyone – not even her family.'

The two of them said nothing.

Glean narrowed her eyes at Flick. 'And whatever *you* are, little girl, you are something that has not been seen for a long time. I would watch your back.'

An icy shiver ran over Flick's skin.

Glean turned away from them. 'Are all the First Class here?' she asked the room of Thieves.

'We are, Overseer.'

She nodded. 'Today we take the first step towards freedom. Join me and be free of the dread that lies over this world. And know that you will be safe.'

There were determined nods all around. The Thieves were prepared to do whatever their Overseer wanted of them. Flick wondered if they were too afraid to refuse or if they too truly wanted this.

Glean knelt and opened the latches on the case. The lid sprang open and a smell of cold air wafted out. Uncertainty crossed her face for the first time.

'We simply . . . step in?' she asked.

Jonathan stepped forward again. 'Please. Overseer Glean, listen to me. You owe it to the people of Five Lights to tell them what is happening. You can help heal this schism you fear so much. Please!'

'I owe this place nothing. You have given me a whole new world,' Glean said. 'And it is mine for the taking.' She stepped into the case.

And then everything seemed to happen very fast . . .

Pinch, Lute, Hid and Swype all rushed forward, towards the suitcase. It was as though they were attached to Glean by a string and had no choice but to follow her.

The Thieves didn't pause to consider the strangeness of climbing into another world through a suitcase. They jumped in, leaping in quick desperation. Their red coats vanished into the suitcase one by one—

Hid, the last to get in, maliciously knocked Jonathan to the floor as he passed him. An anxious look crossed

Jonathan's face and he tried to scramble up, reaching for the suitcase . . .

Flick gasped, understanding smacking her in the face.

Of course. If the Thieves pulled the suitcase through with them, they could come back to Five Lights anytime they liked. And if Jonathan couldn't convince them to stay and heal the schism, he wanted to make sure the Thieves would not come back to damage Five Lights further.

CLOSE IT! Flick's brain screamed at her. She leapt forward, throwing herself on the floor, skidding towards the case –

As the last scrap of red coat twisted into the suitcase, Flick stuck her hand inside. She felt the handle in the other world and she grabbed it.

She pulled.

Please! she thought desperately. *CLOSE!*

The suitcase came back with her, pulling out of itself, turning inside out as it turned the right way in, popping into the City of Five Lights as it closed in the world the Thieves had so carelessly leapt into.

Flick was sealing them in and there was nothing they could do about it.

She fell backwards as the suitcase lifted from the

ground. She landed hard, next to Jonathan, who, despite it all, was grinning at her like he'd witnessed the world's best magic trick. The suitcase landed with a *THUD* on the floor beside them.

They sat in silence for a moment. The room felt incredibly still and quiet.

Tentatively, Flick lifted the suitcase lid. A tartan fabric interior stared back at her, with a little pocket for socks or keys. There were some old straps hanging in the main body of the case; the elastic had long since lost its tension. There was no other world. No schism. Nothing unremarkable at all. She tapped the bottom of it. It was very solid and very ordinary.

'I broke it.'

Jonathan made a small noise of surprise. 'What do you mean?'

She showed him.

He didn't smile. 'I see. Well. I suppose we shan't be using that any more, except perhaps to carry books around.'

Flick stared at it. 'Where did they go?'

'The last place they'll have wanted to go,' Jonathan sighed. 'An island, surrounded by deep ocean.'

Flick's mouth dropped open. 'They're going to be stuck there? Forever?'

'I hope so,' Jonathan said ruthlessly. 'But I'm not certain of anything.'

Flick touched one of the straps in the suitcase. The Thieves had been extremely nasty, but to leave them stranded like that . . .

'I did tell them not to use it,' Jonathan said, as if he could read the small print of her thoughts.

'Yes,' she admitted with a sigh. 'You did.' She remembered the piles of bottled magic in the cabinets. 'What happens to this world? To all the bottles?'

'They're stuffed full of magic,' Jonathan said. 'We need to release it.'

'Will the other Thieves let us?'

'I doubt it.'

As if on cue, there was a sudden thundering of footsteps and Flick turned just as the heavy door behind them burst open, letting in several dozen Thieves, all looking ready for a fight. One of them, at the front, even had a mace in his hand. Flick jolted to her feet before she realised the Thieves weren't looking at her and Jonathan.

They were looking for Glean, Flick realised. They were on their side.

'Where did they go?' Nicc pushed people aside and came to the front. 'Did we miss the fight?'

Flick couldn't help grinning in relief and happiness at a familiar friendly face. 'Wasn't much of a fight, actually.'

'Oh. That's a shame. I was looking forward to it.' Nicc winked and turned back to her makeshift army. 'They're gone, everyone. You can relax.'

There were groans and clanks as the Thieves put their weaponry away.

Nicc came over, her boots scuffing the expensive carpet. 'Now what *did* happen here, Flick?'

Flick looked at Jonathan. 'I don't know if you'll believe it.'

Nicc folded her arms. 'Try me.'

*

'We'll smash all the bottles,' Nicc promised. They were in the Thieves' dining room on the top floor of the Order office, drinking hot chocolate so thick it was practically cake. 'Turns out there are more in the walls than we knew about. And under the floors. The magic is everywhere except where it needs to be.'

'What happened?' Jonathan asked. 'What happened to make the Order so driven by greed?'

Nicc shrugged. 'We used to have a different Overseer. Then about four years ago Glean came along and took over. There are all sorts of rumours about how. Anyway, Thieving changed, after that. The Class system changed from a measure of achievement to a way of controlling who knew what secrets. Only people Glean knew personally got to be First Class.'

Flick put her mug down. 'Where did she come from?'

Nicc made a *who knows* gesture with her hands. 'I don't think anyone ever had the backbone to ask.'

'She said she wasn't from this world,' Jonathan mused. 'We may never know, for certain. Still, I would like to find out. Difficult, though, given her current whereabouts.'

Flick touched the suitcase on the table. 'And I broke this . . .'

'Mm. I didn't exactly plan for *that* to happen. Not that I'm complaining.'

Nicc looked at Flick, impressed. 'Is it true you broke out of another world into this one?'

Flick felt very uncomfortable. 'Yeah. I don't know if I could do it again.'

'I hope you can,' Jonathan said. 'Because your gift seems to be one that keeps on giving, Felicity.' He smiled. 'Now, not to panic you or anything, but I believe we may have outstayed our welcome.' He tapped his watch.

Flick put her hands to her face in horror. 'Oh my god. What time is it? Back at Strangeworlds, I mean?'

'Um. It's tomorrow,' Jonathan said guiltily.

'Tomorrow?!'

'About five o'clock in the morning,' he said. 'With that in mind, shall we make for home? Quickspark's isn't too far away.'

'Wait,' Flick said. 'I want to check something.' She held her hand out.

Jonathan stared at her palm for a moment, then wordlessly took the tiny brass magnifying glass from his pocket and handed it over. 'If you're sure.'

Flick nodded. 'I want to know what we're dealing with.' She went over to the window and put a hand to the glass. Outside, the sky was baby blue, marked with only a few white clouds.

'Flick,' Jonathan called. 'There's such a thing as knowing too much.'

'No, there's not,' Flick said. 'That's just something people tell you when they're afraid, and they think you will be, too.' She kept her hand at the window and raised the tiny magnifier to her eye.

The effect was thrilling and terrifying. A filter of darkness descended over Flick's vision, turning the sky outside from blue to black. The air swirled with glittering golden magic, and above the tops of the tallest buildings . . .

A jagged rip in the atmosphere hovered above the city. It was golden-white and glowing monstrously, seeming to pulse as bits of magic steadily drifted into it like water running downhill.

Flick realised she was crying. 'It's . . .'

Someone put their arm around her. 'Is it as bad as we thought?' It was Nicc.

'I don't even know how anyone could fix . . .' Flick stopped as a sudden light flashed at the bottom of her vision, and a stream of white-gold magic shot into the sky like a firework. It collided with the schism, and as Flick watched . . .

The schism shrank back.

Just a little.

But it shrank.

Flick lowered the magnifying glass. 'They're smashing the bottles, aren't they?'

'I hope so,' Nicc said.

'I saw it. The magic. Going back into the sky. It was healing the schism. It was.' Flick looked back at Jonathan. 'It's going to be OK, isn't it?'

Jonathan's eyes flicked over to the window. 'We can only hope.'

'We can do more than hope,' Nicc sniffed. 'We can do something about it. Even if we have to change the way we live. Nothing's more important than this. This is our home.' She pulled Flick into a hug.

Flick tensed for a moment, then relaxed into it, suddenly feeling completely exhausted.

Nicc let go of her. 'Thank you, Flick,' she said, 'for helping us to save our world.'

CHAPTER FORTY

'Look for a blue case. Light blue, with gold fastenings,' Darilyn said.

They were in the wine cellar of the Wilting Lily, where the casks of ale and bottles of wine shared the cold space with twenty or so suitcases. Flick had been so relieved to see the Quicksparks unharmed that she'd gone straight in for a hug with Darilyn as soon as she saw her.

'I thought Hid had hurt you,' she said, letting go eventually.

'Oh, him?' Darilyn rolled her eyes. 'All bark and no bite. Wouldn't know the right end of a spoon, never mind how to question anybody. He just put a magical lock on the front door. Foolish man. Never even asked if there was a door out the back. How else would we have carried two dozen suitcases out of the emporium without being noticed?'

'We hid them here,' Greysen said, 'because we didn't have a lot of time. And the Wilting Lily is a tavern popular with Thieves. Last place they'd look is under their own nose.'

Nicc grinned from the cellar steps. 'It's fortunate I never knew what they were.'

Darilyn rolled her eyes. 'You keep looking for that suitcase.'

'Will it take us home?' Flick said, searching through the pile.

'Indirectly.' Jonathan sipped from the cup of tea he had somehow managed to acquire. 'We're taking the scenic route home, Felicity. One stop, and then Strangeworlds.'

'How do you know it's safe?'

'I've got a friend waiting for us.'

'I didn't think you had friends.' Flick raised her eyebrows at him.

Jonathan looked contrite, a wine-stain of a blush starting over his white cheeks. 'About that. I was hoping . . . given the circumstances . . .'

Flick sighed. 'Let's do that when we get back.' She examined the cases as Jonathan came closer, picking up one himself. 'Why aren't these cases at Strangeworlds?'

'Oh, you don't put all your bridges in one basket.'

Flick walked away from the suitcase piles, and sat down beside him. 'Glean said something had caused the schisms in the multiverse. She didn't say what it was, but she knew. And you don't.'

'No.' He frowned. 'I don't like not knowing.'

Darilyn pulled out the blue case. 'Here it is, Custodians. Time to go home.'

· 'Excellent. But before we go, I have to ask ...' Jonathan trailed off.

'Your father?' Greysen asked.

Jonathan nodded.

Greysen shook his head. 'Can't tell you much more than we told your friend. I'm just sorry it didn't seem important before. Your father came to us, mentioned a lighthouse, then asked for some privacy in the shop. We never saw him again.'

'And he gave no indication whatsoever about where he was going?'

'He never said where this lighthouse might be, or what he needed to visit it for. Sorry. I don't know anything else.'

Flick saw Jonathan glance at her. 'I see.' He fished the magnifying glass out of his pocket. 'I know this is asking a lot,' he said guiltily, 'but . . . would you mind?'

Flick didn't hesitate. She took the magnifier and looked through it.

The wine cellar had a low-level magical glow about it.

But none of the suitcases sparkled. Not even one.

She lowered the magnifying glass and shook her head. 'I'm sorry.'

Jonathan's face was blank as he took the glass back. 'He must have taken it with him. Pulled it through, wherever he went. If he went at all.'

Flick looked at Nicc. 'Was there any information on Daniel Mercator in Glean's office? Anything you heard?'

Nicc shook her head. 'Last time anyone saw him in the city was months ago.'

Greysen cleared his throat. 'Sorry we can't be of more help.'

'Well, this isn't goodbye,' Jonathan said, looking up with determination. 'I shall come back.'

'We both will,' Flick said.

The Custodians smiled at her. Nicc gave them both a small salute.

Jonathan took the case and opened it. 'Now – the person waiting for us is called Tristyan,' he said to Flick. 'Don't stare at his ears.'

*

Tristyan insisted on cleaning up Jonathan's bloody nose before letting them go. 'Some things never change,' he sighed.

'Unfortunately,' Jonathan said.

Flick sat on the dining chair and watched. They'd exited Five Lights into Tristyan's living room, and he was very relieved to see them. He'd given Flick a warm drink that tasted like medicine and a soft smile that seemed almost familiar. Then he set about fixing up Jonathan's various cuts and bruises.

'Do . . . do I know you?' Flick asked, breaking the silence. 'Tristyan?'

'I was about to ask you the same thing,' Tristyan said, turning to look at her.

They stared at one another. Tristyan tucked his long hair back behind one ear. It was pointed, like an elf's. He certainly wasn't from her world.

'I'm sure we've met,' Flick said. 'But we can't have. Can we?'

'I don't travel between worlds, so it's highly unlikely,' Tristyan said.

Jonathan looked between them both, a doubtful frown on his face.

Flick wished she could think clearly. She shrugged. 'Weird.'

'It is.' Tristyan smiled cheerfully at her again, and Flick was positive she had seen that expression before. It was nagging at her in a way that made her feel slightly nervous, as if she was skirting around the edge of a deep shadow.

Jonathan got up and checked his reflection in the mirror over the mantelpiece. His glasses were still broken and he looked as tired as Flick felt. She wanted to ask if the scrap of information he'd managed to get about his father had been worth it. Somehow, she doubted it. They barely knew any more than before, had gotten themselves captured, and had almost lost an entire world in the process.

Flick tapped the edge of her cup with a fingernail. She'd heard people say *you mean the world to me*, but that couldn't be true, could it? No one loved anyone that much. No one was worth that much to anyone. Were they?

She wasn't sure she knew the answer.

Tristyan moved to sit opposite her and shook her out of her thoughts. 'How does the travel agency suit you, Felicity?'

'Mm . . . It's OK,' she said.

'She's got a gift for it,' Jonathan said, looking at them both through the mirror.

'There you have it, then.'

Flick rolled her eyes. 'Ignore him. He's trying to get back in my good books.'

'I'd say you could do worse,' Tristyan said. 'He would have done almost anything to get you back, I think.'

Flick didn't know what to say to that.

Jonathan picked up the spare suitcase, the one Flick had locked permanently. He had filled it with old Society books from Greysen and Darilyn. 'Ready?'

'Yes. It was nice to meet you.' Flick shook hands with Tristyan, still feeling not entirely sure about him.

'And you. Look after each other. And don't leave it so long next time,' Tristyan called, as the two of them dropped through the suitcase and back into the travel agency.

*

They surfaced half sideways, half upside down, tumbling out at the back of the shop and sprawling in a heap of arms and legs that made them groan and clutch at the bits of themselves that hit the wooden floor.

Flick crawled into one of the armchairs. 'Ow. My . . . everything hurts.'

Jonathan wobbled over to the desk and swapped his smashed glasses for an unbroken pair out of the drawer. 'Agreed.' He collapsed into the swivel chair.

Flick closed her eyes. She was dog-tired, her muscles ached, and she wanted her mum. She'd never wanted her mum so badly in her life. And she wanted her dad, even if he would fall asleep on the sofa. And she wanted Freddy, even if he'd try to eat her sleeves.

She wanted them all.

She had missed them all so much.

Flick pushed herself upright. 'Jonathan . . .'

'Let me go first, please.' Jonathan sat up and looked at her. 'I am sorry, you know. I am so . . . so sorry. I lied to you – kept the truth from you. You're a better person and a better travel agent than I could ever hope to be. But you don't have to come back ever again. If you want, this can be where your story ends. And, if this is goodbye . . .' He held a hand out. 'If this is goodbye, I am not sorry at all to have met you, Felicity. You're what this world needs. I am very glad you're back in it.'

Flick stared at his hand, then shook her head. 'It's not goodbye,' she said. 'Not yet.'

Jonathan smiled.

Flick sighed. 'Adventures. Who'd have them.'

'Well, since you're asking . . .'

They stared at each other. Then dissolved into tired, aching laughter.

CHAPTER FORTY-ONE

Three Days Later

'Knock, knock,' Flick said, pushing the door open. 'That's not traditionally how knocking works,' Jonathan said, looking up from the huge book he'd been reading. His legs were up on the desk again. So was the magnifying glass.

Flick grinned and put a box of tea onto the desk. She took the book out of Jonathan's hands and read the title page. '*A Study of Schisms?*'

'I thought I should at least try to learn what my dad failed to teach me,' he said. 'And it's interesting.' He gave her a cautious smile. 'How are you?'

'Better, I think.' She put the book down and picked up the magnifying glass, twirling it in her fingers.

'What did you tell your parents about where you were, in the end?'

'Nothing. I figured it would be easier not to answer any questions than to try and keep a lie straight. My dad went absolutely off his trolley. They'd had the police out, and everything. I'm grounded for the next thousand years.'

'And yet, here you are.'

'Yeah, well, they've got to leave the house sometime.'

The argument had gone on for almost four hours and ended with everyone in the house crying, including one of the police officers. It had almost pulled Flick apart, but she knew that having the internet cut off until she was twenty-five was a small price to pay for keeping Strangeworlds a secret. How could she make her parents understand she had come so close to losing them when she couldn't tell them what had happened? The pain of keeping everything a secret – of keeping what made herself special a secret – hurt her down to her bones.

She helped herself to one of Jonathan's biscuits. Jonathan deftly fished the magnifying glass out of her fingers as she did so, putting it pointedly down on the desk.

She tutted, mouth full of biscuit. 'You can trust me, you know.'

He took his legs down off the desk. 'I know. I do trust you. Honestly. I suppose it would be a fine thing if you could say the same about me.' He picked at his cuff.

Flick waited a few seconds before shrugging. 'You know, if you'd just told me that I'm different I probably would have helped you anyway.'

'Really? But why?'

'Because that's what people do for their friends,' she said. 'They help them. And they tell them what it is that makes them special. Even if what makes them special is their ability to drive you absolutely mad.'

They were quiet, then. The sounds of the road outside drifted in under the door, and there was nothing in the room except breathing and thinking and the gentle ticking of the dozens of clocks. It was so comfortable they both might have fallen asleep.

'Will you come back, then?' Jonathan asked. 'Properly?'

Flick snorted. 'As if I could walk away now. I know too much, don't I?'

'Well, quite. But for what it's worth I should hate to see you decide to walk away from Strangeworlds. It might be selfish of me, but I like having you around.'

Flick raised her eyebrows. 'To pass on what you know?'

'No. I *thought* that was why I liked having you around,' Jonathan said. 'But, really, it's because of who you are as a person. It's nice to have . . . well, to have a friend I suppose. I'm sorry – I've never been very good at this. You'll have to forgive me if I'm making a hash of it.'

'No.' Flick smiled. 'You're better at it than you think. I'd rather you said you wanted me to hang around as your friend than as your student.' She prodded him on the arm. 'No more secrets though, yeah? If I ask a question, you give me the truth. No lies.' She stuck her hand out.

'No lies,' he agreed, shaking it.

'And . . . what about your dad?' Flick asked.

Jonathan looked down at the desk. 'I . . . would like to continue that search.'

'What if he's dead?' Flick asked. 'I'm sorry to be blunt, but it is possible.'

'I don't know,' Jonathan said, without looking up. 'I just hope.'

Flick nodded. She understood that. There was always hope.

It wasn't enough, though. There was also action. You had to have both, in the end.

After that, there were biscuits and more tea, and the two of them barely had to say anything at all. When

Flick's phone beeped with the alarm to say she needed to leave in order to beat her dad home, Flick went to the door. Then paused.

'Jonathan . . .' she started.

Jonathan knew the start of an awkward question when he heard it. 'Mm?'

'That picture on the stairs. The one of the boy in school uniform?'

'Yes?'

'Is that of your dad?'

He nodded. 'Oh. Yes, it is.'

'That's nice,' Flick smiled. She opened the door, then looked back at Jonathan. 'You look exactly like him, you know.'

Jonathan didn't answer. He looked as though speaking would break him.

Flick's alarm buzzed another reminder in her pocket. 'I need to go.'

'Wait,' Jonathan got up and took the magnifying glass off his desk. He held it out to her.

'You're serious?' Flick took it quickly, in case he wasn't.

'I'm serious. It's more use to you than me. Keep it. You'll be back, won't you?'

'I'll have to be, now,' she said, putting the little brass instrument into her pocket. 'As soon as I can.'

Jonathan took the door and held it open for her. 'Safe journey, Felicity.'

She stepped through the door of The Strangeworlds Travel Agency, out of one world and into another.

ACKNOWLEDGEMENTS

This book would never have been written, let alone published, without the support and encouragement of my wonderful agent, Claire Wilson. Thank you for helping Flick and I take our first steps together, for being my knight in shining armour, and for pointing out I was about to pour salt into my tea that one time.

To my editors at Orion Children's, Lena McCauley and Samantha Swinnerton, I thank you both to the stars and back again. Most people are phenomenally lucky if they get one awesome editor, but I had TWO! Thank you for putting The Strangeworlds Travel Agency in business, and for all your wonderful work.

Thank you to the whole team at Hachette Children's Group, including the Rights team for all their hard work sending Flick and Jonathan around the world, to Dominic Kingston for PR, and to Samuel Perrett and Natalie Smillie for designing and illustrating a cover so beautiful I'm thinking of having it tattooed on my back.

Shoutout to Nicole Jarvis, who let me Charles Dickens my way through the first draft by sending her 200 words at a time to read over Twitter DMs. To Darran Stobbart and Melinda Salisbury, for keeping secrets and donating your names so I could turn them into candy. A thousand thanks to Steve Jones, Peter L. and Gabriel Wulff for being wonderful sensitivity readers. Thank you to my writing tribe on Twitter, including Alice S-H, Alice Oseman, Laura Steven, George Lester and Jo Hogan. And thank you to Steph Elliott, Jo Clarke and Louise Inniss for being the best cheerleaders an author could hope for.

Kudos to the entire AO3 community for being a bottomless pool of stories, feedback, hope and support – keep writing, everyone. Thank you Lia Louis for putting up with stressful text messages about eye-bags and eating packet-ham out of the fridge, and to Nick for being my best friend in the whole multiverse. And a special mention to Oliver Clark and Sana Aslam, who have been there since the start.

To my wonderful family... Thank you for putting up with me. Thank you to my parents for giving my imagination the space to grow along with me, and for pretending you didn't know I was reading under the covers every single night. And to Anton and Joseph... You are my world, my home, my multiverse. I love you so much.